THE RISING TIDE

The Lindisfarne Series
Book Four
(Prequel)

BY THE SAME AUTHOR

THE RISING TIDE

THE LINDISFARNE SERIES
BOOK FOUR
(PREQUEL)

JOHANNA CRAVEN

-

ISBN: 978-1-7638694-0-0

HOLY ISLAND OF LINDISFARNE

DECEMBER 31st
1694

CHAPTER ONE

This house is not haunted.

Footsteps, though—yes. Tapping and crunching, somehow both inside the house and out.

But this house is not haunted. The past does not linger here, at least not outside of imagination.

Abigail Blake is thinking of the past tonight, feeling it hover around her. Echoes of her husband's voice, so loud inside her head it might well be coming from the halls of Highfield House. But her husband Samuel is lying in his grave now, buried in the churchyard of Saint Aidan's, across the water in Bamburgh.

Is that why her thoughts have gone here, to a terror of her own making?

Little wonder: fuming pots are still smoking on side tables, thickening the air with cinnamon and rosemary—forever more the smell of death. Windows cracked open to let the frigid air in and keep the smallpox at bay. More than a month since Samuel had fallen ill; since that dreadful morning he had woken dizzy with fever. In little more than a week, he was gone.

Has enough time passed to be certain none of the children will suffer the same fate?

Abigail had kept them all out of their father's sickroom, had stood firm against their protests—mostly from Nathan, who had been particularly close to his father. But she herself had been in and out of that room, ferrying water and cloths and colourless soups, praying at her husband's bedside. Speaking gentle words to keep his spirits high, until the fever closed in and stole him away.

This would be the worst of things, if her sons and daughter were to fall ill on account of her and her unheard prayers. Unheard? Undeserved, perhaps.

But she is weary of these thoughts now, this fear. Doesn't have the strength, or the will, to keep carrying it. In this whisky-tainted half-light, she is ready to turn their lives over to chance. If the illness is to come for them, let it come. She is too exhausted to fight it any longer.

A sound comes from outside the parlour window. The crunch of footsteps in snow. Glass still in hand, Abigail goes to the window and lifts the curtain. Peers out at the silver-white landscape.

Snowflakes patter silently against the dark glass, the dunes of Emmanuel Head transformed into moonlit white rises. The silence is profound now. Surely the footsteps were nothing but imagination. It's a sound that does not belong out there, not on a night like this.

Tonight, those north of the border will celebrate the coming of the new year. They will be sweeping their hearths and hanging holly to welcome the Hogmanay night. Here in

England, with their antiquated calendar, the new year will not arrive for another three months. Here, they are still languishing in the year she buried her husband. A year she can't quite grasp the edges of in order to see it clearly. Abigail closes her eyes. Lifts the glass to her lips. Her husband's whisky. Remnants of him.

The liquor slides hot down her throat. Does little to lighten the weight of her grief, or of this shadowed, creaking manor. Highfield House seems to have come alive in the four weeks she has been a widow. Become filled with more empty places, more echoes, more memories. It had not felt quite so big or haunted when Samuel was here.

In any case, she had stopped believing in ghosts many years ago. Stopped believing out of necessity when she had moved up here to Lindisfarne, to become the mistress of this monolith. And now what is she? Caretaker, she supposes. The house is hers but not hers. A roof over her head, yes, but she has no rights to sell this place. When he comes of age, her eldest son Oliver will be king of this castle, lord of these un-haunted, haunted halls.

The clock on the mantel chimes. Midnight. A new month, at least. To those north of the border: a new year.

When the twelfth chime falls silent, Abigail hears the footsteps outside again.

She sets her glass on the side table and takes the lamp from the mantel; tries to take her courage with her. She needs courage now, doesn't she, widow and caretaker that she is.

She goes first to the upstairs hallway to check on her children. Opens one door, the next, the next. Nathan and Eva are both sleeping deeply, small bodies rising and falling with breath, undisturbed by the pale beam of her lantern.

Oliver's blankets are tossed messily across the mattress and the curtains are parted, letting a stream of moonlight shaft across the empty bed. She is not surprised to find him missing. Her oldest child is an eternal challenge. Eleven years old, and razor sharp.

There is no way he ought to have made it out of his room without her being aware of it. Her sleep has been fragmented since her husband's death—no doubt fatigue is beginning to cloud her mind. Still, this old, groaning house makes late-night escapes difficult, at least from up here on the second storey. The window is too high, the stone wall unscalable. To have made it to any of the downstairs exits, he would have had to come down the only staircase. She had not heard him do so.

She peers through the curtains. At once, she knows the footsteps outside the house belong to Oliver. Because out in the dark bay beyond the house, lamps light up the shape of a ship. She has no idea who owns the vessel, or why it is here. But Oliver will have been fascinated by the sight of it from his bedroom window. Will have gone outside for a closer look.

She hurries downstairs, snatching her cloak from the hook beside the door and stepping out into the night. Her breath plumes out in front of her, silver against the black of the cloud-banked sky. Snowflakes glitter in the globe of lamplight, the moonscape of snow giving the dunes an otherworldly glow. The sea sighs as it pulls the pebbles of the embankment below the surface.

She calls Oliver's name, her voice disappearing, unanswered. Intrusive in the snow-hushed stillness. A distant wooden clatter floats across the water from the ship.

Abigail steps carefully down the path in front of the house, her feet sinking into the snow, dampening her stockings at her ankles. She steps out on the dunes, skirts and cloak sighing. Tiny steps, so as not to lose her balance on the ice. She calls for her son again. Pans her lamp through darkness. It's answered, suddenly, by another shaft of lamplight.

"Madam?" The voice that comes back is not her son's. It's smooth and deep, tinged faintly with the rolling vowels of the north. Similar to the way her husband had spoken. "Is everything all right?"

She lifts her lamp. The light picks out a tall man wrapped in a long black cloak, face half hidden by a cocked hat pulled low.

Shock rattles through her at the sight of him. There is no good explanation for any man to be out here on these dark dunes, whether he came from that ship in the bay or not. This wild top end of Holy Island is empty but for her and her children and their unquiet house.

"Stay away from me," she hisses, charging further onto the dunes and panning her lamp around in a wild arc. She calls Oliver's name again.

For several minutes, she loses sight of the man as she rounds the house. Snowflakes sting her cheeks, obscuring her vision. She squints into the darkness beyond the reach of her lamp, searching for her son.

She turns the corner of the house and meets a fresh flare of lamplight. There is Oliver, the man from the ship with a firm grip on his wrist. Abigail thrashes through the snow towards them. She grabs her son's wrist and yanks him out of the man's grip.

"How dare you lay a hand on my son?"

"Forgive me," the man says. "I was only trying to keep him safe. His lamp had blown out, and he was far too close to the edge of the headland." The clouds part slightly, and a sliver of moonlight lets her glimpse a little more of his face. He is close to her age, she guesses—a few years past thirty. But there's a searing aliveness in his eyes that Abigail does not remember feeling for years.

"Stay away from us," she hisses. She turns away and begins to march back to the house, tugging Oliver along beside her. An unlit lantern dangles from his free hand.

"There's no need to act so hysterical, Mama," he says casually. "I just came out to look at the ship." As though it is the most normal thing in the world for an eleven-year-old boy to be prowling through the snow so far past midnight.

"How did you get out of the house?"

He doesn't answer. Not that she expected him to. When it comes to Oliver, there is a time and a place for truth telling, and it is not here or now.

As they reach the front door, she finds herself looking back over her shoulder. Back towards the man with the cocked black hat. Back towards the ship.

Nothing, now. No footsteps, no voices, and they are alone on the headland once again.

Abigail slides her key into the front door of the house and shoves it open. Tries to convince herself that this silence, this emptiness, is what she has been seeking all along.

CHAPTER TWO

Sometimes, when he wakes, Nathan forgets his father is no longer here. Sometimes, when his mind is still bleary with sleep, he expects Da to come striding down the hall, throw open the bedroom door and say *Up you get, my lad, it's a bright morning for living.*

Other times, he dreams he is standing at his father's grave, watching his coffin being lowered into the earth. It's a dream that comes in vivid colours; a dream in which he is wearing his mourning clothes—tight-buckled breeches and the silk band that itched at his throat, the too-big black justacorps hanging off his shoulders. On the nights he has that dream, he wakes with the knowledge that Da is gone, fresh and clear and aching, and he wonders how he could ever have forgotten.

This morning, the knowledge of his father's death is sitting dully at the back of his mind the moment he opens his eyes. Da won't come in here to make sure he is awake in time for breakfast. Won't come in smelling of rosewater and tobacco, or with the cold sea air clinging to him.

Pale pink light is creeping through the gap in the curtain. Nathan remembers suddenly that it had been snowing last night, and the knowledge softens the edges of his grief. He scrambles out of bed to look at the freshly coated landscape. The snow reaches right up to the edge of the embankment, where it has been bitten into by the in and out of the sea. Everything is clean and vivid again, the bleak mud-streaked snow of yesterday now dazzling white.

A creak of the floorboards from Oliver's room next door draws Nathan's attention away from the window. He tiptoes out of his room and presses his eye to the keyhole of his brother's bedroom door. Oliver pulls out the chair at his writing desk and sits. Dips a quill into ink and begins to scrawl something down on a piece of paper, his blond head hunched over the page.

Nathan wonders what he's writing. Copying something from a book, maybe—he has seen Oliver do that plenty of times. Pieces of information he finds most fascinating, wants to store away and never forget. Oliver knows so much about everything, especially the Viking raids that happened here on Lindisfarne more than nine hundred years ago. Oliver knows all the details: about the great famine that came before the raid, and the lightning and whirlwinds and dragons that the chronicles say came before the attack. Nathan loves hearing the stories of the Viking raids. At least until the part where the monks' blood is splattered on the walls of Saint Cuthbert's church.

"I can hear you out there, Nathan," Oliver says, not looking up from the desk.

Nathan backs away from the keyhole. He hears footsteps

come towards the door. Feels the quickening of his heart. Oliver throws the door open and stands leaning against the thick wooden frame, arms folded across his chest.

Nathan dares to look up at him. He is never quite sure which version of his older brother he is going to get. Sometimes, Oliver dishes out a look that says he wants Nathan gone; other times, he's welcoming, like when he has a new game to play, or a new story to tell. Today, there's a look of bored indifference on his face.

"Have you come to see the hole in the wall again?" he asks.

Nathan nods. It's not entirely true; he's more intrigued by his brother than he is by the hole in the wall—but only by a little. The hole in the wall is definitely worth his fascination.

Oliver had shown it to him a few days ago. Nathan had had the sense that his brother had known about it for some time; had only just decided to share this piece of knowledge with him, for some hidden purpose of his own. But he didn't care. Oliver had let him into the secret now, and that was all that mattered.

Oliver steps aside, letting Nathan into the bedroom. "Do you remember where it is?"

"Yes." Nathan pushes on the panel to the right-hand side of the fireplace. The panel swivels beneath his hand to reveal the small, dark hiding place behind. He peers into it curiously. He has no desire to go inside; the last time he had done that, Oliver had insisted on coming with him, and closing the panel behind them. They had sat side by side in the tiny space, enclosed by a darkness so thick Nathan could not see his hand in front of his face. Oliver didn't speak, just sat there listening to their breathing. Nathan's shoulder pushed hard against the brick wall and he could feel his lungs growing tight. Could feel the warm, earthy air gathering in his throat. He had felt a very pressing need to get out of that hole in the wall—not that he would ever let his brother know that, of course. He had been more than a little relieved when Oliver had grown bored with whatever it was he was doing, and had pushed the panel in the wall open again.

A thrill in small doses, maybe.

Like he does each time he sees the hiding place, Nathan wonders why it is there. It's a deliberate hole, he knows that much. Not like the time he and Oliver had been playing in the cart shed and had accidentally rammed Da's caulking mallet through the wall. This is a different kind of thing altogether.

The day Oliver had first shown him the hole, Nathan had asked him if he knew who had put it there and why, but Oliver had just stood silently behind him. Then he'd said, "You're not to tell anyone about this, do you understand? Not Mama, or Eva, or Mrs Calloway."

Nathan had promised—not a word. He liked the thrill of keeping his older brother's secrets. When Mrs Calloway, their nurse, had asked him what he had been doing that afternoon, Nathan had said, *Nothing much, just keeping to myself,* as casual as you like, and had been proud of himself all evening.

Oliver had made him promise not to say a word about the knife he'd found in the water off Saint Cuthbert's island either. A Viking knife, he'd said. Left behind after the raids. Nathan had believed him then, back when he had just turned seven. But now he's almost eight, he's starting to wonder if that might not be so true.

"Come and look at this," Oliver says suddenly. Somehow, he's at the window—Nathan had not even heard him move from behind him. He's pulling back the curtain and peering out over the water.

Nathan joins him at the glass. There's a ship out on the water. Not a herring boat—much bigger, like a merchant ship or a pirate galleon. Nathan has seen plenty of ships like this: in the Lindisfarne anchorage, and out in Beadle Bay, but he's never seen one moored outside his house before. He wonders how he had missed it when he had looked out his bedroom window earlier. He supposes he had been too entranced by the fresh snow. Or the thought of Da being gone.

"Came in last night," says Oliver. "I went to have a look."

Nathan can't wait to be like his older brother. To think to himself, *I'm going to go have a look at that ship*, and just off and do it, without a care in the world. Nathan knows that if he tried such a thing, Mama or Mrs Calloway would catch him before he even made it down the staircase.

"Is it a navy ship?" he asks. "Or a supply ship? Or are they pirates?"

Oliver shrugs. He moves from the window and takes the page sitting on his desk. Shoves it into his pocket. "We'll find out."

———————— ✦ ————————

Last night feels strangely dreamlike, the edges of his memories frayed by the dark, by snow, by the long, slow and sleepless voyage up the coast of England.

When he had returned to his ship last night, after rescuing the boy from the headland, Henry Ward had fallen into the deepest sleep he had had in weeks, a dram of Hogmanay whisky pushing against the edges of his dreams.

It had been a fleeting, instinctual decision to moor his ship on the far north side of Holy Island, rather than in the village anchorage. Instinct, perhaps. Six years as a privateer, and fifteen years on merchant vessels before that, and Henry Ward has relied on instinct a lot. More often than not, it serves him well.

There is no action to be had here on Lindisfarne, of course—he is here to sell the cargo he had taken from his latest seizure—an uneventful haul of sugar, molasses and coffee. But a habit for secrecy had taken over and directed him to moor the ship in the darkness beyond the uninhabited north side of the island.

At least, he had assumed it uninhabited. He had not expected to see a house on the headland. It was old and wind-pressed—he guessed it had been standing there for decades.

Ward had seen the boy's lantern moving through the dunes, and suspicion had drawn him out into his longboat to see who was moving through the darkness. His distrustful mind had imagined thieves and pirates and Frenchmen, and anyone else who might see fit to take a piece out of the cargo he has brought up here to sell. Distrustful, yes, but Ward can't deny he was glad to have gone out there. The boy's lamp had burned out while he was climbing the rugged scarp of the headland, and Ward had only just made it to him in time to light his way back down to the dunes. A few seconds later and he could well have been searching for the child in the cold black-ink water of the high tide.

This morning, he has taken the longboat to the village to face the questioning of the harbour master, and collect the deposit for the cargo. Once the money is in his hands, he will have his men deliver the shipment. His young cabin boy is with him to show him the way to the street housing his buyer's new office.

Finn is quiet as they climb up the beach from the anchorage into the village. He has been this way since Ward had told him they'd be visiting Lindisfarne. Eyes constantly drifting out towards the shadow of the Farne Islands. Ward follows his gaze across the leathery grey water.

"Your father still over there, lad?"

"I think so." Finn looks up at Ward, his brown eyes wide. "You're not going to send me back there are you?"

"No. Unless that's what you want?"

Finn shakes his head, looking at his feet. "No, sir."

"Good. I've no desire to look for another cabin boy."

Ward feels the eyes on him as they turn into the cobbled warren of the village. Reluctant though he might be to be here, Finn has done a good job of directing him straight towards the main street, where their buyer is located. Not that there are all that many wrong turns for him to have taken.

Ward knows himself an anomaly in this small village. A child of Newcastle, he had been out to Lindisfarne a few times in his youth. His buyer has since moved from the mainland to the island—and is willing to pay a good enough price to make the journey up here worth it. Ward can't deny there's something faintly pleasant about returning to the county in which he grew up. Not that that familiarity makes him feel like any less of a stranger here on Holy Island.

Beside him, Finn is walking with his head down, woollen cap pulled low to hide his face. He watches his feet, shoulders rounded. Afraid to be recognised, no doubt, by anyone who might tell his father they have seen him. Ward walks close, doing his best to shield him.

Ward halts in his step as a tall, blond-haired boy appears at the end of the street. In spite of the darkness last night, he has no doubt it is the same boy he had seen roaming the dunes at midnight. Oliver—the son of the woman who had appeared from the house with an admonishment on her tongue.

The woman who, inexplicably, has lodged herself in Ward's thoughts and is refusing to be relinquished. He can't quite make sense of why. Pity? Perhaps. But he has never really been one for pity. More likely, a sense of being drawn to a woman who had dared to scold him. Because he has never really been one for getting scolded by women either. Usually they are far more accommodating.

Oliver catches sight of him and quickens his pace in their direction.

"Wait here," Ward tells Finn.

Finn glances at Oliver, then nods silently. Steps back to hide himself in the narrow gap between two houses.

As Ward approaches, Oliver stops walking. "Are you to stay moored in the bay tonight?" he asks, not bothering with a greeting. "Outside our house?"

"Yes." Ward folds his arms across his chest, feeling inexplicably defensive. "I trust I'll not find you running about the dunes in the middle of the night again. You could have got yourself killed."

"What kind of ship is it?" Oliver asks. "Are you a merchant? A pirate? I assume you're not navy. Why are you moored at Emmanuel Head, instead of in the anchorage?"

Ward raises his eyebrows, taken aback by the child's boldness. Who is he to ask such questions? He guesses Oliver to be no more than ten or eleven—Finn's age. If his cabin boy ever spoke with such audacity, he'd thrash him into tomorrow.

"I'm glad I finally found you," Oliver continues, when he realises Ward is not going to answer his barrage of questions. "I've been looking for you for hours." He reaches into his pocket and produces a folded page. Holds it out. "This is from my mother."

Ward takes the page curiously, aware of a faint flicker in his chest. He unfolds the paper to find a few lines of small, neat lettering:

Please forgive my behaviour last night. I regret my outburst and hope you can accept my apology.

I would very much like to make it up to you. I do hope you and your officers will accept my hospitality at Highfield House this evening.

Yours faithfully,

Abigail Blake

Ward stares down at the words, caught off guard by the invitation.

He realises the boy is staring up at him, waiting for an answer. Ward clears his throat, in an attempt to buy himself a little time. He cannot accept, surely. It is not the done thing. Given the way Abigail Blake had been striding alone across the dunes last night, he can only assume she does not have a husband with her in that vast hulk of a house. Or at least, if she does, that he is severely incapacitated.

Then again, would it be rude to turn down her attempt at making things up to him? Ward would hate for her to think he sees her behaviour as unforgivable. He cannot tell if this line of thought is valid, or if comes only from the way this woman has worked her way into his thoughts.

"Tell your mother I shall consider her offer," he says finally, feeling a need to extract himself from the boy's rigid gaze.

Oliver hovers for a moment, as though not entirely happy with the response. His lips part, and for a fleeting moment, Ward feels uneasy. Cannot make sense of why.

"Very good, sir," the boy says finally. "I hope my mother will see you this evening."

CHAPTER THREE

Abigail has not told her mother about Samuel's death. She does not want her pity. Does not want her assistance. And she does not want to open the door of Highfield House and find her mother on the doorstep.

Abigail's mother, Susanna, had always kept a tight hold on her. Abigail is not sure if that had caused the problem, or if it had been a result of the problem. All she knows for certain is that once, she had been just as troublesome as her eldest son.

Susanna had been aware of that false-hearted streak inside her daughter long before Abigail herself could truly make sense of it. That unplaceable *something* that made her look at the world through a warped and tinted lens; through distorted eyes that saw only darkness in the world. Made her act accordingly. Made her lie. Speak in sharp, spiteful words— directed, almost exclusively, towards her mother. Broken glass and torn dresses in an attempt to shake loose that restlessness inside her.

It's a part of herself she never wanted; a part she has

always tried to keep hidden, tried to fight. The desire to hurt another, to deceive, to be cruel—these days, Abigail can see these things as separate from herself. Can see them as unwanted thorns that blow in—and will blow out again just as quickly, if she just closes her eyes and allows herself to breathe.

Abigail had not had close friends as a child. Susanna had kept her on a tight leash, in an attempt to tamp down the aggressiveness, the deceit, the destructiveness. Or at least to keep it hidden from prying eyes.

Abigail had kept her dark side hidden from her husband too. Had kept it locked away inside her for more than a decade of marriage, carefully filtering everything that came out of her mouth—impossibly challenging at first, but easier with time—in an attempt to make herself a more decent person.

Now, she has buried that troublesome part of herself so deeply it could almost have ceased to exist—at least it would feel that way if she couldn't see the same darkness in her eldest child.

Abigail was nineteen when her mother had pursued the match with Samuel Blake, a kind and hardworking merchant who had sold some fine imported housewares to her closest friend. To this day, Abigail is not sure if Susanna's enthusiasm over the marriage had come from the thought of her daughter marrying a wealthy and well-respected gentleman, or at the prospect of her being carted off to somewhere as distant an inaccessible as Lindisfarne.

It was a part of the world that was barely in Abigail's consciousness. A part of the world she had no desire to make home. But Samuel Blake was a kind and decent man who brought out the best in her where her mother brought out the worst. She would become mistress of a grand house, he had told her—a wild and windswept place he had unexpectedly inherited after his cousin's untimely death. Abigail had not wanted to leave London. Had not wanted a life on this sometimes-island, in a house that felt heavy with other people's footsteps. But she had seen an escape from the suffocating life beneath her mother's wing. And leaving London, or sometimes-island, or echoing house or not—she had taken it.

Perhaps, she had thought, she might even outrun the parts of herself she did not wish to take with her. The parts that seemed far more glaring when she was in her mother's company.

When she had left London twelve years ago, Samuel's ring freshly on her finger, Abigail had promised her mother she would keep in touch; she was Susanna's only child, after all, and her father had been gone for many years. And for a while, she had. Weekly letters detailing the children's progress, her attempts at turning Highfield House into her home, lengthy descriptions of the island, crafted at her husband's desk, with her gaze turned out to sea.

But the weekly letters had dwindled to monthly, and then once or twice a year. And visits? Well, Abigail has not been back to London since she left more than a decade ago, and it's been years since her mother ventured up here. She's not seen the boys since Nathan was in leading strings; has never laid eyes on Eva.

Abigail knows her mother's distance has a lot to do with Oliver. The last time her mother had been around her son,

Abigail had seen Susanna's unease. Had seen the fear in her mother's eyes that Abigail might have passed her cruel streak onto her son. Well. There is no *might* about it. Nonetheless, Samuel's death is something Susanna ought to know about.

Abigail takes a deep breath and settles into the chair at the desk. Around her, the house is quiet; Nathan and Eva long asleep, and Oliver's footsteps sounding quietly in his bedroom. Rain is pattering against the windows, settling silent against the snow.

The room feels intensely inhabited by her dead husband; his quills still standing in a pot beside the ink, the smell of his tobacco still emanating from the drawer. Desk chair indented with his weight, leaving his ghostly imprint. Abigail closes her eyes. Inhales the fading presence of him. How long will it be, she wonders, until there is no trace of Samuel Blake left in here at all?

A sudden wave of grief surges up on her, tightening her throat and stinging her eyes. In so many ways, theirs had been a good marriage. A strong marriage. Though they had never had the kind of dizzying lust for one another she had read about in histoires, he had always treated her kindly, fairly. Looked upon her as a dear friend; a partner to navigate life with. They had not married for love, but a genuine and natural love had grown out of it. And as Samuel's wife, she had found an anchor, a solidity, that she had never felt before. A solidity that grounded her, made it easier to fight off the unwanted parts of herself. Samuel Blake had been an achingly decent man, and that had made her want to be a good wife to him. He, and later, their children, had been a reason to fight against the restlessness, the darkness inside her. She prays that one day, Oliver will find a similar reason.

Abigail closes her eyes, trying to find the will to write this cursed letter. When she opens her eyes, her gaze is drawn through the open curtains, alighting on the faint rose of lamplight coming from the ship in the bay.

And suddenly her thoughts are back in the dark whisky haze of last night. The man with the cocked hat. The sudden appearance of the ship. Oliver's escape from the house. How he had managed to do so is a question she has not yet found the strength to linger on. But she needs answers from him. Needs the truth.

She shoves aside the blank pages and goes down the hall to her son's room. Opens the door without knocking.

"Get your books," she says. "We're to have a lesson."

Oliver is sitting cross-legged on his bed, whittling away at a piece of wood with the sharp end of a quill. He looks up at her through a thatch of thick ice-blonde hair, a faint smile flickering in the corner of his lips. He does not protest at having a lesson so late at night. No doubt he knows as well as she does that this is not really about his education. It's about hers.

These lessons with Oliver, these times when it's just the two of them, feel like the only times she can ever truly get through to her son. His lessons have become the time in which she pries out the answers she needs. When they are in company, even with just his brother and sister, Oliver is aloof and secretive. But when it is just the two of them, Abigail manages, sometimes, to crack through his façade.

It's a skill no one else has ever had. Not the children's nurse, or Oliver's teachers; certainly not his father.

Abigail tells herself it's because she's his mother.

She knows that really, it's because she and Oliver are so frighteningly similar.

He gets up off the bed without speaking and slides into his desk chair. Abigail drags the armchair over from the corner of the room and perches on the edge. She reaches for the mathematics text from the pile of books on his desk. Opens to a page scrawled with algebraic symbols she has no idea how to decipher. She turns backwards through the book until she finds a page of simple arithmetic. "This page," she tells him.

She has taught him little. In the three months since he was expelled from the grammar school in Berwick they have covered little beyond basic Latin phrases and arithmetic Abigail dug up from her own lessons some twenty years ago.

Oliver begins to work through the sums. Numbers and symbols flow easily from his quill; she knows he finds this less than challenging.

She ought to seek out a tutor for him. He is far too intelligent to be scrawling down childish sums with his mother. Abigail is well aware of his passion for knowledge—has seen him willingly studying algebra, reading Balfour's philosophy, Latin poetry and prose, and his favourite of all: history. His love for knowledge had just not extended to abiding by the grammar school's rules.

Heaven knows he could have a fine profession ahead of him; a finer profession than his merchant father. Medicine, perhaps, or the law. If only he could find a little discipline. Perhaps this dull arithmetic will remind him of the value of what he had thrown away.

Then again, this is not about arithmetic at all.

"How did you get out of the house last night?" she asks.

Oliver dips his quill in the ink. "Through the front door, of course."

Abigail keeps her face passive. Knows that this is Oliver; knows she has to sift through lies—sometimes veiled, other times deliberately blatant, like this one—before she reaches the truth. "I see." She nods towards the next row of sums. "Continue."

This is their unspoken arrangement: a lie leads to more schoolwork; the truth leads to the end of the class. Oliver will get to the truth, she knows. He always does. It's another of their unspoken arrangements. He will be honest with her— eventually—as long as she is honest with him.

His quill scratches across the page, a frown of concentration creasing the bridge of his nose. A log breaks open in the fireplace, sending a volley of sparks up the chimney. Outside, the rain has intensified, throwing itself against the windows and drumming against the roof.

Abigail fixes her eyes on her son, tension crackling between them. She feels an intense sense of connection to him; far more than she feels to her other children. A connection that both scares and comforts her. Nathan and Eva, gentle and compliant, are both entirely their father's children. Oliver is entirely hers.

"There's a passage," he says suddenly. "In the wall."

"What?" It ought to be a lie. Sounds like a lie. But there's a look in Oliver's eyes that she recognises as honesty.

"Behind the priest hole."

"There's a priest hole in this house?"

"You didn't know?" By his tone, she can tell he knew she was completely unaware.

"Where?" she asks.

"In here."

Her thoughts begin to race. Samuel had grown up visiting this house—the house of his uncle. Had he known about this? She thinks of him and his cousin tearing through these passages as boys. It seems impossible that they would not have known of such a thing. But surely if he had, Samuel would not have put their troublesome eldest son in this bedroom. It's possible, she realises, that her husband might not have known of this. Possible this might have been a dressing room, or his aunt's bedroom, forbidden to the boys.

Oliver puts his quill down neatly in the centre fold of his book. "Would you like to see it?"

Abigail nods.

He goes to the fireplace and pushes on one of the dark wooden panels to the right of the grate. The panel twists open beneath his palm, revealing a small dark room tucked into the stone of the fireplace.

At once, Abigail is imagining all that might have happened in this house. Her windblown manor shielding Catholic priests within its walls. She imagines the terror that might have infused this place as priest hunters strode from room to room, hunting for their prey. Little wonder she sometimes finds herself so on edge in here, with so much fear and suffering trapped in the fabric of the house.

She cranes her neck so she is looking deep into the hole. Thick, hot blackness, barely touched by the lamp on the mantel, or the flames simmering in the grate beside them. "I don't see the passage," she says.

Oliver reaches into the back of the hole and pushes against the far wall. This is another wood panel, she realises then; not the unyielding stone of the wall. It turns beneath Oliver's hand, revealing a second, slightly larger brick-lined room. And in its far corner, a dark opening that leads down into blackness. Into the walls of the house, Abigail realises. The sight of it makes something twist in her stomach.

The smell of cold earth rises up to meet them. Abigail can just make out the top rungs of a ladder poking up through the hole.

"It's a double priest hole," Oliver tells her. "We learnt about them at school. The first room remained empty to trick the priest hunters, and the priest stayed hidden in the second room behind the first. And whoever built this one made it so a priest that's hiding could escape the house too. Quite genius, don't you think?"

Abigail swallows heavily. "Where does the passage lead?"

"It comes out right beneath Nathan's window."

Abigail stares into the dark chasm, thoughts racing. She wants to tell Oliver not to use the priest hole anymore. Knows that will only encourage him to do so more regularly. Perhaps she could have Mr Emmett from the village come and board the hole up at both ends.

She can only imagine what Oliver might do in retaliation.

A knock at the front door startles her.

No one ever comes out here—at least, they don't since her husband died.

Abigail stays motionless for a moment. Her daily, Ruth, has long left the house, and it is up to her to answer the door. Perhaps she ought to ignore it. Hope that whoever it is will go away. It's far too late for visitors.

"Are you not going to answer the door, Mama?" Oliver says finally. "What if it's someone in need of help in this bad weather?"

She peers at him curiously, trying to see behind his eyes. It's not like him to care about another person's plight. But he is right—someone could be in trouble out there. And she will not let herself be that person who does not care about others. She has fought too hard to keep that selfish and spiteful woman at bay.

Abigail makes her way down the stairs.

She turns the key and pulls the door open to a bloom of gold lamplight. Finds the man from the ship standing on her doorstep in the rain, with three other men behind him.

CHAPTER FOUR

At the sight of her, Ward feels an unexpected jolt in his chest. He takes her in in the lamplight; chestnut coloured hair pulled back from her face, bundled in a low knot at her neck. Pale cheeks and an even, symmetrical face that ought to be unremarkable, but somehow is anything but. Shadows underline clear blue eyes that carry an expression Ward cannot quite make out. Suspicion? Not quite. Surprise? This is closer.

No doubt she had not expected him to accept her invitation.

He can hardly blame her—Ward himself had not expected to accept it either. And yet somehow, once dark had fallen thick across the island, he had found himself drawn out here with his officers in tow, just as she had requested.

Abigail Blake is dressed in simple black skirts and a house jacket, devoid of embroidery or embellishments. Mourning clothing? Perhaps coming here was an enormous mistake. Still, too late for such thoughts. He can hardly walk away without a word now, not even if he wanted to.

"Good evening," he says.

The surprise in her eyes gives way to the same searing anger he saw from her on the dunes last night. "What do you want? Who are all these men?" It's not just anger in her eyes, he realises then. It's panic.

He also realises she is not about to let them in from this torrential downpour. "I'm sorry," he garbles. "I…" Rain runs down the back of his neck, soaks his shirt. Lost for words, Ward holds out the note Oliver had given him that morning. The note, he sees now, that most certainly was not written by his mother.

Abigail snatches the sodden page. Unfolds it and reads it quickly. She presses her lips into a thin line.

"And you imagined this to be genuine, I assume?" she says icily. "You imagined I might willingly invite a group of strangers into my home while my children are sleeping?" She looks at him for a long second. He can feel her scrutinising him; and beyond that, a faint curiosity. He feels suddenly, intensely vulnerable. A foreign sensation, but not, he realises, an unpleasant one. And that in itself feels unmooring.

Ward hears a poorly hidden chuckle from one of his officers. He clears his throat, feeling embarrassment flush the back of his neck. His sudden vulnerability might not be entirely unpleasant, but he does not like looking a fool in front of his men. And he knows he looks a fool now.

"It was a mistake," he admits. "I apologise, Mrs Blake."

"Yes," she says sharply, thrusting the note back into his hand. "That it was. Goodnight. I trust you can all find your way back to your ship without difficulty."

And the door swings closed, the thud echoing out across

the rain-soaked dunes.

Abigail stands for a moment in the silence of the entrance hall. Her heart is fast and her entire body feels inexplicably hot. She looks up the stairs, searching for Oliver. She cannot see him, but she is certain he has found some hidden corner of the house to peek out from. Some corner she herself is completely unaware of. Like the passage that weaves through the walls of the house. How many more secrets is this place hiding?

The house feels suddenly monstrous, its emptiness heightened by the sudden disappearance of the men's voices. The hollow makes her grief suddenly acute, the fresh holes in her life gaping. She has never felt so breathtakingly lonely.

Before she knows what she is doing, she is pulling her cloak from the hook on the wall of the foyer and swinging open the front door. Striding down the path at the front of the house and out onto the dunes. Rain slaps at her cheeks, running down the back of her neck and soaking into her skirts.

"Wait," she hears herself call. She can see the men up ahead: tall, dark shadows lit only by the faint glow of their lamps. They stop walking almost as one. Turn back to face her.

The man with the cocked hat approaches her, boots sighing through the wet sludge of the snow. She imagines he is the captain of the ship.

"What's your name?" she asks.

He holds out a hand. "Henry Ward." He nods to the men

behind him. "And my officers. Mr Graveney, Mr Hunter, Mr Cook."

She accepts his hand. "Well, Mr Ward. For all his trickery, I suppose my son is right. I owe you a debt of gratitude." She feels not a scrap of gratitude towards him, no. But she cannot spend one more sleepless night walking the halls alone in Highfield House. She doesn't care who is filling that silence. "You and your officers had best come in."

And she hurries back towards the house before she can change her mind.

She is the worst of mothers, Abigail has no doubt. Inviting these men here to assuage her loneliness, it comes from that selfish, spiteful part of herself that makes bad and dangerous choices. With Samuel in the earth, it seem to be tearing itself free.

She takes the men's cloaks and hangs them on the hooks beside the front door. A strange thing, she thinks distantly, to have men's clothes hanging here in the entrance hall again. Feels like a betrayal. Which, she supposes, it is. They're Samuel's children she is putting in danger, after all.

She glances up the staircase in search of Oliver. She ought to be furious with him, of course. But she cannot quite make herself feel the rage she ought to.

Why did Oliver do this? Why invite these men here? For all his disobedience, she knows he never does anything without reason. Never does anything just for the sake of being bad. He's far too intelligent. Far too calculating.

He's enthralled by Henry Ward, she supposes. Wants him at the house, perhaps. Or wants to punish her for the callous way he had spoken to the man last night.

Or perhaps he knows how much she does not want to spend another night in this house with no adult company to speak of.

She hurries into the kitchen, fetching a cloth for the men to dry themselves with. When she returns to the foyer, the smell of wet wool and men has thickened the air.

She leads the sailors into the parlour, trailing her fingertips along the dark wood panels of the wall in a vain attempt to steady herself. Her thoughts are racing. Does she have anything to offer her guests? She has little idea what Ruth has hiding in the pantries. This suddenly feels like the greatest of impositions, for Henry Ward and his men to have inserted themselves into her life like this. Never mind that she had been the one to call them back. Right now, she needs to blame someone other than herself for all this madness. Needs to direct her anger somewhere other than at her own terrible choices.

In the handful of hours since her housekeeper had left, she and the children have managed to turn the parlour into a minor chaos. Abigail has left a poetry book face down on the tea table; Oliver's gloves are on the floor beneath the settle; Eva's doll lying face down beside the hearth. Abigail closes the book and kicks the gloves under the settle. Swoops down to rescue the doll from an officer's stray boot.

Ward's men migrate towards the fireplace, far more interested in the blaze roaring in the grate than in the state of her parlour.

"Please," she manages, "sit." Her polite invitation comes out barbed and coarse, as the two warring parts of herself clash on her tongue. Ward hesitates for the briefest of moments before lowering himself into the embroidered blue armchair beside the tea table. He is looking at her with a look of deep curiosity, the firelight intensifying the sharp contours of his face. His presence seems to suck all the air from the room, forcing Abigail to turn away.

Is it pity that has brought him here? This suddenly seems far more likely than his need for a blazing fire. Abigail suspects she is the kind of woman who ought to be pitied.

She goes to Samuel's liquor cabinet in the corner of the room. Takes out a bottle of brandy and five funnel bowl glasses.

Part of her wants to send these men back out into the night. Wants to return to the quiet stillness of the house. But something nameless, formless, is preventing her from doing that. Preventing her from doing what she knows is right.

The officers are already chatting between mouthfuls of brandy, joking about *better conditions than the tavern* and jibes at their captain's leaky ship. Abigail cannot tell if they are oblivious to the awkwardness of the situation, or simply doing their best to ignore it. Ward gives a half-hearted chuckle that doesn't light his eyes. His gaze follows her around the room.

She garbles something about food, and heads off into the gloom of the house, a strange mix of unease and thrill simmering beneath her anger.

Taking a lamp from its hook in the hallway, she bumbles around the kitchen, finding jars of salted meats and pickled oysters and a bowl of fragrant candied apples. A strange, cobbled-together offering, she knows, but when she takes the bowls of food back to the parlour, the men attack them eagerly.

She takes a shallow sip from the brandy glass one of the

men have left on the table in wait for her. It's enough to settle the tirade of nerves. A small enough mouthful to keep her thoughts sharp. She perches on the edge of the empty armchair opposite Henry Ward.

He is still watching her, a look of uncertainty in his eyes. "This is very kind of you, Mrs Blake," he says. "But you must tell us if we are unwanted guests. The last thing I wish to do is impose on you."

She doesn't look at him. Can't look at him. "You're here now," she says tautly. "You may as well stay." And this anger, she knows well, it's not anger at the men. It's anger at herself. At her weakness for allowing these men into her home while her children are sleeping. While she is still in mourning clothes, with the grief over her husband still so fresh and raw inside her. Anger at her inability to face another night alone in this house. It's foolishness, she tells herself sharply. This is her home. She cannot be afraid of it. Besides, she is never alone in this house. She has three children keeping her company.

Three children she is now entirely and wholly responsible for. What a fine job she is doing.

She takes another mouthful of brandy. And just for now, she thinks, just for now, she is going to push aside the chaos and self-loathing inside her head. And she is going to listen to this chorus of masculine voices that is filtering through her house for the first time in weeks, bringing these midnight hours back from the dead.

"What brings you to Lindisfarne?" she asks, when the men's chatter lulls.

"We've cargo to sell," says Henry Ward. "I've a buyer up here in Northumberland who pays a very decent price. Makes the journey north worth the time and money."

"Cargo? You're a merchant sailor?"

A crooked smile lifts the corner of his lips. "Not entirely. The cargo came from a French vessel returning from the Caribbean."

"A privateer then."

"Indeed."

She is glad of it. For a moment, she had feared *pirate*. And then there would have been no way she could have justified this barely justifiable impulse soiree. But at this sea captain's words, some hidden part of her sparks to life. His words prick at some long-buried fascination with the sea; with lands beyond this one; with lives more than the one she is living. Since she was a young child, she has been intrigued by the lives of seafarers, by tales of Arctic islands and the great south land. In the rigid confinement of childhood under her mother's wing, reading about faraway worlds had made her feel less hemmed-in. Had given her a much-needed gasp of freedom.

It's a fascination she had never spoken of to Samuel. In spite of her desire to do so, she has never learnt to sail, as a number of the womenfolk of Lindisfarne have—has never even learnt to handle that rickety old rowboat that sits on the embankment in front of the house. When the tide rises, turning Lindisfarne back into an island, she is utterly at the mercy of others, if she ever needs to leave.

When Abigail was a child, Susanna had let her know, in no uncertain terms, that seafaring was not a fitting interest for a young lady. An interest a man would not be pleased to hear of in his wife. And so Abigail had tucked it away with the other parts of her that were not fit for a husband's eyes. Had filled that fresh hollow with poetry, and needlework, and a fierce determination to rear a garden on the windblown grounds of Highfield House.

But now these seamen are here—and her husband is not—Abigail wants suddenly to immerse herself in these vast and unreachable places. This world of Caribbean journeys and stolen cargo and privateering fleets tracing the coasts of other lands. Life on Holy Island can feel almost unbearably oppressive sometimes, cut off from the mainland for so many hours of each day. And since Oliver was born, she has been so preoccupied with being a mother—with being *Oliver's* mother—that she has had little time to contemplate what might be going outside the confines of this island. It is oddly blissful to hear stories of the outside world.

The wooden beams above their heads creak loudly as the house shifts in the coldness of the night. Abigail thinks suddenly of her children. Heaven knows Oliver could be traipsing across the dunes right now.

Unlikely, she supposes, given how enthralled he is likely to be by the fact these men are here. Unless he had brought them here so he could disappear without her noticing…

She is rushing towards the staircase as the thought comes to her. Lets out a breath when she spots her son crouched at one end of the hallway, trying to catch a word from the parlour. She pins him with hard eyes. "Go to bed."

A smile flickers on Oliver's lips. A smile that lets her know he has won. The men from the ship are here, just as he intended. Although oddly, right now, Abigail does not feel as though she has lost.

She herds Oliver upstairs and stands in the doorway of his bedroom, watching as he climbs into bed. She peeks into

Nathan and Eva's rooms, then hovers at the top of the staircase for a moment to gather herself against the tumult that is Henry Ward.

When she arrives at the bottom of the staircase, he steps out of the parlour to meet her. Lamplight flickers over his shorn cheeks.

"I'm sorry for appearing on your doorstep," he says, voice low. "It was foolish. I ought to have known your son was behind it."

"And what would have made you think that?"

He hesitates, as though caught off guard by her brittle response.

"My son is a challenging child," she says, before he can find an answer. "He takes some work to get to know."

"I see." Ward catches her eye. He's a strikingly beautiful man, with hooded blue eyes and a sharp jaw. A strong, aquiline nose. Coils of pale, unpowdered hair hang in a long queue down his back. Up so close to him, she feels immensely on edge, her skin heating beneath her mourning gown. She feels that simmering anger bubble up higher in response to her body's treachery.

"He's fascinated by you, I assume," she says. The words come out sounding like more of an insult than she intended. "We don't see many ships like yours here."

"I'm rather grateful to have had cause to visit," he says, sidestepping her sharpness. "Lindisfarne is a beautiful place."

"It is a beautiful place," Abigail admits.

"But not home for you?"

She smiles wryly. "Is it so obvious?"

The corner of his lips turn up, but he doesn't speak. What does he see when he looks at her, Abigail wonders? Can he sense that war inside her: anger and annoyance mixing with the confusing need to keep him here?

"I tried to make it home," she says, hearing her voice soften. "But I still feel like an outsider. They're a tight-knit bunch here. Not so willing to welcome a Londoner, especially one hiding away in such an unsightly beast of a house." She wonders why she is telling all this to a near stranger. She senses some unplaceable danger to Henry Ward—some innate sense that she would be better off keeping her distance from him. But right now, that feels oddly difficult to do.

"This was your husband's home?" he asks, a little tentatively.

"Yes. It was." She nods towards the vast expanse of the house. "This place has been in his family for generations. Samuel was a Northumberland native, but he did not grow up in this house. It belonged to his cousin, and his uncle before that. His cousin died shortly before we married, and the house passed into Samuel's hands."

Henry Ward nods slowly. He has noticed, surely, the way she speaks of her husband in the past tense. Would he be here otherwise? Surely not.

Ward drifts through the foyer, taking in the polished newel posts Samuel had carved by hand, the two portraits beside the front door, the vast painted seascape. He nods towards the artwork. "A Dutch artist?" he asks.

Abigail's cheeks flush. "I don't know," she admits. "The paintings were here when we arrived in the house. I admit I've paid little attention to them."

Ward steps closer, trying to inspect the painting in the dim light. "My mother was very inspired by the Dutch landscape artists. She would have loved this piece."

"Your mother was a painter?"

"Yes. She was very talented. Not that her work ever saw the outside of her workroom. My father had very firm ideas about where a woman's place was, and it certainly was not in an artist's salon." He glances over his shoulder at Abigail. "I'm sure I cannot blame him for having such an opinion. Although I did always think it a great shame that more people did not get to see her work." He turns to look at her squarely. "We shall be gone before dawn," he says. "I will make sure none of the villagers see us here."

She nods faintly. Knows that come the dawn, Donald Macauley and his son will be out on the dunes with hunting rifles; herring fishermen dotting the sea beyond Henry Ward's ship. Abigail can only imagine the stories they would tell if they saw a band of privateers leaving Highfield House.

He is true to his word. At the first hint of light in the sky, he and his men return to their ship. The officers thank her, stumbling bleary-eyed into the pre-dawn chill. Mist hangs over the water, the dawn chorus of birds beginning to reach across the island. Henry Ward lingers on the doorstep. In the pearly half-light, his eyes are almost violently blue.

"Thank you," he says. "For your hospitality. And for seeing past my foolishness."

His foolishness. Abigail had been far too fixated on her own foolishness to be bothered about his.

Still, she supposes, no real harm has been done. She can release her anger now, and her guilt. Because the men are off back to their ship, her children are safe, and no one from the village shall be any wiser.

And perhaps, she thinks, this single night of company

might give her the strength to face the silent nights of Highfield House for a little longer yet.

CHAPTER FIVE

The *Eagle* comes to life slowly the next day. The men are sluggish returning from the tavern, or wherever else they had spent the night—these days, Ward knows better than to ask. He watches the trail of longboats crawl back to the ship as he leans up against the gunwale and brings a cup of watery ale to his lips.

The morning is bitterly cold, but Ward prefers the icy air over the stuffiness of the great cabin. His gaze is fixed on the house, a lonely grey figure against the eternal roll of the dunes. Thin lines of smoke are rising from the chimneys now, and he can just make out glimmers of light behind several of the windows.

When he thinks of last night, he feels a gnawing unease at having turned up on Abigail Blake's doorstep like a fool. No doubt if she had truly wanted his company, she would have made the invitation herself, rather than sending a note into town with her son, on the off chance they crossed each other's paths. Ward knows he had not thought about the issue hard enough, because he had wanted the message to be from Abigail. Had wanted that invitation. Wanted that chance to dig a little deeper into the mystery of her.

In any case, the night is over and done, and he needs to turn his eyes forward to far more important matters. He has learnt the hard way that a man can either commit his life to a woman or the sea—never both.

He tosses back the last of his ale and strides to the helm where Finn is on anchor watch. He is wrapped up in a tarred coat and thrum cap, his youthful alertness a stark contrast to the rest of the bleary-faced crew.

"Did you go to the post house like I asked?" Ward asks.

"Aye sir. There was a letter for you. I think it was from Scotland. It's on your desk."

"Thank you." Ward glances at him. Sees that hollow look behind his eyes. "All right, lad?"

Finn nods, then looks up at Ward, arms wrapped around his chest. "Are we leaving soon, sir?" He's on edge so close to home, Ward knows.

Almost two years ago, he had found Finn sailing alone in Beadle Bay. Had taken him on as a cabin boy with little thought to the consequences. Little thought to who might miss him.

Ward had been in need of a cabin boy, and Finn Murray had been there, guiding his skiff gracefully around the *Eagle*, a look of wonder in his eyes.

Ward had asked cursory questions that Finn had given equally vague answers to. *Aye, sir, I can take orders. No, there's nothing keeping me from coming with you. Aye, I can read and write a little.*

Answers Ward did not care to dig into at the time. Finn

had seemed desperate to take up the cabin boy's post. Desperate to escape whatever life he had come from. Ward had assumed him an orphan. Convinced himself he was doing a good thing by taking the boy to sea and giving him a solid life.

It was not until several months later that Ward had learnt Finn had a father living out on the tiny island of Longstone, setting the shipping beacon alight each night. A father he had left without a word, after a trivial argument. Finn had let the information slip during a sailing lesson one day. Ward heard guilt in the boy's voice. Tried to ignore his own.

Ward knows now it was wrong to take this child to sea with him, at least without asking more questions. He wonders, sometimes, what Finn's father must be going through. The story Finn has painted for him of his life on Longstone is not a happy one. Constant arguments with his father, the two of them prone to flying into a rage. But Ward wonders how much of that is tainted with a childish need to overembellish.

Sometimes, he thinks about doing the right thing and depositing Finn back on his father's island. And then he realises how much he does not want to do that.

Ward tells himself it's because he has no desire to train another cabin boy. He's poured countless hours into teaching Finn the lines and sails of the barque, to navigate by starlight, to write in a legible hand. But he knows there's more to it than that. Knows he has grown too attached to the boy. Begun to see him, sometimes, as the son he never had.

Ward knows how dangerous that is. Apart from anything else, he knows how fragile this life is; how easily Finn could meet his end in a flare of French cannon fire.

Ward leaves the boy on watch and makes his way to the great cabin. The letter is waiting for him in the middle of his desk. He looks down at the seal. Lewis McGowan, Earl of Dunmore. Ward had sailed with McGowan on an East India Company post when they were little more than boys. The Earl had been a skilled sailor—Ward would happily take him into his privateering crew if the man had any desire to leave his life of luxury for the sea.

Lord Dunmore is cunning and charismatic enough to tease Jacobite knowledge out of his fellow Scottish noblemen. Pass it on subtly to men like Henry Ward, who are fighting the Jacobites and their French allies. He's also wise enough to recognise a failing cause when he sees one and privately back the government side.

Ward snaps the seal.

We ought to meet urgently, Henry, the letter begins, in the Earl's ornamental hand. Ward smiles to himself. Just like McGowan to approach everything with a sense of drama. *There are important things I feel you would like to know. Things too dangerous to commit to writing.*

I can just imagine you rolling your eyes at my flair for drama—Ward chuckles to himself at the accuracy of the statement—*but I assure you the pieces of knowledge I have gathered from the Jacobites are worthy of a little drama.*

A morsel of information to whet your appetite: Lord Haver, prominent Whig party politician, is harbouring Jacobite tendencies.

Ward lowers the page, blowing out a breath. All right, so the drama is justified. McGowan has caught him off guard. This is a precious piece of information. And accurate, most likely. Ward knows Lord Haver is a relative of McGowan's—although he imagines there is little love lost between the cousins.

The letter continues, with one sensation after another. Lord Haver's father is not his father at all, but rather, he is the son of a Highlander—*can you imagine such a thing?* in wild, curling letters of excitement. Haver is funnelling Williamite knowledge towards the Jacobites. Too fixated on the promise of power to step away from a political party on the rise, despite his conflicting beliefs.

Damaging information, Ward thinks, if it were to fall into the wrong hands. Lord Haver would no doubt pay a handsome sum to see that this knowledge never made it into the public eye. And what of the Whig party? If they knew such a thing, they would rid themselves of Haver, certainly. But the information could be fatal for a party with grand ambitions. No doubt they too would pay well to keep it from finding its way out.

And if this is merely the titbit McGowan is dangling in front of him to get his attention, Ward hardly dares imagine what else it is the Earl has to say about the Jacobites and their French allies.

He had planned to return to the Channel once he had completed the sale of the latest cargo. But the need to make the journey up to Edinburgh is suddenly pressing. Finn will just have to deal with being so close to home for a little while longer.

At the bottom of the page, McGowan instructs in dramatic, oversized letters: *Burn this once you have read it.*

Ward laughs at the Earl's theatrics. Folds the letter and tucks it in his desk drawer.

CHAPTER SIX

Abigail traipses through the snow towards the village, with her two youngest children running across the dunes ahead of her. She has left Oliver back at the house, with instructions to remove the dead ivy from the outside walls of the manor and feed it into the parlour fireplace for burning. She has no idea if he—or the ivy—will still be there when she returns.

She has said nothing to Oliver about Ward's visit. He has not asked her about it either. The unspoken questions hang in the air between them, thick and heavy. Abigail is grateful not to be in his presence this morning.

Nathan and Eva are barrelling ahead of her in their thick winter cloaks, their giggling rising in the cold air. They follow the trails of deer prints over the dunes, scrambling over the icy rises on hands and knees.

"Be careful," Abigail calls on instinct. She knows there's little need. Knows her children, island natives, are far more sure-footed on the snowy dunes than their mother.

Flushed and breathless, the children slow to a walk as they

reach the village. A horde of fisherman barrel past and Eva hangs back to take her mother's hand, her laughter evaporating. She has become too used to the isolation of the house, Abigail thinks dully. A kitten frozen by the sight of a crowd.

They walk Nathan to the petty school run by the vicar's wife. Watch at the vicarage gate as he heads inside the building with the other young boys. He's the tallest of the bunch now, her long-legged son. He seems a grown-up figure in his breeches and buckled shoes, many of the boys still tottering in snow-dampened gowns. In a few months' time, he will finish his preliminary lessons here; Abigail prays the grammar school that had expelled Oliver will not change their mind about accepting his younger brother.

When the boys have all disappeared inside the vicarage, she and Eva begin the long walk back towards Emmanuel Head.

"Mama," says Eva, watching her feet, "what's your third favourite bird?"

Abigail smiles. "My third favourite bird?"

"Yes."

"Hmm." Abigail takes her daughter's hand. "Maybe a goose."

Eva's forehead crumples as she frowns in concentration. "If you followed a goose, where would you end up?"

Eva is still months from her fourth birthday, but sometimes there's a seriousness to her that makes Abigail wonder at the depth of her thoughts. She wonders how much of her father's death Eva has taken in. How much grief her delicate body is carrying. Like her brothers, she has an innate intelligence; churns out a constant stream of questions.

Speaks with her mother's polished London vowels, completely devoid of the Northumberland roll that surrounds her. But Eva is every inch an island child, entranced by rockpools and wildflowers and the changing hues of the sea. Fearless in the gloomy halls of Highfield House.

Abigail hears someone call her name. She whirls around.

Mairi Mitchell is bundled into a faded tartan cloak, strands of pale hair escaping out the side of a blue knitted bonnet. Her youngest son, just weeks old, is strapped to her front in a woollen cloth.

"I'm sorry," Mairi smiles, "I didn't mean to startle you." Her green eyes take on a sudden seriousness. "Just wanted to see how you were faring. I've not seen you much since Samuel…"

Abigail manages a faint smile. "I'm managing," she says. "Thank you."

Mairi nods in the direction of the vicarage. "Nathan off for his lessons?"

"Yes. He'll be off to the grammar in a few months, God willing." Abigail regrets the words the moment they are out— regrets speaking of such a privileged thing to Mairi. She knows the Mitchells can only dream of sending their sons across the water to the Berwick grammar school.

But the smile Mairi gives her shows no hint of judgement or bitterness. "Do you have some time?" she asks. "Why don't you come back to my cottage a while?"

"Thank you, but I'd best get back," Abigail says. "I've left Oliver alone." The words are instinctive, impulsive. Wrought by the surprise of the invitation. In twelve years, Mairi Mitchell has never once invited Abigail back to her cottage.

"Of course," says Mairi. "I'll walk back to the house with

47

you." Her words leave no room for protest. Abigail realises she is glad for it. Since Samuel's death, adult conversations have begun to feel exceedingly rare.

Then again, her conversations with Oliver often feel far too mature for her liking. Seem to dig further beneath the surface of things than her discussions with Samuel ever had.

She and Samuel had had a strong relationship. But there had always been a limit to how deep their conversations went. Abigail had made sure to keep it that way. Had been ashamed of the cruel thoughts that often came unbidden to her; ashamed of how regularly she had to hold herself back from lying purely for the sake of it, or from thinking unpleasant thoughts about anyone who looked at her the wrong way. She had hated the prospect of her husband seeing that side of her. Had not wanted him to feel as though he had made a mistake by marrying her.

Had not wanted him to know that their son's dark streak came from her.

They leave the village behind, following the path through stretches of snow-patched farmland. Eva trots ahead, stopping to poke at some unseen curiosity in the underbrush. Abigail hopes it's more interesting rock and less dead animal.

"How are the children managing?" Mairi asks.

Abigail digs her hands into her cloak to warm them. "It's been difficult for them," she admits. "Nathan has taken it especially hard. He and Samuel were very close."

Mairi nods. There's empathy in her eyes, if not understanding.

Abigail had met Mairi Mitchell in her first days on Lindisfarne. They have always gotten along, always spoken kindly to each other. But that warmth has never had the space to grow into a true friendship.

Samuel had always been wary of Mairi and her husband, Elias. Wary of the Mitchells' Jacobite leanings; their belief that the Stuarts belonged on the throne—an undercurrent that ran through much of Lindisfarne society.

When the Jacobites had first risen six years ago, in the months after William had taken the throne, Abigail had become aware of a fracturing of the Lindisfarne community. Unspoken, but undeniable. A sense of people becoming more closed off. More suspicious. More divided.

Us against them.

An unexpressed rift in which the Blakes and the Mitchells had always been on different sides. While Samuel had never forbidden her from spending time with Mairi, Abigail had always been able to sense a tension in his eyes, his words, his expression, whenever he saw the two of them together. Ever wary of upturning that precious solidarity she shared with her husband, Abigail had largely stayed away from Mairi. Their friendship has always been a thing of mere pleasantries and passing comments. Conversations that do little to scratch the surface.

Has she ever made anything of a true friendship on Holy Island, Abigail finds herself wondering? Acquaintances, certainly. But she has always had a sense of people keeping their distance. She has always told herself it's because of her eldest son; because of his sharp tongue, his light fingers, his probing eyes. She's lost count of how many times villagers have either cornered her and Samuel in the streets, or turned up on the doorstep of Highfield House, with a list of grievances against their child.

But when she thinks on it now, Abigail realises Samuel had

never had the same difficulty in forming friendships that she has had. Samuel, with his booming laugh and welcoming smile, had always been the life of the harvest festivals, the fairs, the parties, the card games. Constantly stopped in the street for a chat; always off for an ale with this person or that. When Abigail had gone along to such social occasions, she had always had the sense she was only accepted because of whose wife she was.

Oliver is Samuel's son too. Had the village just been less judgmental of his father than his mother? Or is there something else about Abigail that has prevented people from getting closer? An understanding, perhaps, that Oliver might get his delinquent nature from his mother. Or some innate knowledge of how hard she has had to train herself in order to be kind.

Abigail nods towards the baby strapped to Mairi's chest. "How is the little one?"

"An angel," she says. "Can't believe my luck. Even lets me out to work for the cause." She gives a faintly wry smile, running a hand over the baby's woollen bonnet. "Elias says Angus must know in his blood he's a supporter of the true king."

Her words pique Abigail's curiosity. Mairi and her husband have never hidden their Jacobite alliance, even back during the Glorious Revolution when they could have found themselves hanging for treason. Mairi's husband Elias had fought in the lost battle of Dunkeld and had returned to Lindisfarne a broken and unhappy man.

None of this has ever been a secret. But it has been some years since Abigail has heard either of the Mitchells speak so openly of the movement. With her limited knowledge of the situation, she had assumed it had died out several years ago. "The Jacobite movement," she begins carefully. "It's still active?"

"Of course," Mairi says simply. "The Jacobites are passionate men and women. They'd not give up so easily."

They exchange glances, and Abigail reads the unspoken words there: that Mairi knows exactly why their friendship has never grown deeper; that she knows exactly what Samuel Blake had thought of her and her husband.

Abigail imagines, suddenly, a different life; one in which Mairi has always been a far closer friend. A life in which she has never felt that faint hint of scrutiny from the villagers. A life in which Highfield House does not feel quite so isolating and haunted. She imagines Oliver being friends with the Mitchells' eldest son, Hugh, instead of trading insults with him when they cross paths. Imagines Mairi's daughter, Julia, halfway in age between Nathan and Eva, running the halls of the house. How much easier this grief, this sudden forced independence would be for her and her children if they had close friends to lean on.

"What do you do?" she asks Mairi curiously. "When you go out working for the cause?"

"Raising funds," Mairi says. "Calling on wealthy donors around the county. Encouraging them to open their pockets to support the cause. Funding weapons and training and the like." She wraps her arms around the baby. Gives a short laugh. "Elias volunteered me for the position. Says I've a knack for making people do as I please."

Abigail glances back over her shoulder at Eva, who is still fossicking through the snow on the edge of the path. "It must be quite something," she hears herself say, "to be a part of such a movement. To be a part of something bigger. Something beyond yourself."

Her own words surprise her. She had not been aware that such desires were floating around her own head. But they're an extension of her earlier thoughts, she sees now. The need for someone to lean on. The need to care for something bigger, wider, more all-encompassing than her cloistered life, drowning in the echoes of Highfield House.

Mairi's pale eyebrows quirk, and Abigail knows her comment has surprised her too. Mairi looks out towards the clog of clouds on the horizon. "It is something, aye. Certainly. To know you've done your part in putting the world to right. Spreading the word to others."

Abigail glances sideways at her. Was that meant as an invitation? An invitation to further questions, at the very least—if not to more? She doesn't speak, uncertain of how to reply.

The house is upon them now anyway, the pale morning sunlight washing the walls the colour of a stormy sky. Oliver is inspecting the hull of his father's rowboat, which is beached high up on the embankment by the low tide. A small pile of dead ivy sits in coils by the corner of the house, most of it still clinging to the walls. At least, Abigail supposes, her son is still on the island.

Eva breaks into a run to catch up with Abigail, her apron pockets now bulging with pebbles. She takes a fistful of her mother's skirts as she walks down the front path. Stares over her shoulder at her brother, but he doesn't look her way.

Mairi turns her gaze up to the house. "It's been an age since I've been out to this part of the island."

"Most people have little cause to do so." Abigail unlocks

the front door, letting Eva scurry inside with her apron clattering. "Thank you for walking with me," she tells Mairi. "I enjoyed the company."

"Of course." Mairi meets her eyes, and there's a depth in them that Abigail had not picked up earlier. "There's no need to isolate yourself out here," she says. "I hope you know you're not alone." She offers a tentative smile. "Perhaps we've been too long in letting our husbands speak for us."

CHAPTER SEVEN

Nathan is lying in bed, staring up at the darkness that has swallowed the ceiling. Something had woken him from a deep sleep, and now he can hear Oliver moving around inside his bedroom. The fire opposite Nathan's bed has almost burned out, leaving a faint orange glow in the grate. The rest of the house is quiet; just the creaks and groans of the place moving in the night.

Once upon a time, those noises had scared him. Made him think of fairy dogs and redcaps, and all the other terrible creatures from Mrs Calloway's stories. But Da had told him the noises were just the house growing and shrinking as the weather turned hotter and colder. Now, he's not afraid. He likes to think of it as the house breathing.

The floorboards outside his room creak. This is not the house breathing, Nathan knows. This is his brother. The door opens and a faint glimmer of lamplight enters his room.

"Let's play a game," Oliver says.

Nathan scrambles out of bed. "What game?"

"Quiet. You'll wake Mama."

"What game?" Voice softer this time.

"It's called the Viking Game." Oliver is standing in the middle of the room with one arm folded behind his back. Lamplight flickers over his face, turning his cheeks into shadows. "One of us will be a monk from the priory. And the other will be a Viking come to gut him like a pig."

Nathan hesitates. Can't quite determine whether what he's feeling is fear or exhilaration.

"You be the monk," says Oliver. "Go and hide, like they hid in the monastery when the Vikings were attacking. And I'll come looking for you."

Nathan chews his lip. "What happens if you find me?"

Oliver hesitates for a moment. "You have to tell me a secret."

"But you won't hurt me?"

"Of course I won't."

"All right," Nathan says.

"I'll count to twenty," Oliver tells him. "And then I'm coming to look for you." He shifts his hand from behind his back and Nathan sees a flicker of silver in the lamplight. His stomach tightens. "Why do you have the knife?"

"Because it's a Viking knife, obviously. And this is the Viking Game."

Nathan swallows heavily. He doesn't like that knife. But he's sure Oliver is not going to gut him like a pig. At least, he's fairly sure.

His brother turns away and starts counting quietly.

Nathan hurries down the stairs on silent feet. The ground floor of the house is almost completely black, with only faint threads of lamplight from the upstairs hallway straining down into its depths. Nathan reaches out into the darkness, trailing a hand down the wall to keep his bearings. He passes the hallway that leads towards the parlour and dining room. Takes the narrow passage leading to the old servants' quarters.

The blackness is like ink in this corridor, and it smells of dust and forgotten days and nights. The air is freezing, like it's been a hundred years or more since a fire was lit down here. Nathan can't remember a time when these rooms were lived in—as far as he can remember, Mrs Calloway and Miss Ruth have always left the house before night-time. To avoid having to walk back to the village in the dark, Mama had said. Maybe that's true. Maybe they're scared of the redcaps.

Nathan can't help but think of ghosts and goblins and redcaps as he pushes open the door of the first servant's room. Perhaps he'd be better hidden if he went all the way to the back of the passage, where the dark is thickest. But he really, really does not want to do that.

The door creaks as it opens, letting out a breath of air even more cold and stale than the air in the passageway. An icy draught circles his bare legs, his feet frozen against the flagstones. A thin crescent moon is shining in through the uncovered window, and in its fragile light, Nathan can see the outline of a single bed, a wardrobe pushed up against one wall. Considering his options, he creeps over to the wardrobe. Pulls open the door and steps inside.

The faint noises of the house are swallowed, and for long minutes, it's soundless inside the empty wardrobe. How many minutes? Five? Ten? Longer? Nathan isn't sure. He only knows it's freezing in here, and he would very much like to be back under the covers of his bed. But he also knows that

that is not an option. He has agreed to Oliver's game, and he must see it through the to end. That's just the way things are. Have always been.

Finally, there's a sound so faint Nathan is not sure if he's imagining it. Footsteps? Maybe. A line of lamplight shines through the gap at the bottom of the wardrobe door.

He holds his breath. As much as he'd like to go back to bed, he knows this is a good hiding place, and he doesn't want Oliver to find him yet. He wants him to have to search and search for him, and be forced to go down to that blackest part of the corridor. Wants him to think, *well that was a damn good hiding place.*

Footsteps come towards the wardrobe. Nathan sees his brother's eye at the keyhole.

"Found you, monk," Oliver says in a low, slow voice. "Come out and face your maker."

The door flies open, and before Nathan can make sense of what is happening, Oliver has a hold of his wrist and is tugging him forward, out of the wardrobe. He clatters to the floor, knees crashing against stone. Oliver rolls him onto his back and leaps on top of him, knees on either side of his chest. He presses a firm hand to the centre of Nathan's chest and holds the knife to his throat.

Nathan's heart is pounding in a jagged, uncomfortable rhythm, his skin prickling. His knees are throbbing, his breath coming short and strained. Every muscle in his body feels tense, and to his horror, he feels tears threaten behind his eyes. He forces them away. Holds his breath until his brother lifts the knife from his throat.

Nathan feels his body go limp.

Oliver stays looming over him. "Now tell me a secret."

Nathan stares up at his brother's lamplit face. Behind him, blackness swallows the house. He forces his voice to come out steady. "I saw Miss Ruth eating some of our sweetmeats."

Oliver makes a noise in his throat that suggests he's not all that impressed with that secret. "I've got a better secret than that."

"What is it?" Nathan knows the rules to this game: he has to find his brother's hiding place before he gets to hear the secret. But he also knows there is no way Oliver is going to hand over the knife and pretend to be a monk about to be slaughtered. And he can tell from his brother's boasting that, whatever this secret is, he really wants to share it. "Tell me," Nathan pushes. "I found a good hiding place, didn't I? So you should tell me the secret."

Oliver tilts his head for a moment, considering. "All right," he says finally. He clambers to his feet, letting Nathan scramble into sitting. "The captain of the ship was at our house. With some of his crewmen. He was talking to Mama. Sitting in Da's armchair."

"Really? When?"

"Two nights ago."

Nathan is hideously disappointed that he had slept through this. Men from the ship were at the house? What were they talking with Mama about? Did they tell her stories about faraway places and cannon fire? He wants desperately to ask her—secret or no. But he doesn't like the thought of the captain being in Da's armchair. Doesn't like it at all.

"Let's play again," says Oliver.

"I don't want to." The thrill of the game—if that's what it ever was—has been thoroughly washed away by this news. Nathan doesn't care about the Viking Game anymore. All he can think about is the men from the ship. And Da's armchair, with the loose threads on the embroidery and the seat that smells of pipe smoke, positioned just right so you can see out the window and look at the stars.

Besides, he hated the feel of that knife at his throat. Hated the feel of being pinned to the floor, with the air being squeezed from his lungs. His skin feels hot and prickly, and something is crawling inside his belly.

"*I* want to play again," says Oliver. "Go and hide."

"No. I want to go to bed." Nathan dares to look squarely at his brother, and his firmness seems to catch Oliver off guard. Nathan even manages to surprise himself—he knows he is breaking the rules. The game ends when Oliver says so. But he stares his brother down, their eyes meeting, Nathan's heart ratcheting against his chest. Finally Oliver takes the lamp and disappears deeper into the house, leaving Nathan sitting alone in the ocean of dark.

CHAPTER EIGHT

Edinburgh is grey and noisy and crammed with bodies, a stench rising from Nor Loch that makes Ward think of dying things. Shadows of the high-rises in the Royal Mile hang heavy over clamouring streets. Hooves and voices and clattering wheels.

Ward shoulders his way through a throng of people towards McGowan's home behind Lawnmarket. Chimney smoke and breath meeting cold air bathes the city in an eternal cloud.

Ward has not been up here in years. Can't make sense of why McGowan feels the need to plant himself in such a humming and overcrowded blot on the map. Auld Reekie seems to have only gotten madder since William took the throne. He's glad when he wrangles his way through the Earl's front gates and escapes the madness of the street.

McGowan's butler leads him into an elaborate chaos of a parlour, white walls trimmed in gold, and every piece of furniture, from the tea table to the liquor cabinet, festooned with carvings of cherubs and scrolls and delicate chains of flowers.

"Good God, man," Ward blurts, when the Earl comes striding into the room. "What fresh hell is this place?"

McGowan laughs. "Your displeasure breaks my heart." He goes to the liquor cabinet and tugs on a cherubic hand to open the glossy wooden door. "I knew it wouldn't take you long to be on my doorstep, Henry." He gestures towards a plush red-velvet armchair. "Sit down. I've a fine malt whisky that's been awaiting your arrival."

Ward smiles. "With luck it'll make me forget the hideousness of your parlour."

The Earl chuckles. He fills two glasses and hands one to his guest. "*Slàinte mhath*," he says. "To your health."

Ward raises his glass in thanks.

McGowan sinks into the chair opposite his guest, crossing one leg over the other. He's dressed in a royal blue justacorps with gold trimming, large buckles on his breeches and shoes. Long dark wig tied with a black bow. He looks as overdone as his parlour. "How has your journey north been?" he asks. "Did you make the cargo sales as planned?"

Ward chuckles, sipping at the whisky. "Let's not bother with small talk."

"I'd take that personally if I didn't know you better." McGowan goes to the writing desk in the corner of the room and picks up a copy of the *Edinburgh Gazette*. "Heard the news from London?"

Ward takes the paper, the headline catching him by surprise.

The much-lamented death of our late gracious sovereign Queen Mary...

He blows out a breath. "Seems news is slow to reach Lindisfarne." At once, his mind is racing, grappling at what the death of the queen will mean for the war effort. He knows there's every chance the Jacobite movement might see Mary's death as cause for a new rising. "How long have you known of this?" he asks McGowan. "Is it why you sent for me?"

"No. The news only reached us yesterday. But it makes what I'm about to tell you even more pressing."

Ward sets the paper on the tea table. "Talk of a new Jacobite plot?"

"Indeed. Led by one of Parker's men, who fought at the Boyne a few years back."

Ward taps his fingers against his glass. This plot must have been simmering in the background long before the queen had fallen ill. He nods for McGowan to continue.

"He's raising forces around London with a plan to kidnap King William and take him to France."

Ward leans back in his chair, absorbing the information. "'Kidnap.' I assume that to mean 'assassinate'."

McGowan smiles crookedly. "That I can neither confirm nor deny. But I imagine you do not need me to." He brings his glass to his lips. "I'm sure I need not tell you that if the plot succeeds, especially while the nation is in mourning, the monarchy and the government will be out for blood. Mainland France will likely see action again."

Ward nods slowly. "How trustworthy are your sources?"

"I'd not share anything with you I did not believe was entirely accurate."

A broadside of shouting floats in from the street. "How do you know all this information about Lord Haver?" Ward asks. "Did he tell you directly?"

"Not quite. But news finds its way across the family tree."

Ward sips his whisky, enjoying its rich smokiness. "That letter you wrote me about Haver, you know it's damn valuable, don't you. That information gets out and the Whig party would be in disarray. They'd pay a handsome sum to make sure that didn't happen. As would your cousin."

"Aye," says the Earl. "I know it's valuable. That's why I told you to burn it once you'd read the damn thing."

"Surely you know me better than that."

The Scotsman sighs, but there's light in his eyes. "Aye, I do. For all your talk of honour and decency, I know you're not above a little blackmail."

Ward grins. "Only if the circumstances call for it."

***

Abigail pulls a jar of ink from the desk drawer and uncorks it, hoping the morning sunlight will bring her some resoluteness. Just write this cursed letter, she thinks. Get the damn thing over with. She will tell her mother honestly and succinctly of Samuel's sudden illness and passing; will assure her she and the children are well taken care of by his settlement—a settlement supplemented by the income from the tenants of his house in London. Hopefully that knowledge will convince Susanna not to climb into a carriage and come hurtling up here to Northumberland on some ill-advised rescue mission. Dealing with her mother right now is the last thing Abigail needs.

She starts to write. But somehow, the words that spill from her quill are not to her mother. They are to the privateering captain she had found prowling across the dunes last week. The privateering captain she had welcomed into her home. Well, perhaps *welcomed* is not the right word for what she had done. But he had ended up in her home nonetheless.

She does not think as she writes; just lets the words spill from her quill as though they have their own being. They're trite, meaningless words she scribbles down on the page: long, badly formed sentences about the warblers outside her window, and the recent heavy snowfalls, and the roses she managed, against all odds, to grow in the windswept coastal soil of Emmanuel Head. And then, not so trite and meaningless: Samuel's death and the cloud of grief she has been submerged under for the past month. The fragrant smoke of the fuming pots that had filled Highfield House, as she lived in fear of her children following their father, one by one, to the grave. Giving voice, she realises, to the chaos of thought and emotion that has been swirling around her head since her husband has been gone, with no place to put it. She cannot speak to the staff about such personal things as her fears for her children. Is fairly sure Mairi Mitchell has too busy a life to be bothered by birds outside the window.

When she gives a coherent thought to what she is doing, Abigail almost laughs at her foolishness. She tells herself writing to Henry Ward is just an excuse not to write to her mother. But there's something cathartic about putting these words down on the page. Henry Ward will never read them, of course. No one ever will. And that allows her a modicum of honesty that she rarely permits herself.

I fear what the villagers would think of me if they knew of these dreadful thoughts that come and go...

A knock at the door. Abigail drops the quill, splattering

ink over the page, glad for the interruption to this most foolish of exercises. She hears Ruth answer the door. Hears the soft bell-like voice of the visitor, too quiet to make out the words.

Abigail makes her way down the hallway, stopping outside Oliver's bedroom to peek through the keyhole. She is relieved to find him sitting on his bed, hunched over a book. When she can do so without her son catching onto it, she will go to the village and ask Mr Emmett for his help to close up the priest hole. Board up the tunnel that leads out onto the dunes.

Ruth ushers Mairi Mitchell into the foyer as Abigail makes her way downstairs. Mairi is bundled into her cloak and bonnet, her baby squirming in the crook of her arm. Her face is flushed with cold, making the freckles on her cheeks look more pronounced.

Mairi looks about the cavernous foyer of Highfield House, locking eyes briefly with one of Samuel's painted ancestors that looks down from upon the wall. Has Mairi ever been inside the place before? Abigail doubts it.

Mairi smiles at her as she approaches, waving aside the offer of tea. "I'll not stay long." She jiggles the baby gently. "It may be out of place of me to ask. But I wondered if perhaps you might wish to come with me tomorrow afternoon when I go visiting."

Abigail raises her eyebrows. Drops her voice. "When you go visiting? You mean, for the Jacobite cause?"

"Aye." Mairi looks suddenly regretful. "I'm sorry. It was foolish of me to ask. I shouldn't have—"

"Don't be sorry."

Mairi dares a tentative smile. "It's certainly not my intention to force you into anything you don't care to involve

65

yourself with. But if you wish to know what it's like to be a part of something bigger… Or if you just wish for some company…" She shakes her head. "It's mad of me to suggest such a thing, I'm sure. You've the children, and—"

"The children have their nurse." Abigail hesitates, surprised at the voice in the back of her mind that is nudging her to accept Mairi's invitation. That part of her that makes foolish choices seems to be making all her decisions of late.

But this does not have to be a foolish decision. Does not have to be something rooted in darkness and deceit. She is a recently widowed woman in desperate need of friendship. There is nothing dark about that. Heaven knows she could use a little more light in her life.

She takes Mairi's elbow and guides her back through the front door, out of earshot of the housekeeper. Cold wind swirls up off the sea, making Abigail shiver. "You're not putting yourself in danger are you?"

"The movement has been quiet for years. We've been lying low since that dreadful business at Glencoe. These days we can operate safely enough in the shadows."

"And the death of the queen?" asks Abigail tentatively. "Is that likely to change things?"

Mairi hesitates a moment. "I'll understand, of course, if you don't wish to be anywhere near such a thing," she says, gliding past the question. She gives Abigail a bright smile. "I shall leave you to think it over. If you wish to join me, I'll be leaving from the Pilgrims' Way at nine tomorrow morning."

CHAPTER NINE

The next morning, Abigail finds herself striding across the island towards the Pilgrims' Way. She traces the rugged scarps of the northern coast, watching the last of the water drain across the sand connecting Lindisfarne to the mainland. In the low tide, the land feels vast and open, the white sky endless.

Mairi smiles when she sees her. It's an almost conspiratorial look—or perhaps just made that way by the thump of Abigail's heart. In spite of her attempts to convince herself otherwise, she can't shake the thought that she is doing something incredibly foolish. Something that could see her imprisoned. Hanged. See her children growing up as orphans.

She's overreacting, of course. As Mairi said, the movement is quiet these days. There is little chance of being caught. And besides, she's not a Jacobite. Just a woman in need of something to fill the chasm left by her husband's death.

Better this way than with a house full of top-heavy

privateers.

A wagon is waiting at the edge of the path. Ordered and arranged by the Lindisfarne Jacobites? Abigail does not recognise the coachman.

She accepts his hand and climbs into the wagon, Mairi scrambling up behind her and setting the baby's basket on the floor at their feet.

"Will it just be the two of us?" Abigail asks. She is relieved when Mairi nods.

"For today, aye. There are not so many of us working for the cause these days. Only a few of us left on the island."

"Your husband and Donald Macauley?"

"Aye. And a few others."

"Do they know you brought me with you?" For not the first time, Abigail wonders at Mairi's reasons for inviting her along today. Is this an attempt to repopulate the Jacobite cause? Or just an invitation for a little company? An attempt by Mairi to reach out now Samuel is not standing between them.

"They don't know," Mairi admits, lowering her eyes. "I didn't see any reason to tell them."

It feels like a hollow statement. Abigail can tell it was not apathy that had caused Mairi not to say anything to her husband, but rather the knowledge that he would not approve of the situation. Between Samuel's rigid anti-Jacobite beliefs, and Oliver's disobedience, Elias Mitchell has had few good words to say about the Blakes.

"Why am I here?" she asks. "Because your cause needs more people? More support?"

Mairi looks out across the leathery sand of the Pilgrims' Way. A flotilla of gulls shoots skyward as they pass. "The cause does need more support," she admits. "But I…" She shakes her head as though to straighten her thoughts. "Elias was a shadow of himself when he returned from Dunkeld. He barely spoke, didn't sleep, turned to the drink. Barely gave a passing glance to the children. Really, he's not been the same man since." She tugs at a loose thread on her woollen gloves. "I know it's not the same as what you're going through. But I do understand what it's like to feel so lonely. And I thought, if I could take a little of that away for you…"

Abigail manages a faint smile of thanks. She blinks away the tears that threaten behind her eyes. When she trusts herself to speak, she asks, "Where are we going?"

"We'll go south today. Work our way down the coast near Bamburgh. There're wealthy families in the area that have supported us in the past. Some of them fought with Elias at Dunkeld. With luck they'll be willing to open their pockets again today. You needn't have any part of that if you don't wish to," she tells Abigail gently. "You're welcome to just keep me company. Heaven knows I could use a decent conversation."

Abigail returns her smile. "I know the feeling."

The wagon jolts as they leave the sand of the Pilgrims' Way and begin to rattle down the coastal road of the mainland. There is something steadying about the rhythmic clop of hooves, about the innate warmth that Mairi exudes, about the gentle sighs and gurgles of the baby in the basket. Abigail allows herself to sink back against the rough-hewn seats of the wagon. Allows her body to settle into the up-and-down rhythm of the journey.

The sea disappears as the road winds across snow-patched green farmland, the water re-appearing at the foot of

Bamburgh Castle. A dull knot lodges in Abigail's stomach as they approach the village. The last time she had made this journey, it had been to bury her husband.

Without any instruction from Mairi, the coachman continues through the village and rattles the wagon through the iron gates of a property set a few hundred yards back from the coastal road. A large stone manor stands ahead of them; a three-storey palace of glittering windows and polished marquetry that makes Highfield House seem like a windblown relic. Trees grow in neat rows behind the property, their branches skeletal and snow-flecked.

Mairi takes the coachman's hand and steps from the wagon. "Do you wish to wait behind?" she asks. "I'll not be too long."

And Abigail realises she has no desire to sit back and watch. She feels as though she has done that for the past decade, tucked away on Emmanuel Head, peering out at the rest of the world from the salt-stained walls of her tower. In Mairi Mitchell, she sees the tentative beginnings of a friendship. A raft out of her ocean of grief and loneliness. She has no intention of letting that slide away. She says, "I shall come with you."

CHAPTER TEN

Standing on the yardarms of the *Eagle* usually makes Finn feel as though he has climbed to the top of the sky. Makes it feel as though the ocean could go on forever, and as though there is so much of the world to see, he will never manage every piece of it.

Today, he feels none of that. Today, he can't shake the gnawing in his stomach.

He edges along the yardarm, the lines rough against his bare feet and a cold wind howling through his hair. Up here, with the deck laid out beneath him like a tapestry, each roll of the ship feels magnified.

This patch of sea is far too familiar.

Finn hadn't been entirely truthful when Captain Ward had asked him if he wanted to be taken back to Longstone. *No,* he'd said. *No, no, no.* But there's a part of him that longs for it.

Not that he could ever do it, of course. What would Da do if he ever saw him again? Give him the thrashing of a lifetime, probably, then lock him in the cottage so he'd never get out again.

Finn supposes he can't blame him. Because once the thrill of leaving Longstone, of starting this new life with Captain Ward, had worn off enough to become commonplace, guilt had taken root inside him.

His da had never been a worrier—that was his ma's thing. But he is sure that now, two years since Finn has been home, his da is sick with worry for him. Maybe he thinks he's dead.

Sometimes Finn tells himself he and Da are better off without each other. And perhaps there's some truth to that. After all, when it was just the two of them in that cottage, after his ma died, things had been near unbearable. He and Da had barely been able to go a day without one of them erupting at the other over something stupid. Arguments over what they'd eat for supper, over whose turn it was to restoke the firebasket, over the shoes left in the doorway to trip over. Like they took it in turns to blame each other for losing Ma, and the only way to deal with that grief was anger.

Finn reminds himself of the yelling and the anger, and the way the tiny cottage had felt so stifling, on the days he feels most guilty. The days when he most misses his father.

"You half asleep or something, lad?" His crewmate's shout yanks him out of his thoughts. He looks down the yardarm to see the watch leader glaring. Finn curls his body over the broad branch of the yard to fasten the gaskets around the newly furled sail. Tries to focus on the task at hand. Wasn't that the first thing Captain Ward had taught him about climbing aloft? Focus, focus, focus. All too easy to lose your footing and end up splattered across the foredeck like poor old Johnny Greentree had. Then again, according to

Captain Ward, poor old Johnny Greentree had also fallen from the bowsprit and drowned, taken a bullet for sloppy marksmanship, and been hanged for attempted mutiny. These days, Finn is fairly certain Johnny Greentree is just a figment of Captain Ward's imagination, made up to scare his cabin boy into acting right.

Finn knows he's thinking of Da right now because of where they're sailing. When they're out in the North Atlantic and he's scrubbing pots and carrying powder and running messages between the officers, he never thinks of Longstone and the firebasket. Or hardly ever, anyway. He wishes they were out in the North Atlantic now.

But no, they are crawling down the English coast from Scotland, and Holy Island is an ink blot on the horizon.

Finn wonders if they're headed for the big house on the head again. He knows the captain and the officers spent the night there last week. Finn is insanely jealous. He's wanted to set foot inside that house for as long as he can remember.

Captain Ward had seemed surprised when he'd first seen the house on the headland, the day they had come in to Lindisfarne to sell the cargo. Like he'd not expected to find anyone living out there in a place so lashed by sea.

Finn was not surprised. He doesn't remember when he first saw that house, but he remembers asking his da to take him out to see it, again and again. Sometimes Da would grumble and complain he was too tired, or too busy, or that asking to go and see someone else's house was a brainless thing to do. But most of the time, he would take him in the sloop, across the water from the Farnes to that wild top corner of Holy Island where some well-to-do family had made their home.

The Big House, they used to call it. *Da, will you take me to look at the Big House?* Those were the days before he and Da would throttle each other if one looked at the other the wrong way.

When they were back in the cottage on Longstone, Finn would sit around the table with his parents and think about who might live in the Big House with all the chimneys and windows and plants growing over the walls like a runaway forest. *Maybe it's a king and queen*, said his ma. *A pirate that found treasure*, said Finn. Da would just snort and shovel stew into his mouth. He never liked guessing games, or make-believe. Said there was no point to it. *Why pretend the world is anything other than it is?* he would say.

Finn had always found that hard to accept. Maybe because his ma's imagination was so colourful and alive. Back when he was a little child, she would sit on the edge of his bed and tell him stories from the Highlands where she had grown up. Tales of giants and fairies and ghostly pipers, all lit up by the flickering light of the firebasket. She had made life in that little cottage a magical thing—the howling of the wind was the mournful cry of water kelpies, the flitting of seals in the shallows a glimpse of a selkie.

Maybe it was because of all that that Finn didn't want to accept the way Da saw the world. Or maybe because he didn't want to accept that there was only one way to life, one way that things could ever be. That felt far too limiting. Felt like a trap.

Even before Captain Ward had found him that day in Beadle Bay, some part of Finn had always known his life would not be confined to Longstone like his father's was. He had always known he would push and pull, and scrap and fight until the world was something more.

Really, if he thinks about it—and these days, he tries hard not to—he knows it was this that had been at the centre of most of his arguments with his da. Finn had wanted more for his life. Da had believed their sole purpose was to keep the firebasket burning. Stop others from losing their lives in the Farne Islands, the way his brothers had.

Holy Island is so close now, he can see the jagged silhouette of the castle. Beyond it, the dark shapes of the Farnes are dotted on the horizon. If the ship got just a little closer, he would be able to make out the shape of the firebasket from up here. The cottage where Da will be filling his barrow with coal and peat and rattling it over the rocks towards the beacon.

Finn reaches for the ratlines and steps onto the shrouds, doing his best to pull his eyes away.

Ward tells himself it makes sense to stop here at the house. He is travelling south, after all. Passing right by Holy Island.

Makes sense—no, that's not right. Not a part of this makes sense. But there's a pull to return to the house that he can almost manage to justify.

What is it that's drawing him here? Concern for her? Partially, yes. But he knows there's more to it. Much more. She intrigues him because she unbalances him, he realises. At the helm of his ship, he is confident; a natural leader. Around her, he is uncertain. Ward realises he likes the challenge of her.

And that, he reminds himself, is all Abigail Blake can be: an intellectual challenge. The woman is still in mourning clothes, after all. Whatever this restlessness inside him is that comes to life when he's around her, he cannot let it turn into anything at all.

He climbs from the longboat, boots crunching against the shingle on the embankment. A brief visit, he tells himself. For no other purpose than to ensure Abigail Blake and her children are safe and well. He has given the men instructions to prepare for a return to sea immediately—primarily to ensure he has no time to linger in Abigail's company.

He slows his pace as he approaches the house. Oliver Blake is standing in the garden, tearing trails of withered brown ivy from the wall. Behind him, fragile green stalks are straining through a snow-patched garden bed.

Oliver turns at the sound of Ward's footsteps. Watches him with that same shrewd and severe look he had given him in the village last week. The day he had handed over that forged letter from his mother.

Ward strides towards him, ready to scold him for his deception. Before he can speak, Oliver says, "You again." A thread of withered ivy dangles from his gloved hand.

Ward blinks.

"Did my mother invite you here?"

"That's no concern of yours."

Oliver tilts his head. "Are you a pirate?" he asks.

"No. A privateer. Do you know the difference?"

"Of course. Privateers operate legally to supplement the navy's strength. You operate with a letter of marque, signed by the king. You must give a percentage of your earnings back to the monarchy, to help fund the war effort. And you may only operate with a commission. Otherwise your actions are classified as piracy."

"Indeed." The response catches him off guard. Oliver Blake is intelligent and well spoken. It surprises him. Ward cannot imagine this boy paying too much attention during his schooling. An innate intelligence, perhaps. And if this is the case, it would be a great shame for him to be led down the wrong path.

"Do you operate in the Caribbean?" Oliver asks.

"On occasion. I prefer to remain in the Channel or Northern Atlantic. Intercept the French merchants on their way back to Europe. It's a far more lucrative business then venturing halfway across the world."

Oliver nods. "I should like to see the Caribbean," he says. "And many other places besides."

"You wish to be a sailor?"

"I wish to see the world. There's no life to be had here."

Ward chuckles. "That's a definitive statement from such a young man."

Oliver shrugs. "I know what I want."

And Ward believes him.

"All the other boys in the village are earning money already," says Oliver. "It's not fair that I'm forced to endure so many mindless lessons. There are far more exciting things I'd like to be doing."

"You ought to be grateful you come from a family that can afford to educate you. Most are not so lucky."

Oliver snorts. "My mother thinks I ought to be a physician or a lawyer. But I think that all sounds dreadfully dull."

Ward gives him a short smile. "My father wanted those things for me too."

Oliver's pale eyebrows rise. "Really? But you did not want such a life either? You wished to go to sea? Like I do?"

Ward smiles wryly. "I did not have the brains for such an undertaking. My father was most disappointed." Even after twenty years, speaking of it still stings. "He was a seaman himself. Wanted better for me. But he did not get it."

Oliver tilts his head, as though caught off guard by Ward's admission. Ward is caught off guard a little too—it's a thorn he rarely speaks of. But he has some sense—or at least, some hope—that this piece of his past might be of value to Oliver Blake. Might help nudge him in the right direction.

"But you're very successful now," Oliver says. "A privateering captain."

"Yes. I had a lot to prove." The last comment feels too indulgent, and Ward instantly regrets it. Oliver says:

"Will you take me to sea with you? As a part of your crew?"

Ward gives a short smile. "I already have a cabin boy."

Instead of the disappointment he was expecting, something lights behind Oliver's eyes. "So you do take crewmen my age."

Ward folds his arms. "What makes you think you have what it takes to be a member of my crew?"

"I'm smart. Brave. And I'll work hard."

"You are also sharp-tongued and rude. And you knowingly deceived both your mother and me by giving me that forged letter."

Oliver's lips part. His eyes drop downward for a fraction of a second before he looks back up at Ward with a fresh confidence. "Well. If I was on your ship, things would be different."

"Is that so?"

Before Oliver can answer, the front door of the house

groans open and Abigail steps off the doorstep. Surprise flickers across her face at the sight of him.

"I hope I'm not intruding, Mrs Blake," Ward says quickly. "I just wished to call on you before we made our journey south again."

Abigail holds his gaze for a moment. He can read the indecision in her face; almost as though she is trying to determine if she ought to be angry with him. Or her son. Or, perhaps, herself.

"Inside, Oliver," she says finally. "Leave Mr Ward alone."

"*Captain* Ward, Mama."

She doesn't respond, just stares him down, unflinching. Ward watches the boy hesitate, as though debating whether to obey his mother. Then he seems to remember Ward's own presence, and the request he had made about going to sea. He drops the piece of ivy and steps inside without another word.

Abigail watches him disappear into the house. Then she looks back at Ward. "What did he say to you?" she asks, toying edgily with the hem of her dark shawl. A loose strand of hair blows across her face.

Ward fights the urge to touch it. "He was sharing his knowledge about privateering and the war effort. We had quite an interesting conversation. You did not tell me your son wishes to have a life at sea."

Her dark eyebrows rise. "A life at sea?"

"He asked if I would take him in my crew."

Abigail blows out a breath. "My son is not going to sea," she says sharply. There's a cold rigidity to her today, as though she is doing her best not to let him in. As though she regrets the moments of openness she had given him the night he had come to the house.

Ward clears his throat. "I'll not inconvenience you. I just came to thank you again for your hospitality last week. I'm very grateful. As are Mr Graveney and the other men, I'm sure."

Abigail raises her eyebrows—no doubt she can see the flimsiness of his reasoning. Of this detour out to Emmanuel Head merely to thank her for something he has already thanked her for.

"Are you returning to sea?" she asks after a moment.

"Yes. We're to leave this evening."

"Please be careful." The soft-hearted words seem to come from nowhere.

Inexplicably, Ward feels something shift in his chest. Because it does not feel like a throwaway line. It feel as though Abigail Blake truly cares if he lives or dies.

He nods faintly. "I shall."

"Will you be returning to Northumberland?" Abigail asks.

"Yes, God willing. I have a deal in place with our buyer."

She gives him a faint smile. Her face lightens, and for a second, he sees behind her eyes. "Then perhaps we will see each other again."

CHAPTER ELEVEN

The second time she goes out visiting with Mairi Mitchell —
visiting because this is the only way she can put words to what
she is doing—they go straight for the village of Bamburgh.
February now, and the winter is deep and harsh, with a glacial
wind billowing off the ocean and black cloud palling the
town.

Abigail and Mairi stride through the empty streets, holding
tight to their bonnets as the wind tries to whip them off their
heads. Mairi keeps her cloak pulled tight around her body,
shielding her baby from the weather.

They rush past the narrow throat of Castle Wynd, where
Samuel had grown up. Past Saint Aidan's, where his grave
now lies. Abigail is glad to have cause to hurry.

She can just imagine the displeasure she'd see in Samuel's
eyes if he knew what she was doing—and who she was doing
it with. He had seen the Jacobites as criminals;
troublemaking rebels who sought to upturn the balance of
society.

A few hundred yards from the church, they reach a large stone manor house that opens out onto forested land. The seat of the wealthy Headingly family, Abigail remembers her husband telling her.

"Your husband was a Bamburgh native, wasn't he?" asks Mairi, as they hurry up the narrow stone stairs at the front of the property.

"He was." Abigail wonders if Mairi can see the vague unease behind her eyes; that thought that she might be recognised here. Certainly not in a house like this—Samuel's merchant business had never been successful enough for him to rub shoulders with men like Sir Headingly—but she does not know how far down the social ladder Mairi plans on going with her visits.

The baronet is welcoming, and clearly expecting Mairi. He and his wife herd the two of them into the parlour and ply them with tea and honey cake.

"Do sit down and rest a moment," Lady Headingly is saying. "Warm yourselves from that dreadful wind." She ushers them towards the fire roaring in the grate. "I'm sure you've a very busy day ahead of you. And with the little one in tow and all…"

"Indeed," her husband cuts in. "We're so pleased you could make it. I know there are still plenty of us out here willing to give to a meaningful cause." He goes to a shelf and swings down a narrow sword with a flourish. "Have I shown you this before, Mrs Mitchell? My father passed it on to me before he died. Dish-hilted rapier. Quite a fine piece of work. Father used it on several occasions as a duelling weapon but he carried it with him—"

The baby at Mairi's chest lets out a sudden wail. She

mouths an apology to Abigail and disappears out of the parlour. Sir Headingly barely breaks his stride. "He carried it with him while defending Blair Castle. He was far too old to be fighting by that point, of course—as was the sword, no doubt. But he was too passionate a man to be persuaded. He said if he could do his part to see James returned the throne, he would happily die for the cause. Didn't die for it mind you. Heart gave out a few months after he returned to England…"

"I see," Abigail says, at appropriate points in the conversation. And, "Yes, how interesting."

She feels exposed without Mairi's presence to hide behind, but if this couple have any idea that she is the widow of a Bamburgh native—with anti-Jacobite tendencies—they show no sign of it.

She's fascinated that all this might be going on beneath the surface. That all around the country, there might be whispered meetings and stories told, and coins changing hands in wait for the next opportunity for the Jacobites to rise. At least, she hopes coins will be changing hands here. Right now, she's beginning to lose faith that the baronet will ever stop talking.

"Sir Headingly," she says sweetly, when he pauses for breath. "What a wonderful story. I wonder if you might be willing to part with a little of your hard-earned fortune so the Jacobites might one day rise again?"

When Abigail finally emerges from the house, Mairi is walking slowly back and forth along the street, bouncing on her toes to soothe the bleating baby. A cloth pacifier dangles from her free hand. The wind has eased, but there is still a fierce chill in the air, and Abigail pulls her cloak around her tightly.

"I thought you'd never make it out of there," Mairi says with a smile. "Was about to send in a search party."

Abigail laughs. "I'm quite certain you gave Angus a poke to set him off on purpose." She passes Mairi the coin pouch the baronet had given her. It's a ridiculous sum—far more than she collects each month from the rent of Samuel's London townhouse. Almost makes the ordeal of the dish-hilted rapier worth it. "The man can certainly talk," she says. "But he also has deep pockets."

Mairi tucks the pouch into her pocket. "It's the only reason we put up with him." She plugs the knotted pacifier into the baby's mouth. "Must have heard about that damn sword at least six times by now."

Abigail smiles. "Have we other visits to make today?"

"We've three others expecting us, but my Angus seems determined to make things are hard as possible today," Mairi says, running a soft hand over the baby's head. She looks up at Abigail hopefully. "Do you think you might go to Lord Milgate? He's most welcoming. Generous too. And I'll call on the others."

"Of course. If I can handle Sir Headingly, I can handle anyone, surely."

Mairi laughs. She presses a gentle hand to Abigail's elbow. "Thank you. I'll meet you back at the wagon."

Abigail makes her way deeper into the village, following Mairi's instructions to the Milgates' home. It's an uplifting feeling, she realises, to be a part of this. The connection, the sense of involvement; they feel precious. Feel like things she has been craving for longer than she has been aware of. It's far too easy to ignore the danger at the edges.

The exchange is straightforward—Lord Milgate has clearly been expecting her; or rather, someone from the Jacobite movement. She tucks the coins deep into her pocket and begins to stride back towards the wagon, squinting in the pale winter sunlight that has broken suddenly through the clouds. She lifts her face skyward, enjoying the rare feeling of warmth on her cheeks.

A hand reaches out and snatches Abigail's wrist. She whirls around, heart jumping into her throat. In front of her stands a girl of no more than thirteen or fourteen. She holds a thin blade out in front of her.

Abigail feels a flush of rage clashing against her panic. She yanks out of the girl's grip. "What do you want?" she hisses.

"I want the money in your pocket, of course," says the girl. Dirty brown hair hangs loose down her back, falling over her face and obscuring one eye. A birth mark the shape of an apple darkens one cheek. "I thought that was obvious."

It's a bold move, Abigail thinks, for the girl to attack her out in the open street like this. But the girl is standing close, her body angled to hide the blade from any passers-by. She clearly knows what she is doing.

"I have no money," Abigail tries.

The girl's lips quirk, as though she can see the utter untruth of the statement. If she had seen her leaving Lord Milgate's house, Abigail realises, she would know well enough she is not a penniless pauper. And even if she hadn't, her velvet-lined cloak makes it clear she is no peasant.

The girl doesn't speak again; just raises the knife slightly. Enough to make her meaning clear.

In her head, Abigail plays out the events that might unfold. She could run, could call for help, but there is every chance the girl would catch her before she found anyone willing to assist. Every chance she might hurt her.

She could swing a fist; catch the girl by surprise. No. She will not be that person. Will not give in to the rage simmering beneath her sense of reason.

She could empty Lord Milgate's coins into the girl's hand. Admit to Mairi what happened.

This is the most sensible course of action, surely.

But something stops her.

If she returns to the wagon with empty pockets, will Mairi believe she has been robbed? Or will she think Abigail lying? Accuse her of taking the money for herself? It's a believable thing, she knows—the new widow, with three children and an enormous old house to wrangle into some kind of order. And in spite of the tentative friendship the two women have been able to cobble together these past few weeks, Abigail knows there is enough lingering distrust between their two families for Mairi to doubt her.

Abigail takes out her coin pouch, heavy with the sum Lord Milgate had handed over. She doesn't take her eyes off the girl's knife. "I shall give you half of what I have," she says. "And in return, I'll not tell the constable I saw at the harbour where you're hiding. Or what you look like."

The girl considers her. Abigail can almost see her thoughts turning over, trying to determine if she is telling the truth about having seen the constable.

"All right then," she decides. "Half. But you keep your mouth shut. You don't tell a single soul you saw me. And you come back here at the same time next month and give me the same amount again."

Abigail almost laughs at the girl's foolishness. Does she

truly imagine she might just come strolling back down the Wynd at the same time next month to empty her coin pouch into this child's hands? "Very well," she says evenly. "As you wish."

The girl reaches into her pocket and produces a grimy hessian bag. She opens it out in front of Abigail, nodding expectantly. Abigail pulls out half the coins from the pouch and tosses them into the bag. Rage flickers under her skin. And a hot pull of embarrassment. Never in her thirty-two years has she been robbed before. Has always considered herself too wise for that. And now, in her first months without her husband, here she is handing over a small fortune to a child barely older than her son.

She clenches her hands into fists, forcing her anger down. She has gotten away with only giving the girl a fraction of the money, at least. She has to consider that a victory. Not to mention the fact that she has come away from this unharmed.

That knowledge does nothing to slow the thud of her heart, or the anger blurring her vision. Teeth clenched, Abigail turns and begins to walk away. The thing is done now. Over and gone. Walk away.

"You're Oliver's ma, aren't you," the girl says suddenly.

Abigail's whirls back around, stomach diving. "How do you know my son's name?"

The corner of the girl's mouth turns up. "See you next month, Mrs Blake." She turns and disappears into the shadowy snarl of the Wynd before Abigail can question her again.

CHAPTER TWELVE

Mairi is waiting inside the wagon, Angus now fast asleep against her chest.

Abigail stops walking for a moment before Mairi sees her. Draws in a breath to steady herself. To remove any lingering anger and panic from her face.

She cannot say a word to Mairi about what just happened. She had promised the girl her silence. Half the coins in the pouch in exchange for keeping her mouth shut. And while there's a part of her that wants to believe one girl with a knife is nothing to be afraid of, Abigail knows she cannot take the risk. Because that one girl with the knife knows her name. Knows her son. And that means there is every chance she knows how to find her family.

Her and her sons and daughter, in their vast, fatherless house.

There is every chance the girl with the knife could appear on the doorstep of Highfield House, demanding payment, when Abigail does not return next month to give her the rest of the money she had promised.

And she will come back—Abigail sees that now. She will stand at the corner of the Wynd where the street narrows and darkens, and she will wait for the girl with the apple-shaped birthmark. She will drink noblemen's tea and eat honey cake, and put more of the Jacobite funds in this child's hands. How can she risk doing anything else?

Mairi's face breaks into a smile as Abigail climbs into the wagon. "How did you get on?"

Abigail reaches into her pocket and hands over the coin pouch, mumbling some garbled response she herself can barely make sense of.

She holds her breath, waiting for Mairi to question it. *Oh, Lord Milgate usually gives far more.* But she just tucks the money into her pocket and smiles. "Well done, Abigail. You've a knack for this. We're lucky to have you."

"I'd like to come with you again," Abigail blurts. "If you'll have me?"

"Of course."

"The same time next month?"

Mairi smiles. The wagon jolts forward and begins to rattle over the cobbles. "I'll look forward to it."

The reprieve feels all too fragile when Abigail is sitting around the dining table with the children that night, bowls of pottage steaming in the candlelight and sleet tapping against the glass. The fire roaring in the grate fails to reach the far corners of the dining room, and they are all bundled into padded house jackets, scarves and shawls at their throats.

Abigail's eyes dart constantly to Oliver. She knows she

needs to ask him about the girl with the knife. But of course, she cannot do so now; not with Eva and Nathan here.

This tree-trunk of a dining table feels so empty without Samuel's chair filled. As though he had taken up far more than just that one place at the head of the table. With just her and the children here, their small bodies dwarfed by the high-backed chairs, the dining room feels cavernous and hollow. The four of them sit at one end of the table; the boys side by side opposite Abigail, Eva sitting up on her knees beside her mother.

"What did you learn at school today, Nathan?" Abigail tries to keep her voice level. Tries to make it seem as though there is nothing untoward going on here. Never mind about the girl with the knife.

Nathan shrugs, dragging his spoon mindlessly through his pottage. "Some things."

"What things?"

"Please may I have more bread?" Eva cuts in before her brother can speak.

Oliver leans over and whispers something in Nathan's ear. Abigail's eyes dart between them as she cuts a slice of bread in half and places it on Eva's plate.

Nathan presses his lips together. Sinks lower into his chair.

"Are you all right, Nathan?" Abigail reaches out to cover his hand with hers.

He nods, eyes down. Slides his hand out from under hers and clenches his fingers around his spoon.

Something has passed between him and Oliver, Abigail is certain. She is also certain Nathan will not tell her what. He is fiercely loyal to his older brother, for reasons she cannot quite make out. She is certain Oliver has never done anything to deserve such devotion.

When she had returned to the house that afternoon, the boys had been up in Oliver's room. *Playing a game*, Mrs Calloway had said. Abigail regrets not digging deeper.

"You can tell Mama about our game, Nathan," Oliver says, shovelling a spoonful of pottage into his mouth. "We were just playing hide and seek. Weren't we."

"I can play hide and seek," Eva says brightly.

Oliver glances at her, as though he had forgotten she was there.

Nathan says, "Not hide and seek. The Viking Game."

Abigail feels a pull of unease. "What is the Viking Game?"

The boys eye each other. Neither respond.

Abigail tries, "Did you enjoy that game, Nathan?" Her thoughts go to the priest hole in Oliver's bedroom wall. To that ink-black passage that leads down into the walls of the house. She hopes with every inch of her that the boys have not been playing in there. For not the first time, she tells herself to have someone come and board the damn thing up.

"Nathan?" she presses, when he doesn't speak. "Did you enjoy playing with your brother today?"

"Yes." He doesn't look at her. Doesn't look at Oliver.

Abigail doesn't push the issue. She takes a sip of her wine; closes her eyes for a moment. Yes, she thinks, she can convince herself that Oliver was a caring older brother today, just as she can convince herself there is nothing untoward about the fact that he knows the girl with the knife. Right now, she needs to convince herself of these things. Cannot find the space for anything else.

After dinner, she takes Nathan and Eva upstairs to bed.

Her saving graces, she thinks, these two almost painfully innocent children. It would do her good to remember that from time to time. Remember that she has three children—not just one.

She goes out of her way to be doting. Sits on the edge of Eva's bed with her daughter's tiny fingers folded through her own. Tells her a half-remembered childhood story she mostly makes up as she goes along. Eva falls asleep quickly, her dark hair messy on the pillow, leaving her mother's voice sounding loud and lonely in the quiet room.

Abigail finds Nathan sitting up in bed, the star maps he and Samuel had always pored over spread out across his blankets. At the sight of her, he folds them carefully and slips them beneath his pillow.

Abigail blows out the lamp. She sits on the edge of his bed in the fresh darkness, the last glow of the fire giving the room a soft rusty light. She knows she needs to ask again. Nathan deserves more than her silence.

"What is the Viking Game?"

Nathan fiddles with the stitching on the hem of his blanket. "Just hide and seek. That's all."

Abigail hesitates. "Did Oliver show you the hole in the wall?" she asks carefully.

For long moments, Nathan doesn't speak. She can sense him deliberating about whether telling the truth will get his brother in trouble. Finally, he says, "Yes."

Abigail considers her next words. She suspects that Oliver will not have told Nathan about the hidden passage. The pieces of knowledge Oliver shares with his brother are for his benefit alone. And Abigail knows he will not share such a precious secret as a way to escape the house. "Did he do anything you did not want him to do?"

"No." This time there is no hesitation. The blankets sigh as Nathan rolls onto his side to face her. His blue eyes are dark and wide in the firelight. "Why is it there?" he asks. "The hole in the wall. Who put it there?"

"The people who built the house put it there, I imagine," she says. "Your great-great grandfather and the builders he worked with."

"Why?"

She hesitates, debating how much of the troubling history to share with him. "It's a priest hole. A hundred years ago, people were hunting down the Catholic priests because of their views on God. But there were people who wanted to save them too. They hid them in their houses. In priest holes like the one Oliver showed you." Abigail had known nothing about the threads of Catholicism in her husband's family. She wonders if Samuel had been aware of it. Wonders how many generations ago the papistry had died out. Wonders if anyone in his family had lost their life upon the gallows for it.

"A priest hole," Nathan says carefully.

"Yes." Abigail pauses. "You know you can tell me, don't you," she says finally, "if your brother does anything to you that you don't want him to do. Anything to hurt you." She puts a soft hand to Nathan's shoulder. Feels him flinch slightly beneath her touch.

When she emerges into the lamplit hallway, Oliver is waiting for her, leaning up against the wall. He holds her gaze, and for a strange, fleeting moment, she sees Samuel. It catches her by surprise. She's never seen more than a flicker of his father in him before.

"Something happened to you today," he says. "I can tell."

"Everything is fine." Abigail doesn't look at him as she strides down the hallway to the staircase. She's not surprised, really, that Oliver has picked up on her unease. Her encounter with the girl in the alley has left her with a restlessness beneath her skin that she has been unable to shake.

Oliver hurries after her. There's a faint look of hurt in his eyes that she might be refusing to answer him truthfully. Because this is not what they do, is it? An unspoken agreement. A truth for a truth.

But right now, she cannot honour that agreement. Because she does not want to face Oliver's truth. Does not want to know how the girl with the knife had known she was his mother.

She is adept at this; at pushing aside pieces of her son's life. She knows she cannot ignore it forever. But she will wait until they are next sitting face to face over his Latin texts, and the morning light has strengthened her enough to carry the truth upon her shoulders.

CHAPTER THIRTEEN

"Thank you so much for your support, Mr McBain," says Abigail, in a voice that does not sound like her own. "But as I'm sure you know, the Jacobite cause is reliant on the generosity of men like you to find its feet again. If you could spare a little more, we would be ever so grateful. As would the true king." She flashes him her warmest smile. Hopes he cannot see the unease behind her eyes. Or hear the lack of authenticity in her words. Can he tell she is here on account of her own safety, rather than any belief in the true king?

McBain, a round-shouldered old man with intense grey eyes, hesitates for a moment. Abigail doesn't blame him—he's already handed over enough to feed a small country. He digs back into his pouch and passes over another handful of coin. She thanks him profusely, promises him his money will be well spent, and flies out the door in case he changes his mind.

She strides into the village with her eyes down and her hood pulled up high. Her heart quickens as she approaches the end of the Wynd.

Before she had left the house, she had filled a pouch with her own coins, in case she had not succeeded in wrangling money from the donors today. Now such a thing seems foolish. What if the girl with the knife searches her? Takes more than the sum they had agreed upon? Abigail is fairly certain she cannot rely on her to keep her word.

Handing over the money intended for the Jacobites is bad enough. Handing over her own precious funds is unbearable. She is no penniless widow; Samuel had left her a decent settlement. Enough to give their sons and daughter a good home, a good education, a good life. She cannot risk losing the money intended for her children's future.

When Abigail rounds the corner, she finds the girl with the apple-shaped birthmark waiting. In spite of the sum she had handed over to her last month, the girl is still dressed in the same tattered brown skirts and kerchief, the same dirty coif pulled low on her head. "I'm glad you came," she says airily. "I didn't fancy traipsing all the way out to Lindisfarne to fetch the money you owed me."

"How do you know my son?" Abigail snaps. "How do you know where we live?"

The girl gives a warmthless smile, but doesn't respond.

Abigail realises suddenly that they are not alone. An older woman is watching them from outside a cottage a little further down the lane. She comes striding towards them. She is close to Abigail's age, with the same brown hair and storm-grey eyes as the girl—her mother, no doubt. The woman takes the money and shoves it into the pocket of her apron.

"Well done, Lizzie," she says to her daughter, though her eyes are fixed on Abigail. And then: "When will we be seeing you again, Mrs Blake? Same time next month?"

Abigail tightens her hands into fists. "Why are you targeting me?" she hisses. "Is it because of Oliver? Did he do something to you?"

Lizzie glances at her mother, and for a moment, neither of them speak. "You're a wealthy woman with a pocket full of coin," says the mother. "Why else would we be targeting you?"

It feels like a lie. Doesn't it? Then again, this is the simplest explanation. Perhaps she is looking for entanglements where there are none. Perhaps she has just been unlucky enough to be in the wrong place at the wrong time.

Abigail tells herself she will not stay powerless. But this is a game that needs to be played with care. She is afraid of how much these people might know about her family. Afraid of what they might do if she does not give them the money they are demanding.

And then, suddenly, frighteningly, it sparks inside her, that aggressiveness at her edges. Her body is suddenly hot and pulsing. She snatches the front of Lizzie's bodice, shoving her backwards. Presses her up against the stone wall of the nearest house. Lizzie cries out in shock, and it's seconds before her mother has magicked a knife from within her apron. She holds the tarnished blade to Abigail's throat.

"Let go of her."

Abigail's fingers shake as she tightens them around Lizzie's bodice. "How do you know my son?" she hisses. "How do you know where we live?" She feels the blade push harder against her neck. A fraction more and her blood will spill. She hears her heart ratcheting in her ears.

"Let go of her," Lizzie's mother says again.

Abigail swallows a gasp of pain as the knife digs harder into her skin. She releases her grip on the girl. Tries to find gratitude for the fact she is still breathing.

Abigail is in a daze as they rattle back onto Holy Island, the wheels of the wagon sighing over shimmering grey mudflats. She sits opposite Mairi, her black shawl bundled tight around her neck, hiding what she is sure is a red welt left by Lizzie's mother's knife. Her thoughts swing between telling Mairi about the thieves and keeping silent. She knows she has little choice but to turn up here next month and fill Lizzie's pockets again. It feels as though it will only be a matter of time before Mairi begins to ask questions.

Perhaps she is being foolish by thinking Mairi will doubt her if she tells her about the thieves. Perhaps Mairi has even had her own run-in with them while out raising funds for the Jacobites. And if she pulls down her shawl to reveal the angry red mark on her neck, surely this will go some way to proving she is telling the truth. Proving she has not taken the money for her own purposes.

But speaking of the thieves feels too dangerous. She had promised Lizzie her silence. She is afraid of what might happen if she opens her mouth, even in the privacy of the wagon.

Once again, Mairi had not questioned the limited amount Abigail had handed over, and yes, a part of her is grateful. A bigger part of her is thinking about how Lizzie might know Oliver.

It reminds her that there is so much she does not know about her son. So much he does not tell her. Such as his desire to make a life at sea.

Once upon a time, he had told her everything. An impossible stream of chatter had flowed from his lips, as he had narrated every inch of his day-to-day life to her: the seals he had seen off Saint Cuthbert's Island, the prayers he had learnt at the petty school, the way the he could hear mice in the roof when he lay very still at night. She cannot make sense of when that had changed. It had not been a sudden thing; of that she is certain. Just a secrecy that had seeped in almost without her being aware of it. These days, though there is honesty between them, it's a carefully cultivated thing, restricted to the confines of their lessons. Staged, almost. Honesty, but not openness.

Perhaps she cannot blame him. She had killed his dream of going to sea with a single sentence to Henry Ward.

She hates the idea, of course. Too many men who go to sea never return. But she cannot deny there is a part of her that knows it would be good for her son. The discipline. The hard work. The adventure. Perhaps a stint as Henry Ward's cabin boy would help turn him into a more decent young man.

She shakes the thought away. She cannot allow herself to think it, in case it grows legs and runs away. Oliver belongs here with her. She is the only one who understands him. The only one who can keep him safe.

She is distantly aware that Mairi is speaking to her.

Abigail blinks, trying to force her attention back to the conversation. "Pardon?"

"I said, do you need to get home immediately?"

She ought to get back, of course. She has left Oliver at home with only Ruth at the house. But more and more these days, her worry over her eldest son has more to do with what horrors he will inflict on his siblings, rather than what he will get up to on his own. Right now, Nathan is away at school, Eva in the safe hands of the children's nurse. And that gives Abigail the space to admit to what she would rather deny: that she needs a little space from her son right now.

Before she can really make sense of it, they are back in the village and she is being led into the Mitchells' cottage.

The door opens straight into the single room of Mairi's cluttered home. A large fireplace of blackened bricks takes up much of one wall, large cooking pots and kettles on the hearth, shelves cluttered with jars, and piles of utensils on the wall above the wooden table. The other end of the cottage is a sea of sleeping pallets, and the blanket-lined drawer being used as Angus's cradle.

Two red-headed children come barrelling towards them— Mairi's daughter, and her second son, his wild curls escaping out the top of a pudding cap. Mairi shepherds them away from the fire, smiling up at an older girl Abigail recognises as the daughter of one of the fishermen.

"Thank you for watching them, Molly," Mairi says. "I hope they were no trouble."

Molly smiles. "Same time next month then?"

Mairi walks her to the door, nodding over her shoulder at Abigail. "Sit down," she says. She closes the door behind Molly and bustles back toward the kitchen. "I'll fetch us something to drink."

Abigail sits. Mairi settles Angus into the cradle and swings the boy in the pudding cap onto her hip. She tosses a fresh log into the fire, ushering her daughter away from the grate. Takes a bottle of ale from the shelf and uncorks it with her thumb.

The door groans open. Elias Mitchell and his eldest son stride inside, Donald Macauley behind them. The three of them have wind-reddened cheeks and wild hair, the smell of the sea on their skin. Surprise flashes across the men's faces at the sight of Abigail at the table.

Elias gives her a curt nod. "Mrs Blake." He strides over to the fireplace. Murmurs to his wife in words Abigail cannot quite make out. She hears a sharp, hissed response from Mairi. She presses their son into Elias's arms.

Donald Macauley lowers himself into the chair opposite Abigail, folding his gnarled brown hands on the table in front of him. He inspects her openly, his dark bushy brows poking out from beneath his worn woollen fishing cap. Knowing his stare is intended to rattle her, she forces herself to hold his gaze.

In the twelve years she has been on Lindisfarne, she has had little to do with Donald Macauley and his family. An unspoken rule that the family from the house on the head did not associate with penniless farmers. Or known Jacobites. Samuel had always been nervous that, if the Jacobites found their feet again and he and Abigail were seen in the wrong circles, it could have dangerous consequences for their family.

"Strange seeing you here, Mrs Blake," Macauley says finally. "Didn't think we were good enough for the likes of you."

Mairi slams the ale bottle on the table, her green eyes flashing. "That's enough, Donald," she hisses. "What are you thinking being so damn rude to a guest of mine?"

Abigail stands, almost without the thought entering her head. Perhaps Samuel had been right to be concerned. What has she been doing involving herself with the Jacobite cause?

It was only ever going to lead to trouble.

"I'd best be getting back," she says. "The children…"

Mairi takes her wrist defiantly. "Just a moment now." Her words are not directed at Abigail, but at Donald Macauley's glare. "There's no need to leave, Abby. You're welcome here."

"I really think I…"

Mairi's grip on her wrist tightens. What is she playing at? Is she attempting to show the men that Samuel Blake's wife is trustworthy? That she will not turn them in, regardless of what her husband might have thought of their kind? Perhaps she is overthinking everything. Perhaps Mairi Mitchell just wants to feed her a cup of ale.

Mairi looks pointedly at her husband. "Tell Abigail she is welcome here." A barbed look passes between them.

A stiff smile appears on Elias's lips, but it doesn't reach his eyes. "Of course she is," he says thickly. "Please. Sit, Mrs Blake." He continues to glare at his wife.

Abigail feels pinned into a corner. Cannot tell if she is grateful or angry at Mairi.

She sits.

Mairi sets four tin cups on the table and fills them all from the ale bottle. Elias deposits his son on the floor and slides into a chair, stretching his long legs out in front of him. Abigail bundles her skirts tightly around her legs—an instinctive urge to make herself smaller.

Mairi sits opposite Elias, pinning him with fiery green eyes. "We had a productive afternoon in Bamburgh today," she says.

Abigail cannot help but feel as though she is caught in the middle of something between Mairi Mitchell and her husband. Cannot help but feel as though her presence here has been carefully cultivated. She knows Elias has always disliked her family. Is this an act of defiance on Mairi's part? Abigail can't help but fear what Elias might do to his wife once the visitors are gone.

She sees the looks pass between Elias and Donald Macauley. She knows there is nothing accidental about Mairi having dropped this piece of information into the conversation. Mairi wants the men to know that Abigail is involved in the Jacobite cause. Wants them to know she is trustworthy, perhaps?

Is she trustworthy? Even Abigail herself has no idea.

This is what she wanted, she reminds herself. To be a part of something bigger. To have her life expand beyond the walls of Highfield House. But as she brings her cup to her lips, she finds herself shrinking under the scrutiny of the two men. Can't finish her ale quick enough.

CHAPTER FOURTEEN

"You can wipe that sour look off your face now, lad," Ward says to Finn. "Lindisfarne is long behind us."

Finn is sitting at the table in the great cabin, his arithmetic text spread out in front of him and a scowl on his face like an infant who's tossed his rattle out of the cradle. "I don't like arithmetic, is all."

Ward snorts. "Rubbish. You've been out of sorts for weeks." He closes his logbook. Slides it back in his desk drawer and joins Finn at the table. "I know being in Northumberland has bothered you."

Finn keeps his eyes down. "Well, it's like you said, it's behind us now, aye?"

"Yes." If he's honest with himself, Ward has been out of sorts too, but more so for leaving the place. He can't help but think of her.

It's madness, he knows. He has learnt all too well that there is no place for a woman in the life he has made. At least not if he is to continue having the kind of success he is accustomed to. In any case, his crew had signed aboard his ship expecting action and good pay. Not to be languishing in some Northumbrian outpost while he attempts to pursue a woman still in her mourning clothes.

"What's it like?" Finn asks suddenly. "The house?"

Ward looks up, surprised at the question. "Old," he says. "But quite fine. If a little dark and gloomy."

Finn mumbles something into the pages of his book that Ward can't quite make out.

"Speak clearly, lad."

"I said, will we be going back? To Lindisfarne, I mean. To sell more cargo?"

Ward hesitates. Whatever the answer is, it's far too complicated to share with his eleven-year-old cabin boy. "Perhaps," he admits. "But things have changed of late. We need to be prepared to adapt our plans as necessary."

"Because of the queen's death."

"Indeed." Ward is grateful for an excuse to pull his thoughts away from the dangerous topic of Abigail Blake. "Why do you think the queen's death affects us so?"

Finn puts down his pencil, the bridge of his nose creasing in thought. "There's only one monarch now," he says. "Instead of two. Maybe the Jacobites will think the Williamite cause is weakened. They might act again. With their French allies."

Ward smiles. "Good." It's a thoughtful answer—brings him a swell of fatherly pride he is not sure he ought to be feeling. "We'll make a sea captain of you yet."

Finn looks up at him boldly. "If I was a sea captain, I'd have no need for arithmetic. I'd just make my navigator do all the calculations."

Ward lets out a short chuckle. Raps his knuckles against the pages of the arithmetic text. "Another chapter for your smart tongue."

***

Abigail sits on the stool in her dressing room, pulling a brush through the dark hair spilling over her shoulders.

Tonight she will ask him. Tonight she will seek answers. Whatever Oliver has got himself involved in, she needs to know.

Right now, she misses Samuel with an ache that feels almost unbearable. She wishes she did not have to carry this alone. But really, what would Samuel have done? He had had no control over their son. Had tried every approach, fluctuating between threats and beatings, to calm and logical explanations of why Oliver's actions were wrong, and heaping praise for the smallest of good deeds. Nothing seemed to make a difference. Far from the reverence a son was expected to give his father, Oliver had paid Samuel nothing but coldness and disrespect. Abigail is the only one who has ever had a thread of control over their son.

Still, Samuel was the only person she has ever been able to speak to openly about Oliver. And right now, she would give anything to share this burden with her husband.

Movement in the mirror catches her eye. She sees Nathan huddling behind the doorframe, peeking into her dressing room. She flashes him a smile, too grateful for the sudden company to be irritated that he is out of bed. "All right, my love? There's no need to hide."

He emerges from behind the doorframe and perches on

the edge of the chair in the corner of the room. He chews at the cuff of his nightgown, a habit he had left behind years ago.

Abigail puts down the brush and turns to face him. "All right?" she asks again. She slides off her stool and kneels in front of him so her eyes are level with his.

He nods, his thin fingers curling around the arm of the chair. Abigail covers his hand with her own. He pulls away sharply.

She frowns. "Did I hurt you?"

He looks away. "No."

A knot begins to tighten in her stomach. "Are you hurt?" she asks again. And then, with a growing sense of dread, "Did your brother do something to you?"

"No."

She had expected the response, of course. But she knows her younger son well enough to read beneath his words.

"Were you playing the Viking Game again?"

"No."

She puts her hands to his shoulders, preventing him from turning away from her. Feels him flinch, and then tense beneath the gentle curve of her hands. She pulls her hands away. "You don't want me to touch you?"

He squirms under her scrutiny.

"Are you angry with me?" she tries.

Nathan shakes his head, faint. Almost imperceptible.

Is it the loss of his father that has caused this behaviour, this need for distance? Perhaps. It's been four months since Samuel's death. Still, she knows how close Nathan was to his father. A delayed reaction, perhaps. Or perhaps something else.

Just a phase, she tells herself. But her words of self-reassurance do nothing to placate her.

Once she has returned Nathan to bed, she hunts through the house for Oliver. She finds him on the floor in the parlour, hunched over a pile of knucklebones.

"Get your books," she says. "We're to have a lesson." She blurts out the words on a burst of courage, before she changes her mind. She could attempt a normal conversation, of course. A simple conversation between mother and son that does not involve Latin lessons and thinly veiled manipulation.

But she knows she would not get the answers she wants. Needs. This unspoken arrangement of theirs, it must be honoured if she is to get to the truth.

Oliver looks at her intently, but it is not with surprise. "It's late," he says.

Abigail stares him down. "Get your books."

She waits in the parlour as he disappears upstairs. Tracks his footsteps up the staircase, down the hallway to his bedroom. She half expects him to disappear out of the house through the passage, but no, here he is, returning to the parlour with his French text in his arms.

Abigail clenches her teeth. Oliver is far better at French than she is—and he knows it. She knows there's no accident to his having chosen this subject tonight.

He sits cross-legged on the floor beside the tea table. Abigail sets him to work copying down a page of conjugations. Watches him intently as his quill scratches across the page. Every few seconds, his gaze flicks up to her, but neither of them speak.

Finally, Abigail says, "There's a girl in Bamburgh who knows you. A thief. Her name is Lizzie."

He looks up at her; a passive, even look that gives nothing away.

"Do you know her?" she asks.

"I know Lizzie."

"How?"

Oliver sets down his quill, carefully, so as not to drip ink on the page. "How do *you* know Lizzie?"

Abigail feels hot and unsteady. How can her eleven-year-old son always unbalance her like this? She leans forward, meeting his eyes. "No games," she says. "Not tonight. Just the truth."

"Just the truth."

She nods.

"I caught her trying to pick my pocket outside the church the day of Da's burial. I told her she was too sloppy. I told her the best way was to create a distraction, then adopt a little sleight of hand."

Abigail forces herself not to react. She knows this is what he wants. She ought to ask, of course; ask the question he has guided her towards: whether or not he too is a petty thief like Lizzie. She'll not give him the satisfaction. Not tonight, at least.

"She knew I was your mother. How?"

"She saw me with you in the churchyard," Oliver says airily. "You were talking to the vicar with Nathan and Eva. After I spoke with Lizzie about thieving techniques, she suggested we try it on you. I told her not to. I said you were my mother, and you had just buried Da." There's a look of expectancy in his eyes, as though he is waiting for her praise, her thanks for steering Lizzie away from her.

Abigail knows she ought to put an end to this, to make her son see right from wrong. Any decent mother would, surely. But Oliver needs a different approach. The only way to manage him, she knows, is to let him in. Make him feel willing to share.

"How do you know Lizzie?" he asks again.

Abigail hesitates.

"Mama. Just the truth, remember?"

Abigail fiddles with the silver ring on her finger. "She accosted me in Bamburgh one day last month. Tried to rob me of everything I was carrying. She agreed to take half, on the condition that I return the following month to give her the same sum."

Oliver snorts. "That was foolish. You ought to just have given her everything that first time. Then it would all be over and done."

Abigail forces down the rage-filled response that rises to her lips. Half this anger is at herself, she realises. Because she knows Oliver is right.

"You gave her Da's money?" He sounds indignant.

"No. Money that was meant for someone else. Something else."

Oliver tilts his head, taking her in. Suddenly, there's a look of concern in his eyes that seems utterly genuine. "Be careful," he says. "You can't tell anyone about Lizzie, Mama. She won't like it."

"She's just a petty thief. I'm not afraid of her." She cannot tell if this is a lie.

"You ought to be."

"Why?" Her anger flares, stoked by the look of smugness

that suddenly overtakes his concern. "Why should I be afraid of her? Is that what you want? For me to be frightened?" She lets out her breath. "You dreadful boy."

Oliver stays sitting cross-legged beside the tea table, not rising to her outburst. "I shall tell you why," he says, "if you calm yourself first."

Abigail closes her eyes. Clenches her teeth until pain shoots through her jaw. Oliver has always been the one most able to bring her spiteful side to the surface. Tonight, with fear at her edges, it is far too difficult to keep her anger and frustration inside. But anger will not get them anywhere. Tonight, she needs answers.

She sits back in the chair, clasping her hands tightly in her lap. "Forgive me," she says tautly. The back of her neck feels hot and prickly, the coarse wool of her robe irritating her forearms. "Why should I be afraid of Lizzie?" she asks stiffly.

Oliver twirls his quill between his fingers. "Because Lizzie... she's not the only one..."

"I know," Abigail says tautly. "Her mother—"

"No," says Oliver. "It's bigger than that." He hesitates. "They're part of a thieving ring."

Abigail swallows heavily. "A thieving ring?" She wishes very desperately that she and Oliver were in a situation that would allow him to lie to her.

"Aye. They operate out of Bamburgh and target the nearby areas. Lizzie says she and her ma have been a part of it as long as she can remember. She says there's maybe thirty or more people in it. They pool their takings and share it between them all. Her ma joined it after her da died at Killiecrankie."

"Killiecrankie? She's a Jacobite?"

"Not any more. Lizzie says they were all Jacobites once, all of them in the ring. But they turned against the cause after all it took from them."

Abigail's stomach rolls.

Why are you targeting me? she had asked Lizzie's mother. Does she have her answer? It seems too coincidental for Lizzie not to know she had been out raising funds for the Jacobites. But how could she know such a thing? Unless Mairi…

No. Abigail cuts off the thought before it can properly form. She will not let that deceitful, untrusting side of herself accuse Mairi Mitchell of delivering her into the hands of the thieves. In any case, the Mitchells are devoted to the Jacobite movement. Mairi is out raising money. It would not make sense for her to throw Abigail in the path of someone who is stealing from the cause. She curses herself for even allowing such a thought to enter her head.

"How do you know all this?" she asks Oliver.

"Lizzie told me. I think she was trying to impress me. Or frighten me. Or maybe she wanted me to join them because I know so much about pickpocketing. I don't know. Anyway, she told me everything." He leans back on his elbows. "Probably told me too much, really."

Abigail stares into the dancing light of the fire. She imagines the thieving ring growing in the years since those bloody battles at Dunkeld and Killiecrankie; since bodies littered the snow at Glencoe. Imagines widows and orphans and maimed men seeking a way to fight back against the life they had been handed.

She has no thought, of course, of how deep this runs. She only knows that by collecting coins from Jacobite supporters, she has made herself a target for the thieves.

What will happen now if she does not turn up next month with the money Lizzie had demanded? Thirty or more people involved, Oliver had said. Thirty or more people who would have little difficulty finding Highfield House if they chose to hunt her down.

And what choice does she have but to keep doing what she is doing?

Skim the top from the Jacobite funds, and no one need be any the wiser.

CHAPTER FIFTEEN

Henry Ward is pleased to be breathing Northumbrian air again. Never mind that this drumming rain feels far closer to midwinter than the late spring the calendar claims it to be.

Ward's pockets are heavy from the sale of a captured French brig, sold at auction in London. He'd lingered around the capital for several weeks on Lord Dunmore's advice, but the pull to head north had been too strong to ignore. He's not missed the grumblings of the men who had signed on for another voyage into the Atlantic.

"This is foolish," his boatswain, John Graveney had said to him outright. "You'll find a buyer in London. This crew signed on expecting action."

"It would take me just as long to find a new buyer as it would to sail back to Holy Island. Besides, I've a deal in place with our Lindisfarne buyer. I've no intention of letting him down."

Graveney did not argue the point, but Ward suspects the man is not fooled. John Graveney had come to the house that first night—Ward suspects he knows exactly why his captain is insisting on returning to Northumberland. There's a faint pull of embarrassment there, yes. Henry Ward has always been able to offer his crew far more than an uneventful jaunt up the coast of England. It's why he never has trouble filling his ship. He would hate for his crew to find out he is making this journey based largely on the mirage of a woman. He hopes his officers have the good sense to keep their mouths shut about Abigail and their visits to the house.

And the house is upon them now, rows of dark windows looking out towards a gunmetal sea. Through the eye of his spying glass, Ward sees rain rolling down the windows and spraying off the tiles of the roof. Trails of smoke rise from the chimneys and melt into the grey afternoon sky.

He feels an odd unease that has little to do with the weather. A thrill, perhaps. He has no idea what kind of reception he is going to get from Abigail. He is dimly aware that that is part of the allure.

When the ship is moored in the bay beyond Emmanuel Head, Ward releases the men not on anchor watch. In spite of the downpour, the crew make for the longboats and disappear around the point towards the village. Ward pulls on a thick broadcloth cloak and cocked hat before making his own way ashore. Over the embankment to the house.

He knocks on the door. Waits in impatient anticipation as footsteps click on the other side, rain pummelling the back of his neck.

The housekeeper looks faintly surprised to see someone braving the terrible weather.

"I'm here to see Mrs Blake," Ward tells her.

The young woman looks him up and down, a frown of

what looks like disapproval creasing her face.

Ward smiles inwardly to himself at his unease. After the life he has lived, there is certainly something humorous about feeling the scrutiny of Abigail Blake's housekeeper.

"She's just left for Bamburgh," calls a voice from behind him, before the woman can speak.

Ward whirls around to see Abigail's eldest son approaching from the direction of the outbuildings. He is wearing a dark cloak with the hood pulled up over his fair hair. He jogs up to the awnings of the house to shelter from the rain.

"Bamburgh," Ward repeats. He is dimly aware of the front door closing.

"Aye."

"Why would she go out in such dreadful weather?"

"She had pressing business," Oliver says. "Business that couldn't wait. Besides, it wasn't raining like this when she left."

"What kind of business?"

Oliver pauses for a moment, seemingly aware that Ward is hanging on his every word. "It's not my place to say."

Ward swallows down his annoyance. "Do you know when she will be back?"

"I don't know. But if I were you, I'd go over there and find her. She could be in trouble."

Ward frowns. "What do you mean? Why is she in trouble?"

"She's caught up in some unpleasant things. Thievery."

Ward's thoughts begin to race. He had not imagined Abigail to be a lawbreaker. Wonders what could have driven her to do such a thing. A meagre settlement from her late husband, perhaps. The pressure of three growing children and an aged and groaning house. Or perhaps he has just completely misread her. He hardly knows this woman, after all. "Are you telling the truth?" he asks Oliver.

"Of course."

Ward knows, from his few dealings with Oliver Blake, that the boy is not to be easily trusted. But he cannot shake the nagging worry. If Oliver is telling the truth and Abigail is in trouble, he can hardly stand by and do nothing. And if he is lying? Well, then, what harm will a detour to Bamburgh do? Better to be safe, surely.

Ward turns his gaze back out to sea, where the ship is just visible behind sheets of silver rain. Most of his crew has just absconded to the tavern. But he can sail the barque with a handful of men.

"I told her I ought to go with her," Oliver continues. "To keep her safe. She wouldn't hear of it."

It's blatant, the boy's attempt to paint himself in a good light. Make himself into a loyal and obedient cabin boy. Ward is not swayed—but it does make him suspect Oliver is telling the truth about his mother being in Bamburgh. About his mother being in trouble.

Rain drips off the brim of his hat and pelts into the mud of the garden. "Whereabouts in Bamburgh can I find her?"

"I don't know for sure," says Oliver, "but perhaps you might try the harbour first. She paid one of the Lindisfarne fishermen to take her over there. No doubt she'll be looking for someone to bring her home when she's done."

Ward nurses the *Eagle* over to Bamburgh with the anchor watch. Moors her in the shadow of the castle and takes a longboat to shore.

In spite of the rain, the harbour is bustling, with a small army of ketches and sloops riding the choppy surface of the inlet. Wind skims across the water, making lines clatter noisily. Bodies swathed in dark cloaks and hats dart between the anchorage and the village, horses spraying up water as they clop across the cobbles. Ward leans up against the wall of the Rose Tavern, trying to huddle beneath the meagre awnings. Through the steamy window, he can see a fire raging in the grate. He briefly considers going inside to warm himself.

No, it's too risky. He won't have a clear view of the street from inside. Does not want to miss Abigail if she passes.

As he waits, wrapping his damp cloak around his body in a meagre attempt at warmth, he asks himself why he is doing this. Returning to Northumberland, sailing out here to Bamburgh, had not felt like a choice. It had felt like a necessity. Abigail Blake has been at the back of his thoughts—and more often than not, at the front of them too—since he had met her that Hogmanay night. He has found himself replaying their conversations in his head, found himself picturing her face when he closes his eyes. Found himself sifting through her guarded words, her unreadable looks, to determine whether she sees him as a welcome addition to her life, or as a hindrance.

Perhaps he will get the answer to that if she sees him here today.

In many ways, he feels like a fool—not least because he knows he has not kept this infatuation entirely hidden from his crew. He'd never speak of it openly, of course. Not even to himself. Once and only once he had allowed himself to care for—love—a woman.

Amelia was the daughter of the navigator on Ward's final East India post. Ward had just secured a ship and commission, and was about to embark on his first privateering voyage. He had assumed that Amelia being the daughter of a seaman gave her an insight into what their life together would be; assumed she understood that he would spend much of each year on the water, loving her from afar.

But in the opening months of the war, she had asked him to choose. Her or a life as a privateer. Ward's one and only response had been anger. How could she pressure him into making such a choice? He had been trying to make a life as a privateer since the days of the Child's War. She knew all the details: long and tedious negotiations with ship-owners and potential sponsors, the challenge of filling his crew as a new and untried captain. Her ultimatum had been completely unexpected.

Ward had sailed into the Channel without dignifying her request with an answer. Had fully expected to find her waiting when he returned to London months later. Instead, it was a letter waiting, curt and succinct, notifying him of her marriage to another man.

The sight of Abigail jolts him out of his thoughts. She is walking briskly towards the anchorage with her hood pulled up and her cloak tight around her slender body. She looks up briefly to find her way and her eyes catch his, sending a frisson of energy through him.

She changes course to march towards him. "Are you here waiting for me?" Her voice is sharp and accusatory.

A hindrance, then.

"Yes." He dampens the urge to take her elbow and pull

her into the shelter of the tavern's awnings.

Her eyes dart. "How did you know I was here?"

"I went to the house. Your son told me where I could find you. He said you might be in trouble."

Something passes across her eyes—something he can't quite read. For a moment, he hesitates. Has he been misled by Oliver Blake once again? Is his coming out here the last thing Abigail wants?

"I see," she says finally. She looks at him for a fleeting moment, and that look is enough to convince Ward to keep persisting. There's something beneath her eyes, something faint, that—what? Wants help? Wants to be open with him? Wants to tell him what she has entangled herself in? He cannot quite tell. But it is *something*.

He hesitates, debating whether to ask her about the thievery her son had claimed she was a part of. Instead, he says, "My ship is in the inlet. Perhaps I might take you back to Lindisfarne? When you're ready, of course."

Her eyes dart again and her lips part, her response hovering unspoken. Ward realises he is holding his breath. Finally, she gives the faintest of nods. Allows him to lead her back towards the water.

Abigail wishes she wasn't quite so pleased to see him. Wishes this didn't feel quite so much like a dashing rescue.

She does not want to be the kind of woman who has to be rescued.

Nonetheless, the sight of Henry Ward waiting outside the tavern had loosened a scrap of the unease that had come from handing over the money to Lizzie today.

That morning, Mairi had sent a message to Highfield House with her eldest son, telling Abigail she would be unable to make the trip out to Bamburgh today as they had planned.

Without Mairi, Abigail had not dared call on the donors, in case word got back to Elias Mitchell and the other Lindisfarne Jacobites, and she had resorted to handing Lizzie a pouch full of her own coin.

The exchange has left her even more angry and bitter than usual, and she is glad for at least the illusion of protection against the thieving ring that Henry Ward might provide.

Not that she has any intention of letting him know that.

The last thing she can afford to do is let her guard down around him. Allow herself to rely on him. She must keep him at a distance—not least because it has been mere months since her husband's death. Never mind that he makes her heart quicken—surely that's nothing more than a thoughtless reaction to the prospect of having a man in her life again. Because if there's one thing Abigail knows for certain about Henry Ward, it's that he will not always be here. She will blink, and he will be back out in the Channel, fighting the French and the Jacobites, and there is every chance he will never return. She will not allow herself to grow close to anyone else, only to lose them again. Will not put herself in a position to have the ground shaken beneath her once more.

But for all that, he is here now, helping her into the longboat lying on the sand of Bamburgh beach. Shoving the boat into the water. Pulling on the oars and drawing them both out towards the ship.

Away from Lizzie. Away from her mother. Away from the thieving ring hiding in Bamburgh, intent on tearing down the

Jacobite movement from the shadows.

The oars sigh softly as Ward pulls them through the water. Abigail can feel his eyes on her. There's something oddly thrilling about being trapped beneath his gaze. She is not sure a man has ever looked at her this way before. And for all her feverish talk about not letting him beneath her skin, she knows he is already halfway there.

She is beginning to regret her decision to climb into this longboat. Because he is going to ask questions, surely, about what she has been doing in Bamburgh, and she can tell him none of it. Not a piece. She has not seen any evidence that Lizzie and her mother have an entire ring behind them— today, Lizzie had been waiting for her alone at the end of the Wynd, and the exchange had happened with barely a word. But it is not something Abigail wishes to test. She trusts what Oliver had told her about the ring. And she does not dare imagine what might happen if anyone from the thieving ring found out she had been speaking of them—especially to a privateer with a loaded pistol. How much had Oliver told Ward about what she was doing when they had spoken at the house earlier today?

Abigail shivers. The rain is beginning to ease, but water has soaked through to the velvet lining of her cloak and she feels waterlogged and frozen. A stilted silence hangs between her and Ward, and Abigail can tell he is waiting until they are aboard the ship before he asks his inevitable list of questions. Her mind struggles to cobble together a believable story.

She draws her eyes downward. His enormous presence seems to engulf her, unbalance her, tighten her lungs.

The longboat bumps into the hull of the ship, the vessel looking enormous above them. Ward hollers up to his men and two lines appear over the side of the ship. He hooks them to the bow and stern of the longboat. Abigail feels a strange sense of weightlessness as the boat is winched from the water.

Accepting Ward's outstretched hand, she steps carefully onto the deck. For a moment, her breath leaves her. For all her fascination with the sea, she has never set foot on a ship like this before. She is surprised by its solidity; surprised by how close the three masts seem to come to disappearing into the clouds. Surprised by how insignificant she feels standing beneath the broad branches of the yardarms. Out ahead of her, she sees the majestic wings of the eagle figurehead, hovering forever above the water. The ship is no monstrous galleon, but it feels powerful. Strong. And—naively, she knows—unbreakable.

Apart from the handful of men who had winched the longboat from the water, Abigail can see just one other man aboard. He is standing at the front of the ship with a spying glass in hand and an enormous tarred coat wrapped around his broad shoulders. He glances her way. Gives her a curt and curious nod. When was the last time a woman stepped aboard this ship, she wonders? Perhaps she is the first to do so.

Ward marches over to the man on watch and rattles out a murmured list of instructions. Then he leads Abigail through a narrow doorway into the saloon. Down a shallow staircase and through a long hallway with closed doors lining each side. Their footsteps echo, and a deep wooden groan comes from somewhere within the ship. Ward pulls a key from the pocket of his justacorps and unlocks the door at the end of the passage. Ushers Abigail inside.

The cabin is larger than she expected, with a wide bank of windows at the stern and a narrow bunk against one wall. A long wooden table takes up much of the centre of the room, the unlit lamp above swinging gently with the movement of the sea. A rolltop desk sits in one corner, quills and inkpots lined up in neat pots in the corner.

Ward locks the cabin door and turns, leaning his back against it, eyes meeting hers.

She wants to be angry. Angry at being led down here, at being entrapped in this cabin like an animal. But there's a thrill about being locked away with him like this. Her heart is thumping with something that is only fear at its edges.

"Are you safe?" asks Ward. And at this moment, there is nothing heated or predatory about his gaze. There is just concern. That look in itself manages to take away a fraction of the weight that has pressed down on her shoulders since her husband's death. It's a dangerously addictive feeling.

She nods. "I'm safe." She does not know if that's true. But right now, inexplicably, she feels safe. Feels, locked inside this cabin, that the rest of the world does not exist.

Ward takes a tinderbox from the drawer of the desk and lights the lantern above the table. A soft orange light lifts the gloom of the wet afternoon.

Abigail unhooks her waterlogged cloak and slides it off her shoulders. Though the air inside the cabin is stale and sea-soured, she is grateful for the warmth. Ward takes her cloak and hangs it over the back of his desk chair. He takes off his own, slinging it onto a hook beside the door. Passes her a cloth from beside the washbin.

"Here," he says. "Dry yourself. I'm afraid I cannot offer much in the way of a fire."

Abigail gives him a faint smile. "The worst enemy of a ship."

"Indeed."

She uses the cloth to dry her face and hands. She can smell him on the fabric—maleness and sea. She sets the damp cloth on the edge of the table. Nods her thanks.

Ward has removed his wet justacorps and stands before her in his shirtsleeves and waistcoat. He takes a step towards her and his hand closes daringly around her wrist. "Is there anything I can help with?" he asks. His eyes are probing, full of questions she can tell he is desperate to have answered.

"No," she says. "Thank you. There's nothing to concern yourself with. My son just tends to worry for me unnecessarily."

Ward raises his fair eyebrows, and she can tell he does not believe her.

She needs to give him something, she realises. A piece of the truth at least. After all, he has clearly come traipsing out here to save her. That should annoy her, but somehow it doesn't. And it's *that* which annoys her, she thinks dully.

"I…" she begins, then fades out, unsure of where to start. How much to share.

She realises suddenly that she wants to tell him everything. Wants to tell him about Lizzie, and her mother, and her father lost to the Jacobite cause. Wants to tell him about Oliver's warning that she has entangled herself in a thieving ring, with thirty or more souls who could appear on her doorstep if she tries to step away.

She knows it's dangerous to speak of such things. To risk anyone from the thieving ring turning out in retaliation. But somehow, it feels as though nothing she says or does in this cabin will ever find its way out into the light.

She slides onto the long bench at the table in the centre of the room. Curves her hands around her knees. Ward slides in beside her, close, his shoulder pressing softly against hers. She can smell rain and the ocean on his skin. Feels his knee brush against her fingers.

He nods faintly at her, encouraging her to speak.

"I've done something foolish," she says, trying to determine the best place to begin. "I'm not a Jacobite. I've never supported their cause, or even given more than a passing thought to who is sitting on the throne. But since my husband died, I've felt the need to be a part of something... more... Something bigger." The words feel too vulnerable, too foolish. They hang heavily in the stillness, punctuated by the groan of the ship as it begins to slide out of the harbour. "An acquaintance—a friend—of mine invited me to go with her to raise funds for the Jacobite cause." She catches a flicker of something in Henry Ward's eyes. Unease? She can't place it. "We've been calling on the homes of noblemen around the villages. Collecting money for the cause. But I've..." She draws in a breath, feeling herself creeping towards the edge of the precipice. "I've not been handing all the money I raise back to the Jacobites. I—"

"Abigail." Henry gets to his feet suddenly. He goes to his desk drawer, then stops abruptly. Looks back at her, indecision in his eyes. His fingers hover above the handle of the drawer. "There's a letter in here," he says finally. "I promised the man who wrote it that I would not show it to anyone." His eyes meet hers pointedly. "But if you were to find it yourself..." He fades out.

Abigail gets slowly to her feet, following Henry's gaze towards the desk drawer. Curiously, she pulls it open. There, at the top is a folded piece of paper. She can see a large crimson seal on the front, snapped open.

Henry nods at her. She takes the letter and sits back down beside him at the table. As she moves to open the page, his fingers come to rest lightly on her wrist. He says, "Nothing in this letter can leave this room."

Abigail nods faintly. She opens the page and reads slowly over the elaborate curls of handwriting. *A morsel of information to whet your appetite: Lord Haver, prominent Whig party politician, is harbouring Jacobite tendencies…*

Lord Haver's name is only vaguely familiar to her, but she can tell this accusation—connection with the Jacobites on account of being the illegitimate son of a Highlander—would be more than a little damaging to all concerned if it were to find the light of day.

The corner of Ward's lips turn up slightly. "Quite an accusation, wouldn't you say?"

She nods. "Is it true?"

"Lord Dunmore, who wrote the letter, is spying against the movement. He assures me the accusation against Haver is true. But that is far from the worst of it." His fingers tighten almost instinctively around her wrist. Unbidden, Abigail feels something flicker in her chest. "Lord Dunmore also tells me the London Jacobites have a plot underway that involves the kidnapping and possible assassination of King William. And if the plot to kill the king is successful, I'm sure I don't need to tell you that anyone involved in the Jacobite cause will be in great danger." He shifts on the bench to meet her eyes. "Whatever ties you have with the Jacobite movement, you must cut them immediately."

For long moments, Abigail says nothing. Does not allow herself to move, or barely, to breathe. She is intensely focused on the warmth, the weight of his hand against her own. Intensely focused on the drumbeat in her chest. Homing in on these things takes the focus away from this dangerous knowledge Henry Ward has just shared with her.

"This money," he continues, "that you have been pocketing from the Jacobite cause... Have you been doing such a thing out of financial necessity? Because of the pressures of being a new widow..." He hesitates, choosing his words carefully. "Perhaps my opinion is of little concern to you, but I just want you to know that I would not blame you for such a thing."

Abigail smiles inwardly to herself. She cannot be surprised at his jumping to conclusions, she supposes. Henry Ward seems like the type of man to prone to conclusions. Assumptions. The kind of man who believes himself always right.

A part of her longs to correct him. Tell him that Samuel Blake had been a better man than to leave his wife with no choice but to steal. But this untruth, it feels safer. Feels believable. Pitiable, even. Not that she wants pity. But sometimes it can be advantageous. Besides, she can only imagine the chaos she would unleash if she set a crew of privateers upon the Bamburgh thieving ring.

She doesn't speak. Does not confirm or deny. But the look in Henry's eyes makes it clear he has decided this is the truth. He squeezes her fingers. "Promise me you'll not involve yourself in the cause any further."

She wants to promise him this, of course. Wants to walk away from the thieving ring and the Jacobite cause, and never look back—especially now, with this new information about the assassination plot. Perhaps such a thing would cost her

her friendship with Mairi, and any chance of being accepted by the villagers—but she would rather spend every day and night haunting Highfield House than risk being locked up for treason. But how can she make such a promise? If she does not return to Bamburgh next month to hand over more Jacobite funds to Lizzie, there is every chance pieces of the thieving ring will turn up at her door.

"Abigail," Henry pushes. "Please. Promise me."

"Yes. I promise." The words fall out without further thought. And they are true, she realises. She will stay away from the Jacobite cause. She has seen what happens to people accused of Jacobite alliance. Imprisonment. Exile. Execution.

And somehow, she will find a way to extricate herself—and her son—from the Bamburgh thieving ring.

Somehow.

"Good," Ward says. Pauses. "And if you are in need of assistance… financially…" He pulls his eyes from hers awkwardly.

She cannot take the lie this far. She may have convinced herself she needs Henry Ward's pity. But she does not need his money. Samuel had made sure of that. "I shall manage," she assures him.

"Forgive my boldness," he says after a moment. "I should not have… It is not my place to speak of such things." He hesitates for a second, as though debating whether to speak further. Without saying more, he goes to the desk and pulls a bottle of dark amber liquid from a cupboard by the desk. He fills two glasses and sets one on the table in front of her. "Here. You look as though you could use this."

She smiles faintly. Takes a grateful sip of the whisky. It's rich and smoky; warms her throat as it glides down. With each mouthful, she feels the tension inside her unravel a little. Allows herself, just for now, not to think about the thieving ring and the way she is trapped in their net. Allows herself not to think of Oliver's friendship with Lizzie. The liquor in her blood unleashes a recklessness that feels almost painfully liberating.

Henry leans back against the desk as he brings his glass to his lips. She can feel him watching her. Through the bank of windows at the back of the cabin, she sees the sharp corners of Bamburgh Castle disappearing into the cloud.

"I'm sorry for my rudeness earlier," she says. "Today, and every other day before that."

A smile lights his face. "I enjoy the company of a woman who challenges me."

"Challenges you, or offends you?"

A chuckle. "I'm not that easily offended."

Abigail smiles. She gets to her feet and moves slowly towards the rain-streaked windows, allowing her body to adjust to the rhythmic up-and-down motion of the sea. She runs her finger over the delicately carved scrolls adorning the window frames.

"It's a beautiful ship," she says. "Is she yours?"

"Yes. I took her as a prize two years ago and kept her as my own. She was once a French merchant. *La Sainte Marie.*"

"Were you not afraid that changing her name would curse you?"

Henry's lips part. Abigail can tell her knowledge of such a thing has surprised him. She sips her whisky self-consciously.

"I had quite an interest in seafaring when I was younger," she admits. "Sailors' superstitions have always fascinated me."

"Just when you were younger?"

"Yes, well." She looks down. "It is not the kind of interest a husband wants in a wife. Not that my husband ever knew of my interest. Perhaps I am being too harsh on him. Perhaps he would have indulged me."

Henry moves towards her, his boots clicking softly against the floorboards. "How long has your husband been gone?" he asks. His voice comes out husky.

"Samuel passed a few weeks before Christmas," she tells him. "Smallpox. It was very sudden. An immense shock."

"You must miss him terribly."

"Of course." She can't look at him. Feels the skin on the back of her neck flush with guilt. Being so close to Henry Ward's sleeping quarters feels almost painfully intimate. Speaking of her husband here feels like a sin.

"And you?" she asks. "A wife? Children?"

"No. I've never felt the need for such a life."

It does not quite feel like the truth. But Abigail does not pry. It feels safest this way.

She picks up Lord Dunmore's letter from the table and reads over it again. She looks at Henry with a crooked smile on her lips. "I see you've not followed his instructions to burn the page after reading."

He chuckles. "That's because I'm not a fool."

"Does anyone else know about this information?" she asks. "Besides you and the man who wrote it?" She smiles crookedly. "And Lord Haver?"

"Hopefully not. The less people who know, the more valuable the letter. The more Haver and the Whigs will pay to keep the information secret."

"My mother likes to say that nothing stays a secret

5

forever," Abigail says. "'Come midnight, all truths will be revealed,' she used to say." The lies she has just let Henry Ward believe prod at her. "I always thought that sounded terribly dire." Those words had always been a thinly veiled threat on Susanna's part; an attempt at scaring her daughter into honesty. Not that they'd done much good, Abigail thinks wryly. Midnight has long passed, and there any many truths her mother is yet to learn.

Henry smiles. "I suspect Lord Haver is doing all he can to prove your mother wrong."

"This letter must be worth a great deal," Abigail says.

Henry nods. "The information on its own is very valuable. But the letter, with Dunmore's seal, makes it even more so. Gives it legitimacy."

"Then surely it's not safe for you to be carrying it on your ship into conflict."

"Probably not, no."

"Have you no safer place to keep it? A home in London?" She smiles. "That does not float?"

He chuckles. "I've little need for a home that does not float at present. The war is keeping me far too busy."

"Then I can keep it safe for you. At the house." The moment the words are out, Abigail can't believe she has spoken them. This is too forward, surely.

Henry doesn't answer immediately. He meets her gaze. Holds it without speaking.

"I would like to make of copy of its contents first," he says. "Ensure I've a written record of the thing. But thank you. I think that would be a wise thing to do. I shall bring it to you later tonight."

CHAPTER SIXTEEN

The knock at the door comes far earlier than she expected. Evening sunlight is still spilling through the high windows of the dining room, and Abigail is sitting at the table with her children, dishes of bread and stew in front of them.

As the sound of doorknocker crashes through the house, Abigail throws down her spoon and leaps to her feet. Eva stares up at her in wide-eyed alarm.

"Stay here," Abigail tells the children. She hurries off to answer the door before any of them ask questions.

She is nervous tonight; inexplicably so. Why should she be nervous? This is not the first time she has had Henry Ward and his men in her home. She trusts—for better or for worse—that they will not do harm to her or her children.

It's not about trust, of course. It's about the undeniable attraction she had felt for Henry on his ship today. An attraction that had managed to blot out the fear and strain of the thieving ring—at least for a few hours. Those few hours have been enough for her crave the feeling.

She cannot let herself act on these thoughts, of course. Not so soon after Samuel's passing. Besides, tomorrow, Henry Ward will be gone; back out into the Atlantic to put himself in the line of cannon fire, and there is every chance he will never return.

Abigail pulls open the door. Silences the part of herself that is glad to see Henry alone.

She glances down at the small brass box in his hand. "What is in there?" she asks, voice low. She knows Oliver will be listening, trying to catch pieces of their conversation.

"The letter."

She raises her eyebrows. "You thought to lock it up?"

"It's very valuable. I would hate for it to fall into the wrong hands."

"Are you sure you trust me with it?"

"Of course."

He passes it to her, their eyes meeting. The box is small and plain; the size of her palm, fastened with a delicate lock that's tarnished at the edges. "Do you have somewhere safe you can keep it?" he asks.

"Yes. My nightstand. It will be safe there."

He nods. Smiles. "Thank you."

"Good evening, Captain Ward," says a voice from behind her.

Abigail whirls around. Oliver has appeared in the entrance hall, Nathan and Eva peeking out from behind him.

Henry looks taken aback for a moment, then his face shifts into an uneasy smile. "Good evening, children."

Abigail tries to hide the box in the folds of her skirts. She flashes hard eyes at her children. "Back to your dinner at once."

They hover in the entrance hall for a moment, Oliver opening his mouth to speak, and then seeming to decide against it. Abigail keeps her eyes pinned to them until they have all disappeared back into the dining room.

Her thoughts knock together. Eva and Nathan will have questions, surely, about this man who has appeared on their doorstep. She has no thought of how much—if anything—Oliver has told them about who Henry Ward is. Will it be less damaging if she brings him inside to introduce them properly? Or should she let him disappear, and hope the children's curiosity vanishes with the morning?

In the end, it's not her children's curiosity that makes the decision for her. It's that treacherous part of herself that does not want Henry Ward to sail back into the Channel without a little more time spent in her company.

"Will you come in?" she asks, before the rational part of her brain can catch up with her. "I'm sure the children would like to meet you properly."

A look of uncertainty passes across his eyes. "Of course," he says finally. "I would very much like to meet them too." He sounds faintly terrified at the prospect.

She leads him down the passage and into the dining room. The children are silent in their seats, watching with wide-eyed expectancy, their spoons lying abandoned on the table and their stew growing cold.

Abigail gestures to Henry to sit, careful to guide him away from the chair at the head of the table—the chair left empty by Samuel's death. He beside her, opposite Oliver. Gives another gawpish nod to Nathan and Eva.

He is uncomfortable around children, Abigail notes. Awkward. Even if he had not shared as much with her already, she would have been able to tell, by the rigidity he shows around her youngest two, that Henry Ward is not a father. He seems to have managed Oliver well enough in their few interactions she has observed. But he seems more than a little unmoored by Eva and Nathan's open-mouthed stares.

Abigail takes a glass from the cabinet and fills it from the wine bottle in the centre of the table. She sets it in front of Henry and slides back into her chair beside him. Manages stifled introductions. My youngest son, Nathan. My daughter, Eva. And of course, you know Oliver.

She swallows heavily. "Say good evening to Captain Ward, children."

It's a dreadful thing to do, of course, to have this man sit down at the dinner table with her children, mere months after their father's death. She wonders if they are still too young to judge her.

Nathan mumbles a greeting, but his eyes are drawn quickly back to his plate. Eva is kneeling up in her chair, small hands curled around the edge of the table.

"Good evening," she says, her seriousness belied by the smear of stew on the side of her mouth. She inspects Ward with critical eyes. "Who are you and why are you in our house?"

Abigail hides a smile at the bug-eyed horror her three-year-old daughter manages to elicit from this privateering captain. "That's not polite, Evie," she says, fighting the urge to watch Henry try and wrangle out a response. She turns to him, mouthing an apology.

"Are you here on business, Captain Ward?" asks Oliver. "I didn't imagine there'd be much call for privateering in Northumberland."

Henry looks relieved at having escaped Eva's interrogation. "Usually no," he agrees. "But I sell much of our cargo to a Lindisfarne-based merchant." He answers a little too quickly. An answer rehearsed enough to make Abigail wonder at its truth. Wonder if Henry Ward might not have made the journey up here for other reasons.

For her.

The thought makes the back of her neck heat. Makes this far too dangerous. She pushes it away.

"I've been reading about Viking shipbuilding," Oliver says. "I was surprised to learn their longboats could travel at speeds close to your barque." He scoops a careful spoonful from the edge of his stew. "At least, at speeds close to what I estimate your barque to travel at. Given I've never been aboard myself."

A smile flickers in the corner of Henry's mouth. "And what is your estimate of my ship's speed?"

"I would assume nineteen or twenty knots under good conditions. Slightly faster than a fully manned Viking longboat."

"A very fair estimate," says Henry. Oliver looks pleased with himself. "I have some books on shipbuilding techniques you might enjoy. They make mention of the Vikings' superior maritime technology. I shall bring them for you next time I come to the house."

"People thought they saw dragons in the sky," Nathan says suddenly, "before the Vikings raided Lindisfarne. And whirlwinds."

Abigail turns to him in surprise. Where had that come from? She had no idea that Nathan had such knowledge. Had he heard of such things from his brother? His father? She is fairly certain dragon sightings and Viking raids are not general topics of teaching at the petty school.

Ward smiles. Sips his wine. "Is that so? How interesting. What do you think it was they were really seeing? Not dragons, certainly."

Nathan cowers slightly under Henry's attention, but there's a small self-satisfied smile on his face. In a soft voice, he says, "I don't know. Lightning maybe. And storm clouds."

"I would imagine that's very likely."

Nathan's blue eyes light as he reaches for his spoon again. He's just as entranced by Henry Ward as his brother is, Abigail realises. Is not sure if this makes her relieved or fearful.

When dinner is finished, she sends the children upstairs. They thunder up the staircase and the ground floor of the house falls quiet. Seems to shift and widen around her and Henry. With her children's sudden absence, she is suddenly, acutely aware of the fact they are alone together.

She walks him to the front door, a rapid thumping in her chest.

"They're fine children," Henry says. "Very intelligent."

"Thank you." Abigail smiles. "Nathan and Oliver both seem fascinated by all you have to say. And Eva is at that age where she is just clamouring for knowledge. I hope she did not offend you."

He laughs. "I told you, I'm not easily offended. She'll grow to be a very bright young lady, I'm sure. She's much like her mother."

Abigail's heart skips at the compliment. "She's her father's daughter."

"I see you in her also."

His eyes bore into hers, making heat flush the back of her neck. She opens the front door, letting sea-drenched air flood into the foyer. She can hear the tide sighing against the embankment. Out beyond the house, the sea shimmers in the pearly light.

Abigail reaches into her pocket and feels for the brass box. "When do you imagine you might need the letter?"

"Perhaps never. With luck the need for it will never arise. But it's reassuring to know it's safe here if ever I need it."

This feels too one-sided. Henry Ward has entrusted her with his most prized possession, and she has not even given him a scrap of truth about all that is going in her life. Has even allowed him to believe the lie he had created about her keeping the Jacobite funds for her own purposes.

She cannot tell him about the thieving ring. But she can give him something.

She looks up at him. "Will you wait here a moment?"

He nods. "Of course."

Abigail darts back inside the house, leaving Henry on the doorstep and the door wide open to let the island evening blow in. She climbs up to the study and pulls the bundle of letters from the desk drawer. Hurries back out to the doorstep and pushes them into Henry's hands before she can change her mind.

It feels like a bold and exposing move; she has filled these letters with so many personal thoughts. Each time she had sat down to tell her mother about Samuel's passing, she had found herself writing to Henry instead; speaking of her grief, her fears, even her regret at having willingly stepped into the Jacobite movement. Handing them over to him to read, as she had never intended, makes her feel intensely vulnerable. But there is no danger in it. She has not written a word about the thieving ring—has not dared to speak of it even within the safety of these private letters. And she wants to be vulnerable with him, she realises. Wants to be open, and honest, at least more than she has so far. Wants to give him more than lies.

He looks down at the bundle of papers. "What are these?"

"Letters." She swallows heavily, feeling her cheeks colour. "To you. I thought you might care to know about…" She hesitates. Care to know what? The challenge of growing roses in coastal soil?

A sudden wave of regret breaks over her.

But there's a new light in Henry's eyes. A light she hadn't expected. "You wrote to me?"

She can't look at him. "There's no need to read them if you don't wish. But I just felt as though…" She fades out. Feels foolish.

"I very much look forward to reading them. Thank you." He sounds taken aback. As though this is far more than he was expecting. His free hand rises almost instinctively to cup her cheek.

Abigail holds her breath, feeling her heart pounding in her ears. Feeling desire unfurling inside her. She is hot and restless beneath her mourning gown.

This is nothing, she tells herself. This pounding heart, this flush of her skin, it is not for Henry Ward. It is for the possibility he represents; it is a longing for that security, that safety, that solidity, she had felt as a wife. That sense of not having to face the world alone.

But she knows there is nothing safe, or secure about

Henry Ward. He is a man who steals ships and cargo, a man who likely thinks little about taking another's life. A man who justifies it all with a letter of marque. Yes, she has enough knowledge of the situation to know that the line between *privateer* and *pirate* is a hazy one.

Henry Ward is not *safety* or *security* or *solidity*. He is something else entirely.

She ought to step away, yes. Honour her husband's memory. Her husband, who is lying lifeless in his grave. Her husband, who had brought her to live in this faraway house, where no one can see what happens on the doorstep. Her husband who, for all his goodness, had never set her body alight like this.

She feels herself drifting towards Henry, towards the unspoken invitation she can see in his eyes. Feels the tidal pull of him. How easy it would be to reach for him; feel him, taste him, breathe him in. Too easy, here on the doorstep with the great hulk of the house hiding them from the rest of the world.

No one would ever know.

But yes—too easy. This is the act of a woman who had not loved her husband. A woman who has found easiness in her new life as a widow. And Abigail is not that woman. Her head is suddenly full of Samuel. Her kind and decent husband, who had made her into a kind and decent wife. He deserves far better than this.

She steps away from Henry. "Good night," she says, on a breath that barely makes it from her lips. "Take care." And she closes the door before she loses her resolve.

CHAPTER SEVENTEEN

Abigail is at Mairi's door early the next morning. With the bright light of morning, last night's encounter with Henry Ward feels dreamlike and illusory. It has given way to the brutal reality of all he had told her on his ship yesterday. The reality that she has no choice but to step away from the Jacobite fundraising. What that will mean for her entanglement with the thieving ring, Abigail cannot quite yet make sense of.

What will happen when she does not appear at the end of the Wynd next month, to hand over the required funds to Lizzie and her mother? Abigail has no thought of how deep the ring goes—and how much effort they will put into finding her when she fails to appear at the promised hour.

Perhaps she is overplaying her own importance. Perhaps they will simply find another wealthy woman to rob, and they will never think of her again. Or perhaps the Bamburgh thieves will appear on her doorstep, demanding the Jacobite money they see as their owed right for all they have endured and lost. She has no thought of which scenario is the more likely. She only knows she cannot risk being arrested for treason.

Mairi opens the door of her cottage with the baby in the crook of her arm, and another son clinging to her skirts. Abigail shakes her head when Mairi tries to wave her inside. She does not want to drag this out any longer than necessary. Nor does she want to come face to face with Elias or Donald Macauley again.

Mairi steps out into the street with the baby warbling under her arm. She pulls the door closed behind her to pen her other children inside. "Is everything all right? You look bothered."

"I'm afraid I cannot come with you to fundraise any longer," Abigail blurts. In spite of all that has happened, the words are hard to get out. The past months she has spent in Mairi's company have shown her how precious their friendship is. The thought of spending every day and night in Highfield House with just the children and staff for company is a bleak and unswallowable prospect.

For the briefest of moments, the thought of returning to London flits across Abigail's mind. An escape from the thieving ring. From the Jacobites. From Highfield House. The wise option, surely. But that wise option is chased away by the knowledge of how desperately she does not want to be under her mother's influence again. Her mother, who does not yet even know her daughter is a widow.

Abigail knows being around Susanna again will bring out all the worst parts of herself. The anger. The bitterness. The lies, the short temper, the words spoken with the sole purpose of causing offence. These unwelcome parts of herself she can feel simmering too close to the surface after all the stress and sadness of the past months. And she has spent too long outrunning her old self to willingly turn around and embrace her. Abigail will not let her children have that woman for a mother. She does not dare imagine what that might do to Oliver.

Mairi shifts the baby to her other arm. "Is this because of how Donald and my husband spoke to you the day you came here to the house? Because—"

"It's not about that. I just…" Abigail had come to Mairi's cottage with her speech rehearsed. Had planned to blame her reluctance to go visiting on what her late husband would have wanted. Planned to rattle out a trite line about honouring Samuel's memory. But those words die on her lips. They feel far too hollow to be taken as truth. Especially after how close she had come to being pulled into Henry Ward's orbit last night. "I've heard rumours," she says instead, "that the Jacobites are planning something."

Mairi smiles crookedly. "The Jacobites are always planning something."

"Yes, I suppose." Abigail knows she needs to be careful. Cannot step too close to the contents of Henry's letter. She had promised him she would not share a word of it.

But she is worried about Mairi. She knows Henry is right—if the Jacobites succeed in their assassination plot, the redcoats will be on the hunt for traitors. Abigail knows the Mitchells are dedicated to the Jacobite cause. Knows she has little chance of convincing Mairi to step away. But she can at least warn her to be careful.

"I'm worried," Abigail says carefully. "If these rumours are true, the authorities will be hunting Jacobites with a new intensity. And I… Well, I'm all my children have now. I cannot risk anything happening to me. Especially for a cause I've never truly been aligned with."

Mairi doesn't speak at once. "I see. I'm sorry to hear it." Sorry why, Abigail finds herself wondering? Because she will miss her company? Miss her assistance in raising funds? Or because she will miss the sizeable sums she hands over to the thieving ring each month?

A blaze of suspicion comes up on her suddenly, taking her by surprise.

Mairi frowns. "Abby? Is everything all right?"

Walk away, Abigail thinks. She has no proof. Nothing but her own bitter notions that Mairi knows anything of the thieving ring. Notions that are completely unfounded. Mairi is dedicated to the Jacobite cause. Of course she is, of course she is.

But it's a suspicion she cannot shake. After all, Mairi had sent her to Lord Milgate's house that first day. Right into the path of Lizzie. And how else would the thieves possibly have known she was raising funds for the Jacobites? How else would Lizzie have known to specifically demand money on a monthly basis, to align with the schedule of the Jacobite fundraising?

"Do you know of them?" she blurts, unable to hold the words back. "The thieving ring?"

Mairi's pale eyebrows rise. "A thieving ring? What are you talking about?"

Abigail feels her skin prickling beneath her bodice. Regret gnaws at her. The sense that this was a mistake. But it's too late to turn back now. "In Bamburgh," she says tautly. "There's a ring of thieves targeting Jacobite fundraisers."

Mairi pries a strand of her hair from the baby's fist. "Is that why you don't wish to come with me anymore?" she asks calmly. "Because you had a run-in with thieves?" Her words are so logical, so innocent, they make Abigail doubt everything. Make her feel like a fool.

"Yes," she says, unable to cobble together a more adequate response. "I had a run-in with thieves. Who are seeking to steal from the Jacobite cause." She clenches her hands into fists. That gnawing regret turns into a gaping pit in her stomach. She has said too much, of course. Has said far too much. What had she been thinking, letting these baseless accusations come flying out of her mouth like this? She knows how dangerous it is to be speaking of this, even to a friend—although she is fairly certain these accusations have just put an end to her being able to call Mairi a friend.

Mairi lets out an incredulous laugh. "I'm sorry, are you accusing me of sending these thieves out to target you? Thieves that are out to steal from the Jacobite cause, no less." She shakes her head. "Why in heaven's name would I be working with thieves who are seeking to steal from the cause I'm raising funds for? Did you stop for a moment to think about the madness of what you're suggesting?"

Abigail says nothing. After all, what is there to say? Yes, she had stopped for a moment to think. And she had made these accusations anyway. And yes, she can see their utter foolishness. Sees the layers and layers of damage she has done.

"Elias and Donald had their doubts about you," Mairi says coldly. "I told them they were wrong. I told them you we could trust you. But they were right. I ought to have kept my distance." She slams the door and disappears before Abigail can respond.

"We need to make a deal," says Abigail that night. "Neither of us will go near the thieving ring again." She and Oliver are alone in the parlour, the rest of the house quiet around them. Rain is pattering softly against the windows, the remains of a fire popping in the grate.

Oliver eyes her, considering. He runs a hand over the book on the table in front of him. "Lizzie is my friend."

"I don't want you having friends like that."

"She's not a bad person, Mama. She just got caught up in things she didn't wish to. I'm sure you know what that's like."

Abigail inhales slowly, forcing herself not to react. His comment is far too all-seeing. Far too accurate. She shifts awkwardly in Samuel's armchair. "Neither of us will go near the thieving ring again," she repeats.

Oliver sits back on the rug, crossing his legs. He toys with the lacing at the neck of his shirt. "You cannot just walk away," he says. "That's not how this works. You ought to have known better than to fall for such a thing in the first place."

"If they want more money from me, they will have to come and take it," she tells him brusquely. Hopes he can't hear the unease in her voice.

"And you don't think they will do that?"

Abigail doesn't speak at once. She knows just how easy it would be for the thieves to find her. Even if Oliver has not already told Lizzie where he lives, anyone on Lindisfarne could point the thieves in the direction of Highfield House. She doubts there would be too many people in the village willing to put themselves in danger to protect her. Especially after the accusations she had thrown at Mairi today.

Oliver looks up at her, spearing her blue eyes with his. "I will stay away from the thieving ring," he says finally, "if the next time Captain Ward comes to the house, you tell him I would do well as his cabin boy."

Abigail hears her sharp exhalation. She ought to have expected some attempt at manipulation like this. But she cannot make this deal. Cannot condemn her son to a life in which he is unlikely to return home. With every fibre in her body, she knows she will never send her child away to sea with Henry Ward. But right now, she has few options other than to tell him what he wants to hear.

"All right. I will tell Captain Ward." She slides suddenly out of the armchair and kneels on the floor in front of him. Presses her palms to his cheeks. Dear God, she loves him so much, this first-born child of hers. It's an angry, suffocating love, so different from what she feels towards her other children. She loves Eva and Nathan desperately too, of course. But it feels as though Oliver needs something more. As though he needs her to love him as fiercely and violently as possible, to keep him from pulling adrift. "But you must promise me you will stay away from Lizzie," she says. "And everyone else in the thieving ring."

He nods, not breaking her gaze. "I promise."

Oliver stands, and her fingers brush against his hip. She feels something hard and metallic in the side pocket of his breeches.

"What's in your pocket?" she asks.

Without hesitation, Oliver reaches down and pulls out a small, narrow object. Sets it on the tea table in front of them. It's a silver fishing knife, tarnished and bent in places.

Abigail's stomach turns over. So many questions fly at her. The one that makes it out her lips first is: "Where did you get that?"

"I found it in the water when Nathan and I were playing on Saint Cuthbert's Island." The response feels almost painfully innocent. He smirks. "I told Nathan it was a Viking knife. I think he believed me."

"You are cruel to your brother."

"No I'm not." He holds her gaze. "Nathan loves spending time with me. Just ask him."

Abigail makes a noise in her throat. For better or for worse, she knows he is right. "What is the Viking Game?" she asks suddenly.

Oliver shrugs. "Just hide and seek. Nothing more."

Abigail stares down at the knife sitting beside them on the table beside Oliver's inkpot and Latin text. "Why have you been carrying this around with you?" She forces the question out. Is afraid of the answer.

He shrugs again. "It's useful."

"For what?"

"Making repairs to Da's boat. Cutting the ivy from the house. Other chores like that."

She swallows. Thinks of Nathan's new refusal to let anyone lay a finger on him. "Did you hurt your brother with this?"

"Of course not."

Abigail doesn't speak at once. She wants desperately to believe him.

"Did Nathan tell you I hurt him?" Oliver asks.

Abigail glances down, away from his eyes. She knows she needs to tread carefully. Does not want to give Oliver any reason to turn on his younger brother. Not that he has ever needed it.

And not, she realises now, that he even needs an answer to this question. She knows Oliver is well aware of the pull he has over his brother. Surely he knows Nathan would never speak out against him, or put him in any kind of trouble. It's no small part of her that wishes Nathan would learn to stand up for himself a little more. Not that he has ever really had a hope of doing so, with Oliver's shadow having loomed over him his entire life.

"What was in the box?" Oliver asks, veering abruptly away from the topic of his brother. "The box Captain Ward gave you when he came to the house last night."

Abigail knows there's little point feigning ignorance. "Nothing you need to concern yourself with." She slides back into the armchair, suddenly needing to put space between her and her son.

Oliver sits back on the floor beside the tea table and opens his book. "Is it something to do with the thieving ring?"

"Of course not."

He looks at her with intent blue eyes. "I thought we were sharing things with each other. I thought that was what we do."

Abigail reaches down and takes the knife from the tea table. She curls her hand around it, feeling an odd frisson of exhilaration. Power. But this is the kind of power that should not belong to a child. She will lock this cursed thing away. See that Oliver does not go near it again. "We do share things," she says. "But some things are not for you to know."

Oliver exhales loudly through his nose. He leans forward and turns the page of his text with far more force than is necessary. He picks up his quill and dips it in the pot. Is deliberate in spattering ink across the tabletop.

Abigail watches him for a long time, turning the knife over between her fingers. Finds herself rattling through possibilities of where she can hide the damn thing so he does not find it. Perhaps there's little point. He clearly knows the house and its hiding places far better than she does. And if he wants to carry around a knife, there are far too many other places he could find one.

She sets the blade back on the table.

"I told Mairi Mitchell about the thieving ring," she blurts.

Oliver looks up. "I don't think you ought to have done that."

"I know. It was a mistake."

"Why did you do it?" There's a genuineness in his face now. Concern. Kindness. Abigail is glad to see this side of him. It's unspeakably precious. And tonight, she needs it.

"I accused her of sending me into Lizzie's path. I was with her just before it happened."

Oliver frowns. "I don't think Lizzie knows Mrs Mitchell."

Abigail smiles wryly. "No. I'm sure she doesn't. It was a foolish thing to do. Mrs Mitchell was very upset at my accusations."

Oliver sits up on his knees. "What will you do?" he asks. "Will you ask her to stay quiet about what you told her?"

Abigail lets out a humourless laugh. "I think such a thing might only encourage her to do the opposite."

CHAPTER EIGHTEEN

The white flag droops at the top of the French ship's mainmast, barely lifted by the breeze. Surrender.

Ward feels a familiar humming beneath his skin. That acute sense of aliveness that comes with conflict; comes whenever the prospect of death draws a little closer.

It's an easy prize; the ship is far smaller than the *Eagle*. Eight guns at most. The warning shots the *Eagle* had fired across their bowsprit had been enough to send the white flag flying up the target's mast before they even managed to get any of their cannons clear.

The unfortunate *Fortune* is a naval ship, fitted en flute— less guns and more men. There'll be little in the way of cargo aboard, Ward knows, but he's sure they'll find provisions for the French sailors that he can commandeer for his own men.

Of course, they'll also find a crew of enemy navy. It will fetch a fine ransom from the French Government.

Ward stands at the gunwale beneath a thick bank of cloud. Watches as Hunter, his quartermaster, gathers the boarding party. The two vessels are roped together, grinding against each other with each roll of the sea. Half Ward's crew of eighty-five men will board the prize. Men to ferry her provisions back to the *Eagle*. Men to lock the French prisoners in the hold.

The other half will stay aboard. Keep their ship protected.

Murmurs of anticipation ripple through the boarding party. Pistols and cutlasses in their hands. Bands of red fabric knotted around their upper arms so they can be easily identified as allies should any trouble arise.

Ward keeps one hand curled around a loaded pistol. He watches as his men file over the gunwale and onto the prize ship. The sky splits open, and fat beads of rain begin to bounce off the deck. Ward waits, watches as his men disappear into the forecastle of the French ship. The *Fortune's* crew have retreated to closed quarters, and he listens intently for the sound of gunfire. Muffled shouts drift across the water. Orders. Not conflict. Above his head, the yardarms groan.

When the stillness thickens enough to convince Ward the *Fortune's* crew have not retaliated, he calls to Finn with instructions to send the navigator to the ward-robe. Ward climbs through the saloon and down into the ship, plans of ransoms and Northumbrian journeys beginning to take ship in his mind.

The navigator is leaving the ward-robe with instructions to plot a course for London when Hunter strides through the door, Graveney and Cook close behind. The three them smell of action: sweat and sea and the lingering punch of gunpowder that seems to have infused every corner of the ship.

Ward nods at the folded pages in Hunter's hands. "The ship's papers?"

"Aye sir. All look legitimate. A hundred and ten sailors returning to the Continent from Saint Kitts."

Ward takes the papers, reads carefully over their contents. "Good." He takes the wine bottle from the centre of the table and fills three cups for his officers. "She'll fetch a fine ransom from La Royale." He sinks into the leather-padded chair at the head of the ward-robe table. A pleasant exhaustion is weighing down his body. He sips his wine, stretching his long legs out in front of him.

"What of her crew, sir?" asks Graveney, sliding into a seat at the table.

Ward glances down at the papers. "A hundred and ten men. Are they all accounted for?"

"Aye sir," says Hunter. "All locked below."

Ward looks at Graveney pointedly. "Then they will fetch a fine ransom from La Royale."

Graveney rubs his narrow chin. Glances at Hunter, as though seeking support.

Ward leans forward in his chair. "Something to say, Mr Graveney?" He keeps his voice level, despite the irritation gnawing beneath his skin. He has always prided himself on being a fair captain. On letting his men have their say. And he wishes that, whatever it is John Graveney has to say, he'd just come out and say it.

His boatswain hesitates. Takes a gulp of wine, as though to fortify himself. "We've held vessels for ransom in the past, sir. Never seen the need to hold the whole damn crew hostage. Why not just hold the captain and master?"

"We've held merchant ships for ransom in the past," Ward says pointedly. "A naval crew will fetch far more."

"We're ransoming the vessel," Graveney says tautly. His dark eyes spark suddenly. "Since when do we barter with men's lives?"

Ward straightens, eyebrows rising. "Careful, John. That sounds a little too much like a pro-French sentiment to me."

Graveney's neck reddens beneath the dark bristles of his beard. "Pro-French?" he snorts. "You think I'd be sailing with you if I'd a pro-French bone in my body? This ain't about supporting the French. It's about common decency, and you know it." He tosses back another mouthful of wine. "You're heading a little too close to piracy if you ask me."

Ward tightens his fingers around his cup, inhaling to settle the anger simmering beneath his skin. *Heading too close to piracy* is a barbed insult—he has always been careful never to cross that line into lawlessness. This is wartime. Ransoming the crew of the *Fortune* is a privateering act of patriotism. Any man who steps onto a French naval vessel must do so knowing he is taking the risk of imprisonment. Who in hell does Graveney think he is, speaking to his captain in such a manner?

Nonetheless, Ward can't deny there's an uncomfortable gnawing beneath his skin. A quiet voice inside his head asking him if perhaps John Graveney is right. Perhaps this is not an act of war, but an act of greed. And it's this, Ward realises, that is irritating him most of all. He does not like being wrong.

"Your opinion is noted, Mr Graveney," he tells him sharply. "Thank you." He flashes his eyes at his boatswain, a heated look that makes it clear his company is no longer welcome. "I wish you a pleasant evening."

John Graveney strides up onto deck, glad to escape the tension of the ward-robe—and the captain. He draws down a long breath. The air smells of gunpowder and that hot, acrid stench of death. Just his imagination, surely—they had fired little more than a smattering of warning shots, and no one had been killed on either side. He puts it down to the uncomfortable stirring beneath his skin.

The French prisoners, yes. But that is not all of it. The French prisoners are just the tip of a far deeper thorn he's been doing his best to ignore.

He's always been an ardent supporter of his captain. Has been privateering with Ward for more than four years—has signed on with him for commission after commission. Graveney has always found him to be fair and decent—if not a man to leave much room for error. But in the past—how long? Months? Year?—John Graveney has been questioning his captain more and more.

No, that's not right. He's been questioning *himself*.

Coming of age as the son of a penniless bladesmith in London, Graveney had always agreed blindly with his father, his uncles, his friends. The French were bastards; the Jacobites hopeless fools. He'd never stopped to consider for himself what he really believed. Had only ever been towed along the path of those around him. Believed what he was told to believe.

And in these past months—year?—he has felt that begin to change.

No. The uncertainty about the timing of this is a lie.

Because if he stops to think about it, which he is trying his best not to do, he can pinpoint exactly when and where this unease had taken root inside him.

A boarding of a merchant ship in the North Atlantic. She'd been carrying a French crew and a handful of Jacobites Graveney guessed had been exiled from England. The *Eagle* had come only for the French ship's cargo—Ward had had no interest in the old, slow merchant vessel, or the men on board.

Graveney and several others had held the crew at pistol-point while the rest of the boarding party had emptied the ship of its silks and spices. And as the men had looked down the barrel of Graveney's pistol, he'd seen fear in their eyes. Had heard a murmured prayer, spoken in English. He saw rosary beads pass through trembling fingers. And for a fleeting moment, Graveney was a child again, hearing his own mother speak these same forbidden prayers in their creaking Broad Street garret. Watching her pass those same forbidden beads through her own trembling fingers.

His mother had been gone for many years. Two decades and more. Her dangerous, lingering Catholic beliefs had not been spoken of by anyone in Graveney's family since her death. But suddenly those beliefs were at the forefront of his mind. The sound of the Catholic prayer, murmured by a frightened Jacobite on some plundered French ship in the rolling North Atlantic, seemed to reach down into a distant, unremembered part of him. Unbidden, he felt a sudden, unwelcome connection to these men; these enemies. Felt the pistol waver in his hand.

Graveney looks across the dark water to the slim figure of the *Fortune*. She is flying over the water in the hands of the men from the *Eagle* Hunter had instructed to stay aboard as a prize crew.

Perhaps even more unwelcome than the connection he'd felt to the Jacobite on that cursed French merchant brig, Graveney is feeling that same connection to these Frenchmen they locked into the hold of their own ship today. A flimsy connection, yes, but he can't deny it's there.

He wishes this was not a part of him; or at least that it was a part he could forget existed. Because these Catholic beliefs of his mother's, they are also the beliefs of the French enemy. The beliefs of the Jacobites.

And they're beliefs that don't align with a man paid to fire broadsides at those very same people.

Walk away. The thought comes to him suddenly. A laughable thought because he cannot walk away from this ship, either literally or figuratively. Never mind that they're out in the middle of the Atlantic; this is his only way of making a decent living. And Graveney has been in far too much debt for far too many years to pretend he does not need this commission. Owes almost fifty pounds to cursed Amos Sheffield alone, after far too many bad decision at the card tables.

Perhaps he could find a berth on a merchant ship, a vessel not so actively involved in the war. He'd put himself at the mercy of French privateers—and what a damn irony that would be after all this handwringing and foolishness. But more pressing than that: he'd throw away the chance of another promotion; a senior officer's position on Henry Ward's ship that would pay well enough to finally put his debts behind him. Live a better life than his drunkard of a father ever had. A life that, for the first time, has almost begun to feel within reach.

He's clambered his way up to boatswain. Knows he has the knowledge and skills—and the respect of the crew—to be quartermaster when withered old Abe Hunter finally falls off the perch.

He's just not sure he has the right thoughts in his head.

Graveney curls his hands around the railing and lifts his face to the sky. The last faint mist of rain dampens and cools his cheeks. He doesn't want to be thinking like this. He wants his old, predictable way of thinking—that black and white view of the world where there are good men and bad men and nothing in between.

The beliefs are inconvenient, irritating. And they're beliefs that need to be conquered if he's to have any future as a member of Henry Ward's crew.

CHAPTER NINETEEN

"May we speak a moment, Mrs Blake?" Mrs Calloway asks from the doorway of the parlour. The children's nurse, a small, rounded woman in her late thirties, is looking at Abigail with the same gentle, pitying expression she gives Eva and Nathan when they've tripped on the stairs or spilled their ale.

The request makes a too-familiar pull of dread tighten in Abigail's stomach. Usually, when the children's nurse seeks her out like this, it's to tell her of some godawful thing Oliver has done. Abigail has long given up expecting the nurse to exert any kind of control over her eldest son, but Oliver still manages to insert himself into her periphery from time to troubled time.

She puts down the letter from Samuel's accountant outlining the monthly funds from the tenants in the Chelsea house. Stands from the armchair and ushers the older woman into the room.

Mrs Calloway perches on the edge of the settle, folding her weathered hands in front of her. Seems to consider her words.

"Just tell me what he's done," Abigail blurts.

The nurse's eyes soften. "I'm not here about Oliver, Mrs Blake. I'm here because I'm concerned about you."

"Concerned about me? Why?" It's a foolish question, Abigail knows—comes out sounding forced.

She has kept to herself for weeks. Has stayed hidden from Mairi, from the rest of the village. Has had Mrs Calloway take Nathan to and from school. Relied on Ruth to keep them all fed and watered.

The first time she had not gone to Bamburgh to meet Lizzie at the appointed time, she had spent the day in abject terror, refusing to let her children do so much as peek through the curtains. Had kept Nathan home from the petty school; kept Oliver pinned beneath her gaze.

Lizzie had not come to the house. Her mother had not come to the house. Three weeks now, and no one from the thieving ring has shown their face on Lindisfarne. But feeling as though she has gotten away with something feels far too premature.

Abigail spends her days with one eye on the dunes, expecting thieves from Bamburgh; the other eye on the sea—hoping for Henry Ward. Around her, the house seems to hollow and widen, fraying the edges of the courage she has tried so hard to cultivate.

She keeps Eva penned inside, tucks Nathan away the moment he returns home from school. As for Oliver, she knows she has little hope of keeping him close; just has to hope the promise of her putting in a good word for him with Henry will be enough for him to stay away from Bamburgh and the thieving ring.

Mrs Calloway tilts her head, choosing her words carefully. "You seem to be spending more time than ever alone in the house," she says finally. Her gentle Scottish lilt makes her words sound like a lullaby. Abigail bites her tongue to force herself from snapping at the woman's over-the-top gentleness. She's less than a decade younger than Mrs Calloway. She does not need to be mothered. But, Abigail reminds herself, nor does the poor woman need to be snapped at for her kindness.

"Father Dering has been asking after you at church," Mrs Calloway continues, apparently oblivious to the war of good and evil going on inside Abigail's head. "And his wife was hoping to speak to you today at the school, given it was young Nathan's final day."

Abigail lets out her breath, struck with a barb of guilt. It had completely slipped her mind that Nathan was to finish at the petty school today. What kind of mother is she? "Of course," she says hurriedly. "Did he enjoy his last day?"

Mrs Calloway gives her a soft smile, but Abigail can sense—imagines?—a veiled criticism beneath. "I'm sure he will be eager to tell you all about it." The nurse leans forward, her brown eyes meeting Abigail's. "If I might speak openly, Mrs Blake... I know how difficult it is to lose a husband. I know the way the grief can spring back up on you when you think you are past the worst of it. But I know that locking yourself away like this is not the way forward."

How she wishes this was all a simple matter of grief. How much easier that would be. She wishes, too, that she could tell Mrs Calloway the truth: that she is too scared to leave the safety of the house in case anyone from the thieving ring should catch her out on the open expanse of the island. That in a strange sort of way, Highfield House has come to feel like her protector.

Instead, she forces a smile. "You're right, of course." She wants this conversation over. "I shall be sure to venture into the village tomorrow. And I shall speak with Mrs Dering about how Nathan fared at school."

Mrs Calloway looks at her intently for a moment, clearly unconvinced. "Very good," she says, after a moment of hesitation. She stands. "I shall be off home for the evening then, if there's nothing else you need."

In pieces, she ventures out. An afternoon visit to speak with Mrs Dering. A walk with her children to the rockpools in the shadow of the castle. She chooses the brightest, sunniest days, when sunlight spills across the dunes and leaves few places to hide.

The garden flourishes as the days grow warmer and the summer days stretch long and endless across the island. The day she had arrived on Lindisfarne, Abigail had decided to make this garden her project; had been determined to make something vivid and colourful from the jungle of native grasses she had found fringing her house. With an old shovel she had found in the stables, she had set about turning over the earth into garden beds, finding little more than sandy soil that left her first attempts withered and brown.

Now, after twelve years of practice, and countless hours reading up on the subject, the garden is the living, breathing wonder she had always hoped it would be. In the summer warmth, it's an explosion of colour; carefully cultivated lavender and roses, intertwined with native sea-thrift, among the green and gold grasses that run free across the dunes.

Of all things, she is grateful for this garden. Grateful for its colour; so stark a contrast to the dark wood and stone of the house. Grateful for the calmness she feels when she is here among these plants. For the fragrant scent of aliveness; for bees and birds and butterflies.

But this afternoon, it's not calmness she feels. Because there's a flash of movement in the dunes. Large and dark and solid. Abigail feels her lungs tighten like a fist. A roe deer, perhaps. This is the logical solution. But she cannot quite find the space for logic. Instead, she is picturing men with pistols and muskets, and Lizzie's dirt-streaked face with an apple-shaped birthmark.

Her eyes go instinctively to her daughter, who is half-buried in the lavender bush.

"Evie," she hisses. Louder. "Evie. Quickly. Inside."

Eva looks up from the garden, a slightly bewildered expression in her eyes. "Why are you yelling, Mama?"

Abigail tries to level her voice. "I'm not yelling. Inside now, please."

A look of seriousness falls across Eva's face and she trots inside the house.

Abigail follows, locking the door behind them. She hurries to the parlour and yanks closed the curtains. Can't help peeking through them onto the dunes. She sees nothing, no one. But she can see only a small fragment of the island surrounding her. Surrounding them. She feels painfully adrift inside the house.

Eva is watching from the doorway, chewing on the end of her plait, clearly infected by her mother's panic.

Abigail forces a smile. Kneels to take her daughter's soil-covered hands. She smells lavender and sea in Eva's hair.

"Everything's all right, Evie. I'm sorry, I did not mean to scare you."

The pounding of the door knocker echoes through the entrance hall, making Abigail jump. She draws in a breath. "Nathan is upstairs in his bedroom," she tells Eva. "Go up and see what he's doing."

Eva's eyes light, her unease forgotten. She flies upstairs, leaving Abigail alone in the foyer.

Another knock at the door.

She hesitates. Answer? Or hide away and hope the house will keep them safe?

"Who's there?" she calls.

"Mrs Blake? We need to speak."

A woman's voice. It's a sharp and polished voice, her Northumbrian accent far softer than most of the villagers'. A stranger's voice.

Abigail feels suddenly, intensely alone.

But this is not who she wants to be. She will not condemn herself to a life lived in fear. She is stronger than that. At least, she wants to be.

She pulls open the door.

The woman on the doorstep is not a stranger. This woman on the doorstep had stood face to face with Abigail at the narrowest end of Church Wynd and held a knife to her throat.

After you attacked her daughter.

The thought does not bring her the self-loathing she suspects it ought to. It brings her a sudden burst of confidence. She will not let herself be afraid of this woman.

Abigail steps out of the house, pulling the door to behind her. "How did you find me?" she asks. She makes her voice taut and brusque, to match Lizzie's mother's. "Did one of the villagers tell you how to find the house? Or was it my son?"

The woman doesn't answer.

Lizzie's mother is dressed in patched and colourless skirts, the coif on her head pulled almost to her eyebrows. The look in her eyes is solemn and serious, but not as threatening as Abigail had expected. "You made a deal with my daughter," she says evenly. "And you have not kept your word."

"The only thing I promised Lizzie was that I would return the following month and give her the same amount as I did the first time." Abigail grits her teeth. "I did as I promised. Again and again." She lifts her chin. Injects as much forcefulness into her words as she can manage. "I'm sorry. But our arrangement is finished."

A faint smile flickers in the corner of the woman's mouth. "You are not the one who gets to decide that, Mrs Blake."

Abigail's fingers curl instinctively around the doorframe. "I cannot work for the Jacobites any longer," she says, pushing past the threatening edge to the woman's words. "It's too dangerous."

Surprise flickers across the woman's eyes. As though she is taken aback by Abigail speaking aloud of their connection to the Jacobites. Up until this point, it had been a silent undercurrent.

"Working for the Jacobites has always been too dangerous," Lizzie's mother says finally. "Nothing has changed."

Abigail doesn't answer. Lizzie's mother is not what she had expected. This woman is well-spoken and clear-eyed. Clearly comes from a well-off family. Has clearly made some terrible choices. Abigail tries not to focus on how much the woman reminds her of herself.

After several moments of silence, Lizzie's mother says, "If you won't go to the Jacobite donors again, there are other ways you can pay what you owe."

Abigail clenches her fists. "I don't owe you anything," she hisses. "Leave me alone. And tell your daughter to stay away from my son.

A wry smile crosses the woman's face. "Perhaps you ought to tell your son to stay away from my daughter. I don't believe the friendship was instigated by Lizzie." She swats at the bee circling her head. "In any case, we need money from you, Mrs Blake." The words are almost painfully casual.

"No," Abigail snaps. "You don't. I'm not working for the Jacobite cause any longer. I have nothing to give you."

The woman's gaze travels up to the broad ivy-streaked façade of the house. "I can see that's not true. Your husband clearly ensured you were taken care of before he died. Which is more than most of us can say. Most of us widows to the Jacobite battlefields have pennies to our names."

"So you think it your right to take what my husband left me?"

Lizzie's mother shrugs. "My right? Of course not. But people like us, we've stopped caring about what's right and what's wrong. The world has taken far too much from us to bother ourselves with that." She crosses her arms across her thick chest. "You made a deal with my daughter," she says again. "And you will pay us what is owed."

This time, Abigail hears the threat all too clearly beneath the woman's words. "I cannot give you any money," she says tautly. "I need everything I have for my children."

"Well. Like I said, there are other ways you can pay what you owe."

Abigail grits her teeth. "What ways?" she dares to ask.

"Take it from another's pocket. Just as you were doing before."

"Blatant thievery?" Abigail spits. "Join your ring? Do you truly think I will agree to such a thing?"

"I would imagine you might consider it. You're clearly on edge. As though you are expecting us to do something terrible to you and your family."

The accuracy of the words strike her, but Abigail does her best not to react. She will not dignify this outrageous request with anything more than silence.

She unlocks the front door and traps herself inside the house, half waiting for the door knocker to sound again. But there is quiet for a moment, and then the soft footsteps of Lizzie's mother crunching back down the path.

What will the woman do now? Is she returning to Bamburgh to collect the rest of the thieving ring? Are hordes of thieves about to turn up on her doorstep to punish her from stepping away from the ring? Surely Abigail is not that valuable. After all, it had taken Lizzie's mother three weeks to seek her out. Perhaps with time, the thieves will come to see that trying to squeeze money out of the family in Highfield House is a pointless endeavour.

Or perhaps Abigail is just being overly optimistic.

She looks up at the sound of footsteps on the staircase.

"Was that Lizzie's ma?" Oliver asks. "I thought she'd come eventually. I suspected she'd be angry when you didn't go to Bamburgh like you promised."

Abigail says nothing.

"Did you give her money?" Oliver asks coolly.

"Of course not. I'm not going to hand over your father's

money to a pack of thieves."

"There are other ways you can pay what you owe."

Abigail's chest tightens at his use of the exact same words as Lizzie's mother. "We are not thieves," she hisses. "Do you understand?" She presses her hands down hard on his shoulders, forcing him to look at her. "We are going to stay away from Bamburgh and the thieving ring until they decide we are simply not worth the trouble."

Oliver doesn't speak. But the look on his face makes Abigail all too aware of the blind naivety of her plan.

"Flowers," says Eva. "'Flowers' starts with F."

"Very good," says Mrs Calloway as they follow the coast path back towards the house. "And Nathan, can you think of a word that ends with the letter F?"

Cliff, he thinks. *If*, *of* and *kerchief*. Usually, he likes the letter game. But today his attention is snatched by the sight of Oliver out on the embankment beyond the house. He's pushing Da's rowboat through the sand and pebbles on the edge of the beach.

Nathan bursts into a run. Pretends not to hear Mrs Calloway barking at him to get back here this instant and think of a word that ends in F. When he gets to the embankment, Oliver is standing in ankle-deep water, with Da's rowboat bobbing out ahead of him.

"Where are you going?" Nathan asks breathlessly.

"I've something to take care of," Oliver says. "It's very important."

"Can I come?"

"No." But he hovers in the water, one hand on the boat, as though waiting for more questions. Hoping for more questions, maybe.

"Are you going to the mainland?"

"Perhaps."

"To visit someone?"

"Can't say."

Nathan scuffs the toe of his shoe into the damp sand. "Does Mama know where you're going?"

A smile flickers on the edge of Oliver's lips, and Nathan can tell he has landed on the question his brother had been hoping for. "No," he says. "but even if she did, I don't think she would stop me."

CHAPTER TWENTY

This time, Ward knows there's little justification for a journey back to Lindisfarne. This time, he knows it's driven only by his need to see Abigail.

Information on the capture of the *Fortune* and her crew has been sent across the Channel to the Admiralty of La Royale. Ward knows he has at least another week before the letters of credit arrive in payment of his ransom demands.

Enough time for a journey north.

He has left the *Fortune* languishing in the Thames with the prize crew. Had briefly considered leaving the *Eagle* behind too, and making his way northward on a passenger ship without the rest of his men. But no, this crew still has another six months on their articles of agreement, and Ward knows they will not appreciate the lull in action. He'd taken just enough cargo from the hold of the *Fortune* to cobble together an excuse about calling on his Lindisfarne buyer.

At his request, his cook had loaded the ship with fresh meat and vegetables before they'd left London, and now the feast is spread out across the ward-robe table. Ward knows it's a thinly veiled attempt at buying his officers' approval. None of them had been in favour of another trip north.

Tonight though, with their plates wiped clean of even the last speck of gravy, and cards spread across the table in a game of Ruff and Honours, Hunter and Cook seem to have forgotten their grievances. John Graveney is still wearing that pinched expression he's had since they took the *Fortune*. Ward is beginning growing tired of it.

"I assume we'll be getting another night of luxury at the house, Captain," says Hunter, bringing his wine glass to his lips. There's a glint in his eyes that tells Ward he's under no illusions that this journey has anything to do with cargo.

"I'm sure Mrs Blake will welcome you." The words come out more clipped than Ward intended. It feels as though Hunter is encroaching on something private. Ward hates that his crew are aware of his infatuation with Abigail. A part of him despises himself for it. Has he learnt nothing after Amelia?

It's an argument he's had with himself over and over. Each time, he comes to the same glaring conclusion: Abigail is not Amelia.

He drops down the Queen of Spades and scoops up the trick. Draws in a breath before he speaks again, in an attempt to rein in his annoyance. His irritation is not being helped by the windless conditions and the infuriatingly slow creep up the coast of England. He's beginning to feel as though they'll never reach Northumberland. "And with luck we'll have a hefty pay day when we return to London."

Graveney snorts. "You think La Royale will pay to return a ship full of dead men?"

Ward looks at him pointedly. "There's been only three deaths among the prisoners." He nods down at the deck of cards. "Deal."

"Five men," Graveney corrects him, ignoring the cards. "And there'll be far more by the time the ransom money arrives. How quick do you think the fever'll take a crew locked in their own hold?"

"I—"

A knock at the door and Finn hurries inside, collecting their dinner plates from the table. Ward holds Graveney's hot stare. Feels irritation prickling under his skin. A faint nagging of his own conscience. He pushes it away. He did not find the success he has through sentimentality. A nagging voice inside his head reminds him that he did not find it by gallivanting up to Northumberland every time the wind changes either.

Finn clatters the last of the plates together. "Anything else you need, sir?"

"No. Thank you, lad." Ward waits for Finn to leave before turning back to Graveney. "Deal," he says again, rapping his fingers against the deck of cards. "I didn't invite you here tonight to rehash old arguments. The decision on the *Fortune* has long been made."

Graveney opens his mouth to speak again, then seems to change his mind. He picks up the deck and begins to shuffle.

When the game is over and the wine bottle is empty, Ward waits for the other officers to leave. He calls for Graveney to return at the table. His boatswain does not look surprised at the request. He sits opposite Ward, leaning back in his chair and folding his wiry arms across his chest.

Ward doesn't speak at once. He turns his empty cup around, choosing his words carefully. What he wants is to unleash his anger on Graveney. Curse him for his disrespect. For questioning him. For acting in such a petty, childish manner.

But he can also see that anger is going to get him nowhere.

He spears Graveney with hard eyes. "If you wish to be released from your articles of agreement, I'm willing to do so. I'll see to it that you receive your share of the payment from La Royale."

Graveney just sighs.

"I'd be sorry to lose you," Ward continues. "But I'm beginning to think that may be for the best."

Graveney rubs his narrow chin. "And why d'you think that would be for the best, Captain? Because I dared to disagree with you about taking the entire crew of the *Fortune* prisoner?" He gives a short, humourless laugh. "Because I certainly ain't the only person aboard who didn't believe you ought to have done that."

Ward rubs his eyes. "The thing is done, John. The letters have been sent. What point is there in going over and over all this?"

Graveney hesitates a moment. "Well," he says finally. "The situation might come up again, aye?"

"It might," Ward agrees. He toys with the edge of the deck of cards. Chooses his words carefully. "Men change, John. There's no shame in it. If something has caused you to alter your alliance, I will not question it. I just ask that you leave my crew."

"Alter my alliance?" Graveney repeats on a laugh. "Are you asking me if I'm about to jump ship and fight for the

French?" He shakes his head incredulously. "I've given you four years of loyalty and these are the accusations I get in return? All for thinking you shouldn't have locked up all those men and left them to die like rabid dogs?"

Ward hesitates. Has he jumped to conclusions? Is he seeing French and Jacobites sympathies in John Graveney, when all that is there is a scrap of decency? He can't tell if Graveney's words are genuine. Can't tell if he's simply telling his captain what he wishes to hear. His instinct is failing him. Still, Graveney is right: he has given him four years of loyalty. Not to mention the fact he is an organised and thorough boatswain. The *Eagle* has been in fine shape since he had taken up the role two years ago. He would not be an easy man to replace.

"I'm not asking you to leave," Ward says finally. "I'm merely giving you the option. If what we do no longer aligns with who you are."

Graveney stands, making it clear the conversation is over. "I've no intention of leaving," he says. "I was simply making my opinion known. I've every intention of sailing with this crew until the war is over."

Ward is still thinking about *until the war is over* when he makes his way back to the great cabin that night. What he will do after the war is something he usually does his best not to think about. The thought of returning to merchant service, even as a captain, feels almost unbearably dull. And as for the other direction many privateers take in peacetime—piracy— well, that is simply not an option. He's worked too hard to make a name for himself to tumble into infamy. In any case, it's a decision for another day. He's seen little sign that peace is on the horizon.

Ward slides off his justacorps and unbuttons his waistcoat. Rids himself of his boots and shirt and climbs onto his bed in his breeches. Somehow, in the process of undressing, and contemplating the shape his life will take when the peace treaties are signed, he has gone to his desk drawer to collect the pile of Abigail's letters.

He leans back against the headboard, turning slowly through the pages. Lamplight flickers over the curls and scrawls of Abigail's handwriting, and the dimness makes the words blur.

This is far from the first time he has read these letters. Several parts of them, he knows from memory.

Her sentences are often clipped and fragmented, her thoughts often rambling and incoherent. Ward can tell the letters are a way for her to process what's going on in her head. Her fears, her grief, her eternal struggle with keeping the cruel and callous side of herself at bay. Each time he reads these lines, Ward finds himself smiling. Somehow, perhaps foolishly, he likes the dark side of Abigail Blake. Likes the challenge of her. The imperfection. Because that imperfection allows him to be imperfect too. Allows him to acknowledge his mistakes—like holding an entire crew ransom, instead of just her officers.

Abigail's letters, written more than four months ago, when he had last seen her, are interspersed with mentions of her fundraising visits, and her fears that the Lindisfarne Jacobites might discover she is not handing them the full amount that had been donated. How desperately Ward hopes she has done as she promised him and stayed away from the Jacobite cause.

He is well aware that she has not told him the full story. Not given him every piece of why she had ended up with Jacobite funds in her pocket. Not that he needs the full story. It's a common enough tale: a widow left with a miserly settlement and young children to raise. Perhaps he ought to have been more forward, more insistent in helping her financially. That way he would know for certain she has freed herself from the danger of being involved with the Jacobites.

Then again, it has been more than eight months since he had first heard of the kidnapping plot from Lord Dunmore. Perhaps, like so many of the Jacobites' plots, it has just petered out into nothingness.

Nonetheless, the desire to take Abigail's struggle away is immense. As is the desire to be more to her than just a fleeting figure on the edges of her life.

He folds the wad of paper and slips it beneath the mattress. Rolls onto his back, listening to the low groan of the ship on its windless slog northward. Once again, Ward asks himself what he wishes his life to look like once the war is over. And this time, he realises, he has an answer.

CHAPTER TWENTY-ONE

It's Sunday morning. She ought to be in church right now, instead of sitting here in the parlour rehemming her children's clothes. This is far from the first service Abigail has missed. Like she has done most Sundays since she had accused Mairi of being involved with the thieving ring, she has sent Eva and Nathan off to the service with Ruth and Mrs Calloway. Is not sure if her children's presence in her absence will reflect better or worse on her. At least if she is cast down into Hell, she will not take her children with her.

Samuel's rowboat is missing from the embankment this morning. She tells herself she does not know where Oliver has taken himself off to. Is doing her best to remain ignorant. But that is becoming harder and harder to do. Because since Lizzie's mother had appeared on the doorstep and demand Abigail steal for the thieving ring, there have been no more visitors. No more threats. Abigail is doing her best not to consider why that might be. Doing her best not to consider what Oliver might have overheard. What he might have chosen to do on her behalf.

She ties off her sewing and folds Eva's rehemmed smock gown, setting it on the table in front of her. She takes the next piece from the pile, her attention drawn to movement outside the window. Mrs Calloway is herding Nathan and Eva towards the house, Ruth and Father Dering behind them.

Abigail grits her teeth. She supposes this was inevitable, this pity visit from the priest—or maybe *scolding visit* is more apt. No doubt he has more than a few words to say about her neglecting his sermons.

Abigail leaves the sewing on the tea table and goes down the passage to meet them in the foyer.

The children's faces light at the sight of their mother. She ignores Father Dering as Eva barrels into a frantic diatribe about a particularly terrifying seal she saw near Saint Cuthbert's Island this morning. Abigail can feel the priest's eyes on them. Wondering, perhaps, where Oliver is, and why he had not joined his brother and sister at church today.

When Eva runs out of breath, Abigail sends the children upstairs with the nurse and draws in her courage to face Father Dering.

She is expecting fire and brimstone. But his face holds a lingering kindness.

"I know it's a foolish question to ask you if you are all right," says Father Dering. "I know you've suffered a great loss. And I can only imagine the challenge of raising children on your own, especially in a place as isolated as this." She catches the hidden meaning behind his words. Not *raising children on your own*, but *raising Oliver on your own*.

Up close, she notices how lined and weathered the vicar's face is; notices it's a powdered wig on his head, clumsily slapped on over his own thinning hair. Deep folds of skin hang beneath his eyes. He looks older than Abigail assumes him to be. It does not seem that long ago he had been a young man in the pulpit.

She looks past him up the staircase. Nathan is scrambling up the stairs on his hands and knees, Eva copying her brother several paces behind. Abigail smiles faintly.

"Well," she says finally, turning back to the vicar, "of course it has not been easy. But we are managing. It's been many months since Samuel's death."

Father Dering hesitates. "Is there a reason we have not seen you in church for several weeks?" The question feels probing. As though he knows more than he ought to. Has Mairi Mitchell said something to him about Abigail's run-in with the thieves? About the accusations she had thrown about?

For not the first time, the thought of telling the truth about the thieving ring flits into her head. The pull of it is strong. She could return to the village. Attempt to rebuild her friendship with Mairi—or at least beg forgiveness and attempt some kind of civility.

No. It's too dangerous. Silence is the only way. Especially if Oliver has involved himself in thieving because—no, she is not going to think that thought.

"I hope everything is well with Oliver," Father Dering says carefully. "I hope he has not found himself in trouble."

"It's nothing to do with Oliver," she says, making the words sound almost truthful. She sighs. "I know he is a difficult boy. But there's a good side to him. He is very protective of me. Especially since his father has been gone."

Father Dering smiles faintly. "I'm glad if it. And yes, I

firmly believe everyone has decency in them. It is up to us to draw it out."

Abigail's throat tightens suddenly.

"Whatever challenges you are facing, God can help you through them," says the vicar. "You are always welcome at my services." His voice hardens slightly. "Besides, I'm sure I need not tell you the importance of church attendance for the good of one's soul. A true relationship with the Lord is our only way to avoid condemning ourselves to eternal damnation."

Abigail lowers her eyes, biting back an angry retort. She is condemning herself quite enough, thank you very much, without adding the threat of eternal damnation to the pile.

The door knocker thumps, making her heart jolt. The knock sounds aggressive, dangerous—or perhaps just made that way by her sudden racing thoughts. She tries to tamp down her fear. It's just a knock at the door.

Then she hears: "Mama." Oliver's voice, on the other side of the door. He sounds panicked, distressed. Close to tears.

Abigail throws open the door and her son stumbles inside. One side of his face is red and swollen, a long tear in the shoulder of his jacket. The shirt beneath it is stained scarlet with blood. Ruth murmurs in shock as she hurries into the foyer. Abigail hisses out instructions to fetch cloths and water and the housekeeper hurries off towards the kitchen.

Blood has soaked through the sleeve of Oliver's coat, turning the blue wool black. The swelling on his chin is already beginning to darken to bruising.

"What happened?" Abigail demands. Her stomach is rolling. Not least because Father Dering is here to see this. She can feel his presence behind them. Cannot bring herself to look at him.

Nathan pokes his head down from the top of the stairwell, Eva in his shadow. Abigail barks at the nurse to get them out of sight.

"Oliver," Father Dering pushes, "did someone harm you?"

"No," he says shakily. "It was an accident. I slipped and fell on the rocks."

Abigail sees the priest's jaw clench, and she knows with certainty he has not bought the lie. She takes Oliver's uninjured arm and guides him towards the staircase. "Thank you for your visit, Father," she says brusquely. "But I've to tend to my son now."

For a moment, Father Dering hesitates, as though debating whether to argue. Whether to insist on staying. Insist on demanding more truthful answers. Abigail is relieved when he says, "Of course. I shall see myself out."

Abigail leads Oliver up the staircase. Ruth hurries up the stairs behind them with a fresh jug of water and clean cloths in her hand.

Abigail takes them from her, nodding her thanks to the housekeeper and closing Oliver's bedroom door behind her. She helps Oliver sit on the edge of his bed and gently slides off his coat. Eases his bloodstained shirt over his head. She is relieved to see that, though the slash on his arm is long, it does not appear to be deep. He sits shirtless on his bed with his head drooped, picking listlessly at his grimy thumbnail. Abigail can't help but let her eyes linger on him for a moment; on his narrow chest, his long, twig-like arms, the round slump of his shoulders. She cannot remember the last time she saw him even partially undressed. She is struck by just how young and childish he looks.

She empties the jug into the washbin and soaks a cloth. Squeezes it out and hands it to Oliver. "Hold this to your jaw."

He does so obediently. Abigail holds a second cloth to the cut on Oliver's arm, wiping at the dried blood that has trickled down towards his elbow. Focusing on the task at hand allows her, however momentarily, to push aside the questions she knows she must ask. The reality she must face, of what her son has involved himself in on her behalf.

"Who did this to you?" she asks at last. She hopes he will be honest with her, here and now. Hopes she won't have to go through the rigmarole of the lessons in order to get him to speak.

A tearful murmur escapes him. Abigail has not seen this vulnerability from him for many years. Had started to doubt it even still existed.

When he doesn't speak further, she says, "Have you been out picking pockets? Did someone attack you when you tried to steal from them?"

His silence is all the response she needs.

"You promised you'd not go near the thieving ring," she reminds him gently. Tries to keep the waver from her voice.

"I know," he murmurs. "But I was just doing what Lizzie's ma wanted you to do. I thought if I gave the ring what they wanted, they would stay away from you." He rubs his eyes with the back of his hand. "I thought you wouldn't have to lock yourself in the house anymore."

Abigail feels something lurch in her chest.

"I don't understand why they were coming after you in the first place, Mama. Was it because of me? Because I told Lizzie

I was a better pickpocket than her?"

"No." She closes her eyes. How much should she share with him? Perhaps keeping things from him is doing more harm than good. "I went out raising funds for the Jacobites with Mrs Mitchell," she admits. "Lizzie caught me as I was leaving one of the donors' houses. She forced me to give her a cut of the money. They are against the Jacobite cause because it took so many of their husbands and fathers. And they knew I was raising money for the movement."

Oliver doesn't speak at once. Abigail wipes at the blood on his shoulder and wraps a clean cloth around his upper arm. She ties it tightly, feeling him wince.

"Why did you go fundraising with Mrs Mitchell?" he asks finally. "Da hated the Jacobites."

Abigail nods. "I know. But… your father is not here anymore." It's the most rational explanation she can manage. And perhaps closest to the truth. She closes her eyes. "I'm sorry," she hears herself say. "This is all my fault. I stepped away because it's not safe to work for the Jacobites anymore. But I should have kept giving the thieving ring what they wanted."

"It's not your fault, Mama."

Abigail sits beside him on the bed and laces her fingers through his. She feels like a failure. Feels weak. "Whether or not it is my fault," she begins carefully, "it is my problem. Do you understand? It is not for you to solve. You need to keep the promise you made to me and stay away from the thieving ring. I don't want you putting yourself in danger on my behalf."

"And in return, you will tell Captain Ward I will make a fine cabin boy?"

She traces a finger across his thumbnail. Thinks of the tearful waver in his voice when he told her of the attack. The fear in his eyes. She thinks of cannon fire and raging seas and the ever-present shadow of death. "Is that truly what you want, Oliver?" she asks. "Have you truly thought about what that life would be like? How much danger you would be in at times?"

A look of hot surprise flashes across his face. "Of course I have. And of course it's what I want." He pulls his hand from hers. "I'm not afraid," he snaps. "If that's what you think." He stands up and goes to his wardrobe for a clean shirt. He pulls it on over his head, doing his best to disguise a grimace of pain. "The letter," he says suddenly, "in your nightstand. Why is it so valuable it needs to be locked up in that box?"

Abigail's heart jolts. "How do you know it's a letter?" He shouldn't know that. No one should know that. No one except her and Henry.

Oliver doesn't answer. Abigail gets up from the bed and rushes across the passage to her bedroom. Pulls open the nightstand. There is the brass box Henry had given her, with its tarnished corners. Holding her breath, she lifts the lid. The clasp slides easily from the lock, revealing the letter inside.

She charges back to Oliver's room, the box in her hand. Shoves it under his nose. "How did you open this?"

He shrugs. "I've read a lot about lock picking. It wasn't difficult. Hardly worth locking in the first place. Honestly, I'm a little disappointed in Captain Ward." He looks at her squarely. "Why is it so valuable?" he asks again.

"This has nothing to do with you," she snaps. Turns away. For all his bravado, she knows the attack has rattled him. And she also knows that if she is to look at him right now, she will not be able to keep her anger under control. And a fight is the last thing either of them need.

She pulls in a long, steadying breath. It's all right, she tells herself. This is nothing to panic over. What does it matter that Oliver has looked into the box and read the letter? His questions show he knows nothing of the situation with Lord Haver, the Whig party dissenter. Of course he doesn't. He's eleven years old. She forgets that sometimes.

When he returns for the letter, Henry will see that the lock has been broken. Will see that his precious letter has not been as safe here as she promised him it would be. The prospect sits uncomfortably in her chest.

"Is the letter in the box valuable enough to bribe the thieving ring into leaving you be?" Oliver asks.

His words make Abigail whirl around to face him. "What?"

"If it's so valuable, perhaps we could make a deal with the thieving ring."

She grits her teeth. When had her son started using phrases like *make a deal* and *bribe the thieving ring?*

She hesitates for a fraction too long. Enough for him to grab hold of that hesitation. "It's not mine to do anything with," she says. "I'm just keeping it safe." And a fine job she has done of that, she thinks dully.

As much as she does not want to admit it, she knows Oliver is right. The letter would fetch a hefty price, and would be especially valuable to those in the anti-Jacobite movement. Perhaps it *would* allow her to make a deal with the ring. Perhaps it would be a way to keep her and her son safe. She pushes the thought away. The letter is not hers. She cannot let this line of thought progress any further.

As though reading her thoughts, Oliver says, "You don't think Captain Ward would want you to use the letter to get yourself out of trouble?"

How does he see so clearly, she wonders? How is he so all-seeing, so all-knowing?

"He would understand," he continues. "I'm sure he would. After all, I think he loves you."

And of all her son's precocious words, it is these that knock her most off kilter. She busies herself at the washstand, refusing to let him see how much he has unbalanced her. What has he seen, heard, to have jumped to this conclusion? And as for whether or not it is true, she cannot allow herself the space to consider that right now.

"The letter does not belong to me," she says firmly. "And that is all there is to the matter."

CHAPTER TWENTY-TWO

Mr Emmett trudges across the embankment, inspecting Samuel's rowboat that is being lapped at by the tide. "Are you sure you'll not keep it, Mrs Blake?" he asks. "You don't want a way off the island in case you need to leave for any reason when the tide is high?"

"I'm sure," she says. If she ever needs to leave, she will find someone at the anchorage to take her off the island. It's far more pressing to make sure Oliver cannot get to Bamburgh and the thieving ring again. He will be furious when he finds out the boat is gone, of course. But so be it.

"All right, then. As you wish." Emmett scratches his grey beard. And you don't want no payment?"

"No," Abigail says shortly. She doesn't care about the paltry pennies the damn thing will fetch. She just wants it gone. Wants her son to stay away from Bamburgh and its bleak undercurrent of thievery. "Just take the boat, please."

"I've a new game," says Oliver, appearing at Nathan's bedroom door. "It's called Plundering."

Nathan looks up from where he is sitting cross-legged on his bed. He crumples the star map in front of him, hiding its contents from his brother. "Plundering?"

"Aye. Like a pirate."

Nathan chews his lip. He can't deny there's a part of him that's afraid. He had not enjoyed the last game Oliver had invented. Every time he thinks of the Viking Game, he feels a prickling beneath his skin. The last time they had played it, Nathan had hidden in the priest hole. Oliver had taken an age to find him, and Nathan thought he had at last managed to trick his brother.

But then he had grown tired of the priest hole. Grown bored and sore, and a little afraid. Could feel the heat from the fire seeping through the bricks. When he had tried to wriggle out, he discovered Oliver had blocked the hole closed, trapping him inside. Finally, Oliver had pulled him out and murmured *Come out and face your maker*, and had pressed the knife into Nathan's neck so hard it had left a line of blood. The next day, Nathan had been careful to keep his neck cloth pulled up high so Mama and Mrs Calloway couldn't see the mark the knife had left.

They have not played the game since. Have not played anything since. But the Viking Game, and the priest hole, and the fear that swallowed him when Oliver held him down and pressed the knife to his neck have always been on the edge of Nathan's thoughts.

He wants to tell Oliver to go away. Wants to tell him he

does not care about whatever stupid game he has invented this time. But the game is called *Plundering*. It makes him think of pirates and vast oceans, and the man at their dinner table who had come from the ship outside the window. And Nathan just has to know what this game is.

A candlestick, Oliver says. "Fetch it from the dining table. And we're going to pile up our haul here in the priest hole, like we're pirates hiding treasure."

"What are you going to plunder?" Nathan asks.

"The funnel bowl glasses," Oliver says. "From the liquor cabinet." The flickering lamplight makes the bruising on the side of his face look even darker. "Do you think that's a good treasure?"

Nathan nods.

"Good. Off you go."

A candlestick. He can do that. That's not frightening at all.

Nathan hurries out of the room, his stockings sighing against the floorboards. He can hear Mama and Eva chattering in the dressing room; can't make out their words. He creeps past on silent feet. He's not entirely sure what Mama will do if she catches him taking a candlestick from the dining table, but he supposes that a pirate plundering treasure ought to do so quietly.

The fire has burned out in the dining room, and the dark is lit only by a sliver of moonlight that struggles through the high windows. Nathan tiptoes through the shadows. He has to kneel up on a chair to reach the candlestick in the middle of the big table. He hides it under his shirt and rushes back upstairs.

He slips breathlessly back into Oliver's room. Produces the candlestick with a flourish.

"Well done." Oliver nods towards the open priest hole. Nathan sees that he has already added the funnel bowl glasses to their collection. He puts the candlestick down beside them.

"What next?" he asks.

"The pounce pot from Da's study."

Obediently, Nathan races off through the house again. He pulls open the top drawer of Da's desk, ignoring the pull of sadness that arrives with the smell of his tobacco. He hurries back to the bedroom with the pounce pot. Sets it down inside the priest hole with the rest of their treasure.

"Next," says Oliver. "The brass box from Mama's nightstand."

Nathan frowns. "What brass box?"

"In the nightstand," Oliver repeats. "In the drawer." He folds his arms across his chest. "If it's too hard for you—"

"I can get it," Nathan says hurriedly. He rushes out into the passage, breathless, before Oliver can protest.

He slips into his mother's bedchamber. He needs to be very quiet now. He is right next door to the room with Mama and Eva in it. He tiptoes. Holds his breath as he gently tugs open the drawer of the nightstand. It makes a metallic clattering noise as he opens in. Nathan peers inside curiously. He sees a handkerchief scrunched into a ball. A few pieces of jewellery that he has not seen Mama wear in an age. An empty bottle of scent and a few loose coins. Right at the back, like Oliver had promised, is a small brass box.

Nathan grabs it, shaking it curiously. The box is light; doesn't make a sound. There's a lock on it that looks as though it might be broken. He wants to look inside, but is too afraid to open it in case he can't get it closed again. He slides the drawer shut carefully.

Only when he is back in Oliver's room does he let himself breathe. He holds the box out to his brother. "Is this the one? What's inside it?"

Oliver takes it. "That's the one." He opens the lid of the box and peers into it. "The game is over now." And he pushes closed the priest hole, trapping their treasures inside.

CHAPTER TWENTY-THREE

Nathan lies on his stomach on the floor and reaches his arm under the bed. There, at the back, hidden behind a stack of books, is Da's telescope. Well, *his* telescope. Da had given it to him just after his seventh birthday last year. Said he was old enough to take charge of it now. Keep it safe. And that is what Nathan intends to do.

Tonight, he is not interested in looking at the stars, or the sparkling silver eye of Venus that appears first in the sky. Because tonight he can see lights on the sea. It could be the navy, or merchants. It could be the man who had sat at their dinner table and talked about Viking boats and privateers.

He wriggles forward on his stomach and pushes aside the fortress of books until he can reach the wooden box containing the telescope. He pulls it out from under the bed and takes the lid off carefully. Sets the wooden stand up at the window, settling the telescope in the cradle like Da had taught him.

Nathan peers through the lens. At first, he sees only swirls of darkness, interrupted by pinpricks of light. He adjusts the lens until a glow appears in his view. There is the ship. Through the powerful eye of the telescope, he can make it out clearly, with its three masts lit by lamplight like trees under the moon. He can even make out figures moving back and forth across the deck. He wonders if any of them are Captain Ward.

Nathan wants to hate the captain of that ship. Wants to hate him because he comes into the house and sits in the armchair that used to belong to Da.

But he can't hate him. He can't hate him for so many reasons—firstly, that the man in the ship had made his mother smile. And he can't hate him because Captain Ward knows so much about ships and sailing and Vikings. But most of all, Nathan can't hate the man from the ship because he might take Oliver away.

"I'm going to be his cabin boy," Oliver had said at breakfast one day. "He's going to take me to fight the French and see the world."

Nathan pulls his eyes away from the telescope and glances over his shoulder into the darkness of his bedroom. There's a part of him that wants to tell Oliver the ship is here. He knows his brother will be excited. But he also doesn't want to share this with him; wants his own private excitement. Besides, Da had told him to keep the telescope away from Oliver. It's why he hides it underneath his bed at the very back, behind the books, so far away that his fingers barely reach it. Oliver says he doesn't care about the telescope—says he doesn't care that he can't find its hiding place. But Nathan knows he's just pretending.

He is buzzing at the sight of the ship. Can't tell if it's the thrill of having those sailors in the house again, or seeing the smile on his mother's face, or the glittering possibility that the man from the ship might take Oliver away. He can't keep it to himself.

He creeps down the hallway and opens his sister's bedroom door. "Evie," he whispers.

She rolls over, disoriented by the lamplight suddenly spilling in from the hallway. "What?"

"Come and look at the ship."

"What ship?" Her voice is thick with sleep.

"Just come."

She slips out of bed and follows him back down the hallway into his bedroom. At the sight of the telescope set up the window, she hurries towards it. Peers into the lens.

"Can you see the people moving around on the ship?" Nathan asks. "Can you see the lights?"

Eva murmurs noncommittally.

"The man from the ship might come to the house," Nathan tells her. "And he might take Oliver away."

Eva turns away from the glass, dark hair clouding messily around her face. "Why is he taking Oliver away? Where's he going to?"

"To be a cabin boy."

Footsteps make the staircase creak and Nathan herds his sister away from the telescope. Tries to get her out of his room before their mother catches them. They have barely made it to his door before Mama strides inside. She opens her mouth to scold them, but Nathan blurts:

"Captain Ward's ship is here, Mama."

Words die on her lips, and a complicated look falls over her face, as though she can't quite decide what to say. "Are you sure?" she asks finally.

He nods. Sees his mother's gaze drawn towards the telescope. She makes her way towards it. Looks through the window, then bends to peer into the lens.

When she straightens, there's a look in her eyes that Nathan can't read. "Back to bed at once," she says, her words thin and hollow. "Both of you."

———————————◦◇◦———————————

The sight of Henry Ward's ship in the bay has her pacing back and forth across the study, a chaos of emotions rattling through her. Her heart is fast, and she feels more alive than she has in months.

I think he loves you... It's foolish, she knows, to let a child's words unbalance her so much. But as she peeks out of the study window at the lights of the ship, Abigail realises how desperately she wants them to be true. She also realises just how little she and Henry really know of one another. *Near strangers*, she thinks. He does not feel like a stranger.

She knows that, whether he loves her or not, Henry is going to come to the house. She is going to feel that same dizzying attraction she has felt for him since the beginning. And this time, with a certainty that reaches deep inside her, she knows she is not going to have the strength to stay away.

Or perhaps it's like this: she does not *want* to stay away. Because against every grain of sense in her body, Henry Ward has come to represent an escape from this isolated, dangerous life she has built; this life with fear at the edges. It's an escape she needs to take, if only for a night.

Abigail pulls the curtains closed in the study and goes to

her dressing room. She's a chaos of nerves; can barely find a coherent thought in her head. She takes a deep breath. It's late; long past midnight. Surely he will not come to the house tonight. She has a little time to gather herself.

She opens the wardrobe. Finds herself pushing past the dark shapes of her mourning wear to a sky blue mantua hanging at the back. She cannot remember the last time she wore it. She only knows it makes her feel far more alive than the dark clothes she has been drowning in since that bleak, snow-flooded December.

She runs her fingers down the feather-soft silk of the blue gown. The bodice is front-lacing—she could wrangle herself into it without Ruth's help. Could avoid laying herself out to the judgement of her housekeeper. Ought she be judged for wearing something other than her mourning gown? It has been more than nine months since Samuel's death.

Abigail closes the wardrobe door. Henry will not come tonight, she tells herself again. Not so close to dawn, when the secret of them would be exposed to the daylight. The blue gown is a decision for tomorrow. And perhaps if she were to wear it, she could also wear the pearl necklace that has been sitting at the back of her nightstand... She almost laughs at herself. Since when is she the kind of woman so fixated on how she will look for a man? She had barely ever considered such things in the presence of her husband. At least not since they had moved to Lindisfarne and become windblown and wild. But there's a lightness to these thoughts that has been long forgotten. And so tonight, she will willingly allow herself this vanity.

Abigail goes to her bedroom and pulls open the drawer of her nightstand. Reaches in to feel for the necklace. Her fingers graze the delicate pearl strands. But something is missing.

Her stomach dives.

She flies across the hallway into Oliver's room. Tears the blankets from his bed. "Where is the letter?" she hisses, yanking him from sleep. "What have you done with it?"

He rubs his eyes, squinting to make out the shape of her. "I gave it to the thieving ring."

Abigail feels hot, then cold. "Please tell me you are lying."

"I'm not lying."

Abigail's heart thunders. "The letter does not belong to me. I told you, it is not mine to do as you wish with." She scrubs a hand across her eyes. "Who did you give it to? And why?"

"I gave it to Lizzie's ma. I made a deal with her."

"A deal?"

"Aye." Oliver sits up in bed and looks her in the eye. "I gave it to her on the promise that they would stay away from us, Mama. That they would not come after you or me again, or ask us to steal for them. I made her sign an agreement and everything."

Abigail lets out her breath. "Do you truly think they will honour that, Oliver? Do you truly think that's how people like that go about their business?"

He falters. Doesn't respond.

Abigail begins to pace across the dark bedroom. She wants to believe he has done this out of a naïve attempt to help her. But she cannot shake the thought that this is act of retaliation. Punishment for her giving away Samuel's boat. Punishment for her taking away that small piece of his freedom.

Punishment, perhaps, for suggesting he might not have

the strength and courage to be Henry Ward's cabin boy.

"How did you get to Bamburgh?" she asks, her voice catching in her throat.

"I went at low tide, of course. I walked part of the way. Got a ride with a farmer part way." He shrugs.

Abigail goes to the window and lifts the curtain.

"What are you looking at? Is Captain Ward's ship here?" Oliver is out of bed in a second, racing to the window.

Abigail drops the curtain. Holds Oliver back. "Get back into bed," she snaps.

"Is the ship here?" he asks again.

"How can you be excited about such a thing?" she hisses. "I dare not think what Captain Ward will do when he finds out what you did with his letter."

Oliver's eyes flash. "No, Mama. You can't tell him what I did. He'll never let me join his crew!" He lurches forward, trying to grab at her hands. "Please. Just tell him you had no choice because the thieves were after us. Tell him how they were forcing us to steal for them. Tell him you were afraid they were going to come to the house. He'll forgive you. You know he will." He looks up at her with wide, imploring eyes. "I did this to help you."

You did it to punish me for giving away the boat. But no, she won't speak these doubts aloud. Won't give them any form, any life.

"Go back to sleep," she snaps, marching back towards the door. "I need to think about what to do."

Oliver stays sitting up in bed. In the glow of the lamp coming from the hallway, she sees the distress splashed across his face. "You're still going to tell him I would make a good cabin boy, aren't you?"

She doesn't reply.

"Mama? You promised!"

"I promised I would do so if you kept away from the thieving ring. Which you have failed to do. If you cannot keep your word, why should I keep mine?" She grits her teeth, fighting to keep her voice level. "Actions have consequences, Oliver. When are you going to accept that?"

She pulls the door closed angrily and strides back to her bedroom. Thoughts of the blue gown and the pearl necklace now seem painfully trivial. Because tomorrow, when Henry appears on the doorstep, she must tell him his letter is lost. And she must cross her fingers and hold her breath, and pray that his feelings for her, whether they are loving or something far more base and primal, extend as far as forgiveness.

CHAPTER TWENTY-FOUR

The children are lively around the breakfast table this morning; the boys chattering loudly at each other about the ship outside the window, and Eva interjecting with unrelated asides.

Though there is a part of her that wishes they were speaking of anything else—anything that might not cause such chaotic thoughts in her—Abigail is glad she is able to fall unnoticed into silence.

She takes a long, steadying mouthful of tea. After the discovery of the missing letter, she had barely slept, and she does not want Eva and Nathan to pick up on her unease.

Oliver is laughing, talking brashly, behaving as though their conversation last night had never happened. He seems oblivious to the chaos he has thrown her into. No, not oblivious. Just ignoring it. Because now he is looking her way. Catching her eye with a pointed look.

There's every chance he might not even have gone to the thieving ring with the letter, she thinks. Every chance this story about the agreement he had made Lizzie's mother sign is a complete fabrication. He might just have tossed that little brass box into the ocean, or left it lying in the street. She knows he is aware of the letter's value. But she also knows the depth of the deceitfulness inside her son.

After breakfast, she sends him upstairs with a long list of school work to complete, and strict instructions not to show his face until it's done. She takes Nathan and Eva into the parlour to wait for Mrs Calloway to arrive.

Abigail perches on the edge of the settle with her sewing, the children hunched over a game of knucklebones by the hearth. She finds herself looking towards the ceiling. Listening for any sound from Oliver's room. No doubt it will be mere minutes until he has crawled out through the passage again. *Good*, she finds herself thinking. She needs not to be around him today. Needs a moment to breathe. She realises that, somewhere beneath the love and the protectiveness, she is afraid of her son.

Eva lets out a wild shriek, making Abigail's heart jolt. She throws down her sewing and drops to the floor beside the children. Eva throws herself at her, arms cinching around Abigail's neck. Tears are rushing down her cheeks.

"I'm sorry," Nathan is saying beneath his sister's wailing. His own tears spill. "I'm sorry, Evie. I didn't mean to…"

Abigail wraps an arm around Eva's waist. "What happened?"

"She grabbed my shoulder," says Nathan, wiping at his tears with the back of his hand. "And I just… I just… I got scared and pushed her."

Abigail bends her head to meet his eyes, Eva still pressed into her. "You got scared. Why did you get scared? Tell me,

Nathan."

He cries harder. "I don't know."

"Was it your brother? Has Oliver hurt you?" Her voice wavers. "Tell me, Nathan, please. Please. I promise I'll not be angry."

But even as she speaks, she knows this is not the time for interrogation. She doesn't need to hear it spoken to know that Nathan has gotten too entangled in this dark world that Oliver has built for him. Doesn't need the details.

It pains her that he will not let her near him. Will not let her hold him, comfort him. Attempt to make that world a little lighter. But she has let him down enough. Has let both him and Eva down enough.

She knows Oliver is getting worse. Whether a result of his father's death, or Henry Ward's appearance, or just his rapid approach toward adulthood, he is becoming more and more dangerous. Impossible to manage.

Her instinct has always been to keep him close. But perhaps that is just making things worse. Perhaps it's her stifling closeness that has caused him to be like this. Perhaps she has poisoned him with her own darkness.

Perhaps he would be better off on Henry Ward's ship.

She can hardly believe she has allowed herself to think it. What kind of mother is she?

The answer comes just as quickly: a mother who is desperately concerned for her two youngest children.

She knows she is guilty of neglecting Nathan and Eva. When Samuel was alive, it had not seemed quite so dire. They had had an unspoken agreement that she would tend towards Oliver and he would favour the other two. *Favour*—no, it's wrong. Because she does not favour Oliver over her other two children. Does she? No. Not favour—just a different kind of love.

She cannot deny there are moments she is grateful for the children's nurse, for the petty school, for taking Eva and Nathan off her hands. Not because she does not want to be around them, but because once she has given Oliver what he needs, she feels drained dry. Has nothing left to give.

The moment Mrs Calloway arrives, Abigail goes to the village. She has never sought Henry ought before; has always waited patiently—or not so patiently—for him to come to her. But she cannot wait. She needs to do what must be done now, before she loses her nerve.

It has been weeks since she has shown her face in the village. She is wary of seeing Mairi and her husband. Wary of seeing Donald Macauley. Wary of Father Dering, and the barrage of questions he no doubt has for her after she cast had him out of the house with Oliver's blood beading on the foyer floor.

Abigail keeps to the edges of the village at first, skirting the farmland in the shadow of the castle. She looks out at the anchorage, searching the water, the jetty, for any longboats from the *Eagle*. When she sees none, she pulls her cloak tightly around her, puts her head down and enters the narrow coils of the village.

She cannot avoid familiar faces in a place this small. She hands out succinct and flimsy greetings to the vicar's wife, to Mrs Emmett. Pretends not to see Mairi's eldest son as he runs down Church Lane.

Once the boy's footsteps have disappeared, her eyes begin to dart again.

Henry will likely be speaking to his buyer this morning. Or wiping off the remains of a late-night visit to the tavern with his crew.

Or perhaps, more likely, he is still aboard his ship. Perhaps the wisest thing to do is return to the house and wait for him to show himself. She is not sure she can unearth that kind of patience today.

Abigail rounds the village; sees no sign of him. She returns to the anchorage and paces back and forth across the rafts of dried seaweed, the crunch of her shoes lulling her into something trancelike and necessary. He will come to the village, she tells herself. He will come to liaise with his buyer, as he always does when he is in this part of the world. And if he goes to the house to see her instead, Ruth or Mrs Calloway will tell him she is here in the village looking for him.

Finally, she sees him. He and several of his crewmen are seated in the longboat that is rounding around the point. She feels something flip in her chest.

Henry's eyes meet hers while he is still far out on the water, and the moment the longboat knocks against the jetty, he leaps out, striding down the worn wooden walkway towards her. There's a look of concern in his eyes that Abigail can tell is a reflection of her own.

"I need you to take him," she blurts. "Oliver. I need you to take him, before I change my mind."

Henry looks at her squarely. He dares to reach for her hand. She doesn't pull away as his fingers close around hers. "What's happened?"

She closes her eyes for a moment. "I'm scared for my other children," she admits. "And I'm scared for Oliver. I'm scared of where he will end up if nothing changes." Her blue eyes bore into his. "Please, Henry. I'm desperate."

He puts a hand to her shoulder, guiding her away from the jetty, and the eyes of his crew. They stand in the pale shadow of one of the fishermen's huts dotted along the sand. The wind carries a rhythmic wooden clattering across the water from the ships in the anchorage.

"I convinced myself I could manage him," Abigail says. "That I could keep him in line somewhat. But I see now that I've only been fooling myself. I've never had any control over him. I used to criticise his father for that. But I see now that I'm no better."

Henry doesn't speak at once, and a part of her is terrified he is going to refuse her request. A bigger part of her is terrified he is going to agree.

"Will you at least consider it?" she asks. "Please?"

"Of course." Almost imperceptibly, he tugs her closer. His hand slides up her arm. "Are you safe?" he murmurs. "You're not involving yourself with the Jacobite cause any longer are you?"

"No," she says. "I'm not." As for whether or not she is safe, that's a question she does not have room for right now. Because all she knows for certain is that Nathan is not safe. Eva is not safe. They will not be for as long as Oliver is in the house with them.

Henry's rough fingers tighten around her bare forearm, and in spite of the squall inside her, she feels a sudden aliveness beneath her skin. "Come to the house tonight," she says. "You and your officers. And perhaps you might speak with my son?"

CHAPTER TWENTY-FIVE

When Ward gets back to the ship, Finn is still slumped at the table of the great cabin with his head in his hand, and the map Ward had set him to copying spread out in front of him. As far as Ward can tell, he has made exactly zero progress on the work in the two hours he has been away on the island.

He stands over the boy with his arms folded across his chest. "I've had quite enough of this moodiness, lad. I know you don't like being up here in Northumberland, but I've not even asked you to come ashore. No one need know you're here." He had briefly considered leaving Finn in London with the *Fortune's* prize crew. He knows the boy would have preferred not to make the journey back up to this part of the country. But he feels too responsible for Finn to keep him out of sight for so long.

"I know, sir. Sorry." He lets out a hacking cough.

Ward raises his eyebrows. "You're unwell."

"No I'm not."

He chuckles. "What, you think I'm going to toss you

overboard if you're ill?"

Finn looks up at him with watery eyes, then looks back down again quickly. "Maybe. If I have what the prisoners on the French ship had."

Ward feels a tug of unease. He forces a smile. "I don't think so. Just a bad head cold I'd say. I think I'll keep you around for a little longer yet." He nods towards the map. "Finish up what you're doing and go and rest."

Ward holds the door open for Finn, then tucks the map and pencils back in his desk drawer. He pushes open one of the windows at the far end of the cabin, letting a stream of cool air inside.

He thinks of Abigail. Is not sure what to make of her desperate plea for him to take her son to sea. When he had last raised the subject with her, she had been violently against it. He wonders what has changed.

One half of him had told him to refuse; told him he did not want a boy like Oliver in his crew. The other half told him to accept at once; told him to do blindly whatever Abigail asked of him.

And so, caught in the indecision she so often manages to wrangle from him, he had not given her an answer.

He is open to the idea of having another cabin boy in his crew. Less open to the idea of that boy being Oliver Blake. Still, perhaps Abigail is right. Perhaps such a thing will change him for the better.

In any case, if he were to agree, he would offer the boy no more than a brief initial agreement; a month or two at sea at most. Perhaps that would be enough to set Oliver's life on the right track.

As it has done for Finn? Ward is not sure how to answer

that. He'd like to think so. For all this morning's moodiness, he's certainly managed to wrangle some discipline into the boy; stop him from ranting and raving in anger whenever things don't go his way. And he's certainly instilled plenty of nautical knowledge in him.

But Ward can't help but wonder if Finn wouldn't have been better off staying out on Longstone with his father. Safer, certainly. Happier? Maybe.

Ward wonders what Abigail's reaction would be if he took Finn to the house with him tonight. He has never told her that he already has a cabin boy; has always imagined that, as a mother of young boys, she might look down on such a thing. But her request suggests that maybe he is wrong about this. Or at least that she is desperate enough to acknowledge that not everything is black and white.

There's a chance, of course, that Abigail might recognise Finn as the Longstone lightkeeper's boy. A slim chance though, surely. He can't imagine Finn Murray has ever had any reason to associate with the family from the house on Emmanuel Head.

Finn will benefit, surely, from a night in a comfortable bed—a chance to sleep off his illness. More importantly, if he is to consider taking Oliver aboard his ship, he at least wants the two boys to cross into each other's territory beforehand.

It's a little past nine when the knock at the front door echoes through the house. Abigail has fed the children and sent Eva and Nathan up to bed. Exiled Oliver to his bedroom for now—she needs a little space from him to clear her thoughts.

Determine if she is making the right decision in asking Henry to take him to sea. As of yet, she has said nothing to Oliver about the issue. Since he had told her about taking the letter, she has spoken to him in only brusque half-sentences that barely keep her anger at bay. But tonight she will bring him downstairs to speak to Henry properly about his going to sea. Assuming Henry agrees to it.

Assuming he does not fly out of the house in anger the moment she tells him the letter is gone.

Abigail toys with the pearls at her throat as she makes her way downstairs to answer the door. Smooths the soft blue folds of her gown. The coloured skirts give her a much-needed burst of confidence. Out of the dark clothing she has languished in for so many months, she feels more energised, more hopeful. Feels less like she is drowning under the weight of life.

At the back of her mind, she is also aware that the blue mantua is an invitation. A signal to Henry that tonight, if he is willing, she will put the loss of her husband behind her.

She has no idea if, after he hears about the letter, he will still be willing.

The group is a large one tonight. Six men stand on the doorstep, along with a boy who can be no older than Oliver. He's tall and broad-shouldered, but with a smooth, youthful face. Abigail ushers them into the foyer, unable to take her eyes off the boy.

"He's one of yours?" she asks Henry quietly. Knows he can hear the surprise in her voice.

Henry's eyes glide over her, taking in her gown, the jewels at her throat, the cerise powder on her cheeks. Her attempt at snaring his affections—or rather, outrunning her own uncertainties—suddenly feels far too overt. Henry gives her a faint but weighted smile. "He is," he says, as though suddenly remembering the question. He puts a hand to the boy's shoulder; a protective, fatherly gesture. "A hardworking cabin boy, fighting the last of a fever. He's in need of a warm bed for the night."

Abigail nods stiffly. The sight of this child has made her request all too real. This is the life she is sending her son towards. A hundred questions fly at her; questions she wants to ask the boy. Whether he is happy. Whether Henry Ward is a fair captain. Whether it was his own mother who had sent him off to sea as a punishment for not being the son she wanted him to be.

But of course, she cannot ask any of this.

She wonders at Henry's rationale behind bringing the boy here tonight. She knows it's no coincidence that he has done so immediately after her asking him to take Oliver. Up until this moment, she had not even been aware that Henry had any children on his ship.

She gives the boy a thin smile she knows doesn't reach her eyes. "Of course," she tells him. "You can have my eldest son's room. He can share with his brother for the night."

Ward watches after Abigail as she glides up the staircase in a sea of blue silk. He can tell Finn's presence has rattled her. Caught her by surprise. He grips the boy's shoulder. "Behave yourself, lad. Do as Mrs Blake tells you."

Finn nods faintly. "Aye sir."

Ward sends one final glance up the stairs, then follows his

officers towards the parlour, leaving Finn alone in the entrance hall.

The sight of Oliver pressed against the wall in the passageway makes him jump. The boy is shadowed, barely lit by the lamplight spilling from the wall. Ward can tell he has been waiting for him.

"Good evening, Captain Ward," he says evenly.

Ward waits until the parlour door has closed behind the rest of the men. "Good evening, Mr Blake. I'm glad to see you. There's something I'd like to discuss."

A look of hope appears in Oliver's eyes. "Yes?"

Ward tilts his head, considering the boy. Something has happened that has made Abigail desperate for him to take her son. He needs to know what it is.

He could ask her, of course. But perhaps it would be more valuable for him to ask Oliver directly. His willingness to answer—or lack thereof—will tell him plenty about the boy's character.

"You may know your mother has changed her mind about you becoming my cabin boy," he says. "She has asked me to discuss the matter with you."

The glow in Oliver's eyes intensifies. "Has she?" he sounds suddenly innocent, excited.

"Do you know what it was that made her change her mind?"

Oliver pauses. "I can't imagine, Captain. Perhaps she just knows how much it would mean to me."

Oliver Blake is well spoken, certainly. But his words lack genuineness. And, Ward imagines, truth. He stares him down. "I value honesty among my crewmen very highly, Mr Blake."

"What makes you think I'm being dishonest?"

212

The self-assured question catches Ward off guard.

"I'm very honest," says Oliver, before Ward can cobble together a response. "Just ask my mother. We always tell each other the truth."

Ward makes a noise in his throat, unconvinced. He has always prided himself on being able to trust his instinct. And his instinct is telling him to be wary of anything that comes out of this boy's mouth.

Oliver takes a step closer to Ward and something darkens behind his eyes. "I can also keep secrets," he says, voice low. "Such as Lord Haver's connection with the Jacobite movement."

Ward hears his own sharp inhalation. He forces himself not to react. "How do you know of that?" he asks evenly. "Did your mother tell you?"

"No. I read about it. In the letter. In her nightstand."

Inwardly, Ward panics. Has Oliver told anyone else of this? If he has, and this information is on its way to becoming common knowledge, the letter will become near worthless. He had kept it locked up for a reason. Has no idea how Oliver managed to read it. Surely Abigail would not have told him about it.

"I did not know who Lord Haver was at first," Oliver continues, too lightly. "I did not really understand why you deemed the letter so valuable. But I understand now. I can see why you would wish to keep that information to yourself until the time is right."

Why is the boy telling him this? To prove his knowledge? His intelligence? No. Ward sees it then.

Blackmail. He will keep the news of Haver's dissent a secret, in exchange for a berth on the *Eagle*. The outrage that comes up on him is hot and sharp. Ward forces himself to swallow it down. "I am not able to be extorted, Mr Blake," he says firmly. "You can attempt to spread the information you read in that letter, but I'm afraid it will not serve you well."

Panic flashes across the boy's face. "I'm not trying to extort you. I swear it." His façade falls away. "Please, Captain Ward. Give me a chance. I shall be the best cabin boy you have ever seen. And I shall never resort to such trickery again." He looks up at him with wide, desperate eyes. "Please."

Ward's thoughts turn over. He knows he is letting Abigail down. But he also knows he has made the only decision possible. Yes, he wants to help Abigail turn her son into a more decent young man. But he will not do so aboard his ship. There is little point dragging the issue on any further. "I'm afraid not, Mr Blake," he says. "A privateering life is a dangerous one. I cannot have anyone aboard my ship that I do not trust implicitly."

Oliver's face falls. His eyes flash and he opens his mouth to protest. Seems to decide against it. He turns on his heel and disappears down the hallway, without giving Ward another word.

———⊰◈⊱———

Abigail rubs her eyes with impatience. She has laid a bed for Oliver on the floor of Nathan's room, but she cannot find her eldest son anywhere. The last time she had seen him, before the men arrived, he had been in his bedroom. She had made it clear that that was where she expected him to stay.

But now the room is empty. So is the priest hole. Has Oliver gone downstairs to speak with Henry without her knowing? Is he out running wild across the dunes?

As she is making her way back down the hallway towards the staircase, she hears a thump coming from inside Oliver's bedroom. Footsteps on floorboards. She throws open the door to see him pushing closed the panel of the priest hole. His pale hair is windblown, and she can tell he has just climbed up through the passage inside the wall.

Abigail closes the bedroom door behind her. Lifts up the lamp in her hand to illuminate his face. "What were you doing out there?" she demands.

"Nothing."

She can practically see the anger radiating from him. She wonders what has caused it. All she knows is that she cannot send him down to speak with Henry while he is like this; so closed off and angry, with these hot, glowing eyes. If Henry sees this side of him, he will never take him as his cabin boy.

Let him sleep off his rage, at least for a few hours. She can always come and wake him before Henry and the other men leave.

Abigail thinks of the bed she has laid for him on the floor of Nathan's bedroom. No. She will not put him in with his brother. Not while he has this wild look in his eyes.

"You're to sleep in my dressing room tonight," she tells him firmly. "On the settle."

"Why? Why can't I sleep in my room?"

Abigail doesn't respond at once. She senses, instinctively, that Oliver will not take it well to learn that Ward's cabin boy will be sleeping in his bed. The boy who already has the position Oliver is craving. The boy who has already passed

Henry Ward's test.

"Because I asked you to sleep on the settle," she says tautly. "And that is all there is to it." She plants her free hand on her hip. "Oliver? Do you have issue with that?"

He holds her gaze for a moment. "No, Mama," he says resignedly. "I've no issue with that." He turns for her dressing room, without waiting for a response.

Abigail watches after him, trying to steady the unease inside her. She tightens her fingers around the handle of the lamp and makes her way back downstairs. Ward's cabin boy is hovering in the foyer, shifting his weight, his gaze drifting over the seascape and portraits hanging on the wall. He looks uncomfortable, out of place. As though he is waiting for the house to swallow him.

He turns to look up the staircase at the sound of her footsteps.

Abigail stops on the landing and gestures to him to join her. "This way."

Obediently, he scrambles up the stairs behind her. Down the passage. Abigail brings her finger to her lips as they pass Nathan and Eva's rooms, not wanting to wake them. Or is it Oliver she does not want to disturb?

She pushes open the door to Oliver's bedroom. "You can sleep in here."

The boy sniffs. "Thank you."

Abigail nods. Swallows heavily. "Sleep well," she manages. She pulls the door closed. Steps across the passage and peeks in to check that Oliver has obeyed her orders. He is curled up on the settle, the blankets pulled high, so that only his pale hair is visible. She can tell he's sulking.

She hovers in the doorway, debating whether to speak

with him.

"Abigail." Henry's voice is gentle, quiet. Comes from the landing. He has never ventured up the staircase before. She senses that he is not allowing himself to venture all the way up, into this most private part of the house.

At the sight of him, the sound of him, she feels a chaos of emotions boil up inside her. She must tell him about the lost letter, of course. And she must talk to him about Oliver. But most of all, she wants to go back downstairs with him in her blue silk gown and her pearl necklace, and give in to herself. She is craving an escape from the pressures of the last months, the last weeks, the last days—never mind how fleeting and foolish.

She makes her way down onto the landing. Stands close to Henry. A coil of his pale hair has come loose from its queue, and hangs across the sharp plane of his jaw. She reaches out and lifts it lightly from his skin. Lets it trail over her fingers.

"I've sent Oliver to bed for now," she says. "He was not in the right frame of mind to speak with you about such a serious matter."

Ward reaches up to cover her hand with his own. Laces his fingers through hers. "Let's not speak of him now," he says. "There'll be time for that later." He lowers his voice slightly. A deep murmur that Abigail feels inside her. "I've been waiting months to see you. I can't tell you how much I've been longing to be alone with you again."

And it is exactly what she wishes to hear.

CHAPTER TWENTY-SIX

With her hand laced through his, Abigail leads Henry into the dining room. She can hear the distant murmur of voices coming from the parlour, and she is distantly aware that she is being a terrible host. She can't make herself care.

The room is dark, lit only by the lingering glow of the fire. Curtains pulled across windows, hiding the outside world. The air feels warm, pulsing, alive.

Henry tugs her towards him. Plants a tentative kiss on the edge of her lips. Abigail closes her eyes, enjoying the warmth of him. The gentle sigh of breath on her skin.

Voice low, he says, "I want to be more to you than just someone you see on occasion."

Abigail feels a smile on her lips. "I want that too."

He reaches out and tucks a strand of dark hair behind her ear. "I've also been thinking about your financial struggles," he says. "And what you've been forced to do since your husband's death."

Abigail swallows heavily. At once, her heart is pounding

for an entirely different reason. She does not want her secrets and lies brought out into this half-light. Just for now, she wants to forget they exist at all.

"I've opened a bank safe in London," Henry tells her. "An account with the new Bank of England. If it is not too forward of me, I would like to put the safe in your name too. Or rather, your son's. That way, if you are ever in need..."

Abigail hears her exhalation. She cannot believe he would do such a thing for her. She wants to feel guilt—knows it is his belief that she is a penniless widow that has led him to do this. But she cannot quite make herself feel it. Because this gesture, it goes a long way to solidifying whatever this unnameable thing is that's simmering between them. Goes someway to solidifying a future without fear and loneliness and danger.

"Thank you," is all she can manage.

He meets her eye. Trails rough fingertips down the delicate line of her jaw. "I hope it will go some way to showing you how I feel about you. And showing you there is a place for you in my future." He swallows visibly. "If you wish it."

And in that future, she thinks, she will tell him everything. Will tell him every painful truth. And maybe, just maybe, it should not be guilt she is feeling right now, but rather gratitude for all this. For this man who cares for her. Wants to make a future with her. Loves her? Perhaps. But right now, even without the promise of love, it is enough.

There is a danger to Henry Ward, yes. He has harder edges than Samuel had had; has a life scented with gunpowder and defined by the laws of the sea. And perhaps that is why she is drawn to him in a way she never was to her husband. Because she has hard edges too.

But: "You are always at sea," she says.

"I do not have to be." He smiles at her. "I am not at sea right now."

He pulls her close, kisses her hard. His presence feels all-consuming, as though she might drown beneath his weight. It feels impossible that someone as striking, as compelling as him might want someone as plain—and as tainted—as her. Her body comes alive at his touch, and she moves towards him, hands sliding instinctively over his rigid contours.

"Your men are in the next room," she whispers. Her breath strains against her stays, heat unfurling inside her.

His hands grip her thighs and lift her onto the table as though she weighs nothing. He smiles against her lips. "We had best be quiet then."

His mouth is on hers again before she can protest; and nor does she want to. She wants everything this man is willing to give her, she realises. Security, pleasure... and yes, horribly, a life in which her eldest son is no longer her struggle.

He slides his hands up beneath her skirts, pushing reams of blue silk higher until she feels the outside world fall away.

Nathan knows it's very late—could even be midnight. He has not slept for a second.

He knows the privateers are here. Tonight, he had pointed his telescope at the ship and watched as they had climbed into their boats and come towards the house. He had watched the globes of lamplight come bouncing over the dunes like fairy dog eyes. And he had listened as Mama had let the men inside.

Laughter and footsteps and voices.

Mama had come into his room soon afterwards, laying out blankets on the floor. For who, Nathan does not know. He had pretended to not be awake—had not even flinched when Mama had bent over to kiss his forehead. He knows she believed him to be asleep—she would not have touched him otherwise.

There have been lots of footsteps up and down the hallway, lots of shadows moving beneath his door. Mama and Oliver's voices, their words too soft to make out.

It's quiet for a while. Nathan hears the occasional burst of manly laughter floating up the staircase, which makes him think of Da. He wonders if the laughter belongs to Captain Ward, who is going to take Oliver away.

A door across the hallway groans as it opens. Nathan slips out of bed and peeks through the keyhole of his bedroom door. He sees his brother coming out of Mama's dressing room and tromping down the passage, back towards his own bedchamber.

Nathan hears mumbled voices. Someone else is in Oliver's room.

He opens the door to his bedroom as quietly as he can. Steps out into the passage and presses his eye to the keyhole of Oliver's room.

Oliver is standing eye to eye with another boy that Nathan doesn't recognise. The boy is dressed in only his shirt and breeches, his feet bare. His brown hair is all falling out of its queue; messy, like he's just gotten out of Oliver's bed. Does he come from the crew of sailors who are gathered downstairs? Does he, like Oliver, want to be Captain Ward's cabin boy? Perhaps he already is.

Oliver lifts the lamp in his hand, shining it into the other boy's eyes. "Why won't you speak to me?" he hisses. "Are you a half-wit? Or are you scared?"

The other boy is taller than Oliver, shoulders wider. Older? Maybe. It's hard to tell. "Leave me alone," the boy says huskily. "I just want to sleep. Your mother gave me this room."

Nathan feels a sudden, intense need to be a part of this—whatever this is. He wants to meet the boy who sails on the ship with Captain Ward. The boy who has clearly got under Oliver's skin.

Nathan can't bear the thought of staying out here in the hallway any longer. Holding his breath, he slips inside the room.

The boy from the ship turns to look at him, but Oliver gives him little more than a fleeting glance. Oliver sets the lamp on the floor and lifts his other hand, revealing the Viking knife he had hidden in his fist. Nathan feels his heart quicken. He takes a step back, his spine pressing hard against the wall.

Oliver holds the knife out in front of the boy. "Look at this," he says. "It's a Viking dagger. From the days when they raided the island."

The boy snorts. "A Viking dagger? It is not."

Oliver's eyes flash. "Are you calling me a liar?"

"You're lying, aye? Or are you just stupid?"

Nathan feels the air prickle. Feels the rage pouring off his brother. Oliver takes a step towards the boy from the ship. Turns the blade over slowly. Then he looks towards Nathan.

"Tell him, Nathan. Tell him it's from the Viking raids."

Nathan hesitates. He wants to please Oliver, of course.

But he does not want to look foolish in front of one of Captain Ward's crewmen. "I think it's just a fishing knife," he says at last. He dares a glance at his brother. Can tell by Oliver's narrowed eyes that he is unimpressed with this answer. Nonetheless, Nathan knows they have something far more impressive to show the boy than some tarnished old blade from the sea. "But there's a real priest hole in this room," he announces. "Behind the panel in the fireplace." He begins to hurry towards it, but Oliver shoves him hard against the shoulder.

"Get out."

Nathan feels a fizzing blaze radiating across his shoulder where Oliver touched him. The rage in his brother's eyes makes something close in his chest and he hurries out into the hallway. Stands with his back against the wall, staring at the closed door. Perhaps he ought to go downstairs and fetch Mama. But what would Oliver and the boy from the ship think of him then?

He presses his eye back to the keyhole of Oliver's room. Swallows a murmur of fear. Oliver has the blade to the boy's throat. Now, his stomach. He is speaking low, threatening words that Nathan cannot quite make out. And then he catches, *Left them all to die.*

He is speaking of the Viking raids, Nathan knows. Speaking of the monks slaughtered in Saint Cuthbert's church. Whirlwinds and dragons and the blood that pooled across their island.

Come out to face your maker.

Nathan feels frozen in place, his breath rattling against his lungs. He cannot tear his eye away from the keyhole. Cannot go back inside that room. And he cannot run downstairs to find his mother. Even though he is becoming more and more certain that that is exactly what he ought to be doing.

Once, he and Oliver had found a baby bird lying on the ground beneath a tree on the edge of the Macauleys' farmland. Nathan had watched silently as Oliver had pelted it with rocks until it was nothing more than a bloody mess. That had frightened him; made him see the darkness in his brother went deeper than he had first imagined. But surely that darkness doesn't go so far as to cut the throat of the boy from the ship.

Nathan thinks of Oliver trapping him in the priest hole. Thinks of him holding the knife to his throat; hard, too hard. Thinks of that line of blood running down onto his collar, and of hiding the bloodstained shirt beneath his bed beside the telescope so that no one would ever know. And somehow, while he is thinking all these things, he is also not thinking at all. Because there is a part of him that is far too afraid to think. He feels as though, if he thinks the wrong thought, Oliver will push that knife into the cabin boy's neck.

He shifts his weight and the floor beneath him creaks.

"I can hear you out there, Nathan," says Oliver, not pulling his eyes away from the cabin boy's. He doesn't move the knife from his stomach. "Go to bed."

Go downstairs, the voice inside Nathan's head screams. *Get Mama.* But he can't bear to think what Oliver would do to him then. He does not want to be put back in that priest hole.

When he doesn't move, doesn't speak, Oliver turns slightly so Nathan can hear him clearly through the closed door. "Do you want to spend another night in the walls?"

The cabin boy shoves Oliver away. He darts towards the door, but Oliver grabs hold of him, yanking him back. Slashes the knife across his forearm.

Nathan hears himself murmur at the same time as the boy from the ship shouts in pain. He sees the flash of movement pass across the tiny window of the keyhole. Sees the crimson bloom of blood on the boy's arm, stark against the white of his shirt. And Nathan watches the boy from the ship swing a desperate fist. Watches it strike the side of Oliver's head. Oliver falls sideways, his head slamming into the thick wooden post at the foot of the bed. And Nathan is unable to stop his cry from escaping as he watches his brother fall.

CHAPTER TWENTY-SEVEN

Henry's forehead rests against hers, and she feels his body rise and fall with gradually slowing breath. "You are all I think about," he says. "When I'm at sea."

Abigail smiles. "I hope that's not true. That sounds very dangerous."

Henry laughs; a warm honey laugh that Abigail feels inside her. The idea that she might fill his every thought is an impossibly pleasant one. It dulls the ache of these past months, of the thought of losing Oliver to his ship—by her own making. And it gives her the courage to confess to that which has so far been a complete impossibility: that she no longer has the Jacobite letter. No, she is not going to think of that now. Almost, but not quite yet. She is going to let herself get lost in the pleasure of this moment. Enjoy the feel of his body close to hers, for just a little longer.

Loud laughter rises up from the parlour. Drunken laughter, like the men are steadily working their way through the bottles they brought with them.

"You ought to join your crew," she says. "They will be wondering where you have got to."

He chuckles. "I'm fairly certain they know exactly where I've got to. And it's far more pleasant being in here with you."

"Leave them aboard next time," she says, surprising herself with her boldness.

His blue eyes shine. "As you wish."

He is like an illusion, she thinks. She realises she is waiting for him to disappear. Waiting to wake one morning and find he was nothing more than a dream. Never mind that her body is still buzzing with pleasure, and there is a dull ache between her legs.

She hears a cry from upstairs.

Nathan.

She pushes herself from the table and straightens her skirts. Hurries out of the dining room and up the stairs, Henry's footsteps thumping behind her.

She sees Nathan in the passage. He has his eye pressed to the keyhole of Oliver's bedroom door, palms flat to the wall. Abigail can see his back rising and falling with rapid, panicked breath. She hurries to him. Impulsively, she takes his arm, cursing herself when he yanks away. "What's happened? Where's your brother?"

His look of white-faced dread is one she has never seen before. It's going to fell her, she thinks. Whatever is on the other side of this door is going to bring her to her knees.

Henry throws the door open and charges inside, before she can prepare herself.

She stops breathing. Stops thinking. Hears a strangled cry that could be her own. There is no other sound; no sense. The world contracts and there is nothing but her son sprawled across the floor beside his bed. A thick seam of blood runs from his temple, shining in the gold glow of the lamp. Trailing, disappearing, into the dark floorboards. Abigail falls to her knees beside him, and some part of her is present enough to feel desperately for a pulse. But the glassiness in his eyes; the cold, vacant stare. She has seen this often enough—recently enough—to know this is death. Lying on the floor beside him is the thin-bladed knife he had pulled from the sea. She hears a sound try to escape her throat. She pulls it back in as her lungs strain. Presses her hands to Oliver's cheeks. Shakes him. Wills him, blindly, to come back to her.

Henry rushes to the window and wrenches it open. He leans over the sill and peers into darkness. Sea-scented air billows inside. He hollers out into the night, bellowing his cabin boy's name. He whirls from the window. Throws open the wardrobe. Peers under the bed. "Where did he go, lad?"

Abigail is only distantly aware that Nathan is in the room with them. At Henry's question, he edges towards his mother, but then backs away, as though afraid to approach his brother's body. He stumbles from the room and hovers against the wall in the hallway. Shakes his head.

"You don't know?" Henry demands. "How could you not know? Did you not see where he went?"

Nathan murmurs in fear.

"Henry, please," Abigail manages.

She knows, of course. She knows where the cabin boy is. The priest hole; the passage. There is no other explanation.

But something prevents her from speaking.

Ward thunders downstairs. She hears him speak to his men—curt, barked instructions to find his cabin boy. Distant, distorted sounds. The front door slams.

Abigail realises Nathan is no longer in the hallway behind her. She calls for him weakly, his name catching in her throat. She feels a deep cold taking over her body.

Nathan does not appear. Does not come to stand back here beside his brother's body. Does not come to join his mother in this breathless vigil as she sits in a pool of sky blue silk.

Find him.

Every cell in her body screams at her to stay here with Oliver, but she knows Nathan needs her. How many times in her children's lives has she chosen her firstborn over his siblings?

It's the deep quiet that pulls her to her feet; draws her out into the passage, and towards Nathan's bedchamber. Every inch of her is shaking, her vision swimming. The walls of the house feel as though they are tightening around her, forcing the air from her lungs. She stumbles into Nathan's room. Sifts through the shadows, finding the bed empty.

Down the hall to Eva's room. Abigail finds Nathan curled up at the bottom of his sister's bed. Eva is still sleeping, and Abigail is grateful.

Her chest is heaving. Grief is pressing down on her so heavily she can barely lift her head. But she cannot let it out now. Not here. Not around her children. She sits beside Nathan on the edge of the bed. Close. Letting him know she is here. No touching. Hopes the weight, the warmth, of her body beside his own will go some way towards comfort.

Ward pauses at the bottom of the staircase, staring up into the gloomy hallway. A part of him is desperate to go back to Abigail. Another part of him can't bear to face her.

But he knows staying down here is the height of cowardice.

He forces himself back up the stairs. Through the ajar door, he sees her sitting on her daughter's bed, her son curled up beside her. Ward hovers outside the room, feeling like an intruder. Less than an hour since he had imagined a life in which this family might become his own. Now, surely, that imagined future is in pieces.

He continues down the hallway. Dares to step inside Oliver's bedroom. At the sight of the boy's body, he feels a profound hollow yawning open inside him. A deep grief; if not for Oliver himself, then certainly for his mother, and those glittering possibilities that had come alive between them tonight.

He stares down at the knife beside the body, the trail of blood running towards it from gash in Oliver's head. What had happened here? He thinks of Oliver's deceitfulness. Thinks of the temper he has spent the past two years trying to purge from Finn. For a strange, fleeting moment, it feels as though bringing these two boys together was never destined to lead anywhere other than this. The regret is searing. Makes his body blaze.

He reaches down to close Oliver's eyes. The boy's skin is beginning to whiten. Body beginning to grow cold.

A door creaks in the room down the hall and Abigail appears at his shoulder.

"Help me move him," she murmurs. She crouches at Oliver's side, her eyes not leaving her son's face.

Ward bends, scoops Oliver's limp body into his arms. He takes a step towards the bed.

"No," says Abigail. "Take him to my room." She nods to the room across the hall.

Ward nods wordlessly. Carries him into his mother's room and lays him on the bed, his blood beading crimson across the pillow. He smooths the boy's shirt. Ties, pointlessly, the lacing at his neck. And then he turns back to Abigail. Does he hold her? Comfort her? He has no idea. He knows no words, no apology, will ever come close to being enough. But he cannot just give her silence.

"The boy will be punished," he says finally.

Abigail drifts over to the bed and curls up beside Oliver's body. She shows no inkling that she has even heard him.

"I've men out looking for him now," Ward continues anyway. "And at first light I'll go out to Longstone in case he's decided to return to his father."

His words seem to snap Abigail out of her daze. She sits up. "Your cabin boy is the lightkeeper's son? He's the one who did this to Oliver?"

Ward nods faintly. He knows he has done what he had promised Finn he never would—but how can he stay silent?

Abigail lets out a long, shaky breath and turns back to Oliver. Ward dares to press a hand to her shoulder. Feel her flinch beneath his touch.

"Leave," she says.

"Abigail, I…" He scrubs a hand across his face. "You shouldn't be here alone."

"I'm not alone."

"You know what I mean."

But he is not welcome here. That much is clear. He can

see in her eyes that she holds him responsible for this.

And as much as he wants to stay; as much he hates the thought of leaving her here alone, he knows his presence is doing more harm than good right now.

"I'll go to the village," he says. "Send the vicar to the house."

He waits for a response that doesn't come. And he steps out of the house into cold spring darkness that feels impossibly weighted.

⸻ ❖ ⸻

Abigail closes her eyes, Oliver's limp hand held tightly between both of hers. Keep him close, she thinks. Keep him close like she has always done. And somehow, she will change things.

The knock at the door echoes through the house, splintering the stillness. Abigail holds her breath, praying the sound won't wake Nathan or Eva.

The sound is swallowed quickly, the knocking disappearing into nothingness. Barely aware of herself, Abigail gets to her feet, makes her way downstairs. She is distantly surprised her legs have managed to hold her.

Father Dering stands on the doorstep, dressed in a dark cloak and cocked hat. "Mr Ward told me what happened."

She can't find a response; just steps aside to let him into the house. Leads him up the staircase and into her bedroom.

Father Dering approaches the bed. He kneels. Takes Oliver's hand in his and murmurs a prayer. Abigail lets his words wash over her. *Lord, forgive us our sins. Help us in our final hour.* Feels that grief pressing down on her, darkening her vision. No. Not now. She cannot let it out.

"Was this an accident?" Father Dering asks finally. "Mr Ward was unclear on the details. I can see Oliver has hit his head, but…"

He knows, Abigail is aware, of the kind of boy Oliver is. Was. Does not dare think of what questions are circling in his head.

She can only imagine the storm of gossip that will arise if the villagers learn Oliver died from a fight with the lightkeeper's son. It will engulf her house, her surviving children. And it will engulf that tiny spit of Longstone, where the firelight burns to keep men alive.

The truth will not bring her son back. It will only tarnish his memory.

"He fell," she manages. "The bedhead…" It sounds like a lie. Sounds like a story the villagers will poke holes in.

For a long time, Father Dering doesn't speak. Doesn't ask for the missing pieces of the story.

Is this, Abigail wonders distantly, why she had not told Henry of the priest hole, and the passage his cabin boy had used to escape the house? Because even in the depth of her shock and grief, there had been fear of what Oliver might have done in the last moments of his life? And perhaps she did not want the boy she had sent up here to Oliver's room to be hanged for his… what? Crime? Act of retaliation? Self-defence?

One child was dead already. Condemning another to death would not bring her son back.

Father Dering clears his throat. "You know better than anyone that smallpox is rampant in these parts. No one would question…"

Abigail nods wordlessly. Does her son deserve this—for his end to be tidied into something more palatable? She knows the truth will just lead to more questions—questions about what Oliver did to invoke the cabin boy's attack. She knows, because they are questions she cannot help but ask herself.

She knows she could ask Nathan.

Perhaps she ought to. Can't bear to. She does not want to know the answer. Nor will she force Nathan to relive such a thing. She does not want him to speak of his brother any more than he has to.

Perhaps she does not want him to speak of his brother any more, ever. Because she knows that being Oliver's younger brother has left a deep imprint on him.

Father Dering clears his throat. "The watching of the body," he says carefully. "Do you wish to undertake it yourself? Or would you rather he be taken to the church?"

Abigail hears a muffled sob come from her throat. When Samuel had died, she had sat with his body throughout the night with Ruth by her side. Watching over him. Confirming his death. Ensuring he would not mistakenly be sent to his coffin alive. Keeping vigil over her husband's body had taken almost every ounce of her strength. She cannot fathom doing so for her child.

"Take him," she manages. "Please."

Father Dering takes her arm to steady her. "Of course. Is there anyone from the village you would like me to send to the house? My wife? Or Mrs Mitchell, perhaps?"

"No," Abigail says quickly.

"Are you certain?"

She nods.

The rest happens in a haze: the priest wrapping her son's body. Placing him in the wagon to be taken to the church. Father Dering disappearing from the house, the soft sigh of wagon wheels against the path carved through the dunes. They have come to an unspoken agreement that her son has died of smallpox. Believable enough, Abigail supposes. She has barely shown her face in the village for weeks, months; easy for the villagers to believe she was nursing her ill son.

Abigail goes to her daughter's bedroom. Curls up between the shapes of her sleeping children. She presses herself against Eva's tiny body, inhaling her warmth, trying to settle her own breathing into the same steady rhythm as her daughter's. She cannot be alone in the vast expanse of her own bedchamber tonight, with Oliver's blood staining her pillow.

But nor can she close her eyes and let sleep take away this most unbearable of days. Do so, and she sees Oliver's lifeless body on the floor beside his bed. Sees his eyes, vacant and cold, fixed on nothing. Sees the look of dread on Nathan's face as he turned away from that keyhole.

Instead, she lies awake, staring through the gap in the curtains. Her eyes fixate on the tiny globe of firelight spilling from the shipping beacon on Longstone. And she feels the grief tear open inside her.

CHAPTER TWENTY-EIGHT

When dawn begins to lift the sky, Ward climbs into a longboat. He pulls slowly, steadily on the oars, feeling the pit inside him turn into something heavy and hollow. He shivers, a chill going through him that feels far beyond the effect of the cold dawn air.

The island of Longstone emerges from the cloud like ink in water. In the pale morning, the firebasket is still glowing, a gold glimmer against the sea of white. Ward can just make out the crooked jetty, the stone cottage on its raised foundations, bolstered against the sea.

Already, he is perhaps too close. He does not want to be seen. But he needs a glimpse of what is happening on that island.

He and the other officers have been hunting for Finn since they had left Highfield House last night. They had torn apart the island, searching the dunes and coves and the snarls of the village by lamplight. The tide had been high, and Ward had not imagined Finn had battled the ocean to get onto the mainland. But now he has to consider it a possibility. He knows the boy a capable swimmer.

He also knows there is a chance Finn might have found a boat unattended at the Lindisfarne anchorage and fled back here to Longstone. Unlikely, perhaps, given what Ward knows of the tension between Finn and his father. And perhaps more unlikely that he would not flee further afield. Somewhere the shadow of the *Eagle* cannot reach. Perhaps if Finn is to return to Longstone, to the father he had run from, he will do so once the ship has left these waters.

Ward pulls the oars from the oarlocks and settles them inside the longboat. The boat drifts on the water, caught in a deep stillness that the soft lash of the waves against the boat quickly becomes a part of.

Ward squints in the pale light. No movement from the island. He sees only one small sloop tied up at the jetty, suggesting Finn has not returned home.

Ward blows into his gloved hands to warm them. Is he going after Finn out of concern for his safety, or because he wants him punished? He can't tell. The rage in him, the disappointment, is almost unfathomable. But so, he realises, is his fear for the boy's wellbeing. Because when all is said and done, Finn is still just a child. And the thought of him running, afraid, penniless, makes Ward's stomach knot.

There is a part of him that does not want to find the boy. Because if he is to find him, he will have to make this terrible choice of what to do with him. By all rights, what Finn has done ought to be punished by death. The ship's articles say as much—a killing outside of battle or duel is punishable in kind, even if the death was unintentional. Ward cannot bring himself to even entertain the possibility that Oliver's death was anything other than an accident.

He is not sure he would have the strength to mete out the punishment his own articles say Finn deserves. The right thing? Perhaps. What Abigail would want? Surely. Surely if she got her hands on Finn Murray, she would tie the noose for him herself.

Throughout the sleepless night, Ward has been replaying that moment when he first burst into the room to find Oliver's body. The window was closed, he thinks. Jammed shut. He'd wrenched it open it to call out into the night for Finn. *The window was closed.* Which meant Finn could not have used it to escape the house.

But what alternative is there? Had he somehow made it downstairs without anyone noticing? It seems so unlikely.

Or is he wrong about the window? The more Ward thinks on it, the more the memory blurs, and the less sure he is. But what does it matter? Oliver is gone. Finn is gone. And Ward cannot help but blame himself.

Over and over, he has been playing yesterday's choices in his head. His decision to take Finn to the house. His abrupt refusal to take Oliver to sea. His enticing Abigail downstairs when she had been busy tending to her children. How might things be different if, for just one of these instances, he had chosen a different path?

He had meant everything he had said to her about their building a future together. Last night, with her breath on his skin, that future had almost felt tangible. Now, everything has fallen away. Ward wonders if he will ever be welcome at Highfield House again.

He watches the island for a long time, a thousand thoughts colliding inside his head. The sky has lightened completely now, the beacon dwindling against the morning. Ward watches a man—Finn's father, no doubt—emerge from the cottage and trudge across the rocky island towards a small stone shed. As he returns to the house, he seems to catch sight of the longboat loitering on the sea. He strides out across the jetty. Lifts a hand to shade his eyes from the needles of rising sunlight.

He stands motionless for several moments, matching Ward's own inaction.

"Can I help you there?" he calls gruffly. Ward can't tell if the offer is genuine, or a veiled threat.

Ward opens his mouth to call back. To ask about Finn. But something stops him.

Finn is not on the island; this is clear enough. And he has nothing of any use to share with this father who has lost his son. Days ago, yes. He could have told him his boy was safe and well, could have admitted he was the one who had drawn Finn into a life of privateering. But now he has nothing of use to offer his father.

You are a coward, Ward thinks to himself, and the thought is followed by thick pull of self-loathing. But he lifts the oars and settles them back into the sea as silently as possible. Pulls away, averting his eyes from the man standing alone on the edge of that lonely, windblown island.

Which village is this? Finn tries to rattle though the hazy map inside his head. He had passed through Beal after he had swum across from the island, then followed the road north until it vanished into the dark. When dawn had come, he had

kept moving. So maybe this cluster of houses is Ancroft or…
He doesn't know. All he's sure of is that he has never been so
cold in his life.

After he had found the priest hole, and the passage that
led out of the house, he'd run across the island without his
jacket or boots and leapt into the sea to escape Holy Island.
Had spent the night shivering in his wet shirt and breeches.
It's a cold that reaches his bones; that makes his thoughts
sluggish and tangled. His throat is burning and every muscle
in his body aches. The cut on his arm is pulsing. It's stopped
bleeding now, but it's left a battlefield of blood on the sleeve
of his shirt.

Finn crouches behind a low stone fence, staring at the
washing line behind a cottage on a bend in the street. He
knows he needs to keep moving. Keep heading north, where
Captain Ward will not find him. But he also knows that to do
that, he needs boots. Dry clothes. Food.

There's a pair of breeches on the washing line. Shirts
flapping in the breeze. In his fevered state, he thinks of the
ghosts of pipers, and sails luffing on the mainmast of the
Eagle. It's a coat he is craving more than anything, but a dry
shirt and breeches will be a welcome start.

Finn's eyes dart. He can see smoke puffing from the
chimney of the cottage; sees flickers of movement through
the cloth window. Over the fence, in and out, he thinks. And
no one will be any the wiser.

He is nervous. He's never stolen anything in his life—not
if you don't count the French ships and cargo he had been a
part of taking. But Captain Ward always said that patriotism,
not theft, because they had a letter of marque.

Captain Ward would thrash him silly if he knew what he

was about to do. So would Da. The thought makes his chest ache. Because Finn knows he will never see Da or Captain Ward again. How can he? He can never go home to Longstone now. Captain Ward will be looking for him, waiting to string him up for killing Mrs Blake's son and running away from his crime.

He wonders if all the men he had sailed with feel like this after they fire the cannons and pull the triggers on their pistols. Do they feel this same dark and heavy weight in their bellies at the thought of the lives they have taken? When they lift their tankards to celebrate a victory, are they thinking of men who will never celebrate again?

All Finn knows is that he will carry this on his shoulders for the rest of his life. When he is falling asleep, he will feel that blade pressed to his belly. When he closes his eyes, he will see the boy's head cracking against the bed. And he will feel, always, always, always, that terrible guilt and regret that had broken over him when he had seen the boy's lifeless eyes staring up at his. That desperate need for time to reverse. For that impossible chance to do things differently.

And what is a stolen shirt compared to all this? What point is there trying to be a decent person now? The thought makes him dart over the fence and yank the shirt and breeches from the washing line without another second of hesitation. He runs down the street, his bare feet muddy and sore. Hides behind a tree and wrestles off his damp, bloodstained shirt. Changes into the stolen clothes. A man's clothing—the shirt hangs loose on his shoulders and he has to cinch the lacing of the breeches tight to keep them from sliding over his hips. But they are dry and clean, and that is all that matters.

What now? A coat and boots and food, yes, but after that?

How does he go about surviving when he has no place to go and not a penny in his pocket? Finn supposes he will just keep walking. If he keeps going north he will reach Berwick, and that is a town that is big enough to hide in. Perhaps even big enough to find another ship to sail on, or a farmer looking for workers.

He knows Captain Ward has taught him a lot of useful things. Things most lads with his upbringing would never know. Reading and writing, yes, but more than that too: navigation and ship handling and many other things besides. Like how to take orders. And that, Finn thinks, might be the most valuable thing of all.

He puts his head down and starts to walk, his wet clothes bundled up beneath his arm. Just keep walking, he tells himself. Keep walking, and he can put it all behind him: Lindisfarne and Longstone, and his time on the *Eagle*. But the harder he tries to stop the thoughts, the more violently they fly at him, until his mind is full of his father, of Captain Ward, of the boy he had killed. Full of the woman whose son he had taken, and those invisible, sleeping children behind the doors of the house with the passage inside the wall.

CHAPTER TWENTY-NINE

Nathan is wearing his mourning clothes again. They don't hang off his body as much as they did when he was standing at Da's coffin last winter. He can feel his toes pressing into the ends of his shoes now, and his jacket is tighter around his shoulders.

He stands on the edge of the grave with Mama and Eva, just as he had when they had buried Da. Today, though, it does not feel like a mountain is pressing down on his shoulders, or like all the air has gone from his lungs. He wonders if that makes him a bad person. His brother is dead. And yes, he feels a strange hollow, the sense that something has been gouged from his life, never to return. But shouldn't he feel like a mountain is pressing down on his shoulders?

His gaze drifts along the rows of villagers gathered in the churchyard. There are Mr and Mrs Emmett, and Mrs Dering, who had taught him at the petty school. Mrs Calloway is here, dabbing at her eyes with a handkerchief, even though Nathan knows she never liked Oliver. There is Mr and Mrs Mitchell, and Hugh, who would yell insults at Oliver whenever he saw him.

Does Hugh Mitchell feel like something has been gouged out of his life too, now he has no one to yell at in the street? Does he too feel this strange hollow inside him?

Hugh's little sister is standing beside him, winding a piece of red hair around her finger and staring hard at the stamped metal patterns adorning the fabric on the lid of Oliver's coffin. Nathan wonders what she is thinking. She looks up, as though feeling his eyes on her, and Nathan turns away quickly.

Father Dering's robes billow in the wind and make him look like a giant bat. He says, "May God watch over this dear child, taken too soon by a cursed illness."

But Nathan knows it wasn't the illness that had killed his brother. It was the boy from the ship. Oliver had put the Viking knife to the cabin boy's throat, and the cabin boy had swung a fist. Oliver's head had hit the bedpost and—the thought comes before Nathan can catch it—maybe he deserved it. And that, Nathan thinks, definitely, *definitely* makes him a bad person.

Before they had come out here today, Mama had sat him on his bed and pressed her hands down on the mattress beside his, like she was holding his hands but not holding his hands. She was not dressed in the same black gown she had worn for so many days after Da's death. Instead, she was wearing white, because Oliver was an innocent child, or a child at least, and white was the colour you wore when an innocent child was sent back to God.

"Nathan," Mama said, "no one needs to know what you saw the night Oliver…"

Died—he finished the sentence in his head; the sentence she couldn't say.

He just nodded. Did not want to tell anyone what he had seen. The things he saw through the keyhole have been going around and around in his head since that night, and he feels as though speaking about it will give them even more power. He has not spoken about them to anyone. Even Mama has never asked for details of what happened, and Nathan is grateful.

"When people ask, we will tell them Oliver caught the smallpox like Da." Mama's voice was thin and rattly. "Do you understand?"

Yes, he understood. Understood he was to breathe in this lie so much it became the truth. Understood they would not have a wake in the house for Oliver, for people to pray over his body and lay flowers, in case people saw the gash in his head and came to learn how he really died. They would just bury Oliver in the churchyard and the bells would toll, and then he and Mama and Evie would go back to the house to hide away.

Mama tugs him and Eva forward to the edge of the grave. Nods at them to take a handful of the freshly dug earth. Nathan does so obediently, feeling a pull of reminiscence from Da's burial. He looks down at the coffin holding his brother's body. Tries to imagine Oliver inside it. Like being inside the priest hole, he thinks. But forever. That hollowness in his stomach yawns open, and he releases the handful of earth. Watches it flutter down. And as it lands on the lid of the coffin, it seems to make a thud far louder than could ever be possible.

John Graveney leans back against the *Eagle's* saloon and stretches his long legs out in front of him. Blows a slow, steady line of pipe smoke into the sky. A heavy grey is pressing down on the island, and he can't tell if the dampness in the air is trying to be cloud or rain.

He looks up at the sound of approaching footsteps. Quartermaster Hunter grunts like a long-suffering donkey as he lowers himself down beside Graveney, dropping the last few inches with a dull thud.

Graveney chuckles. "All right there, old man?" He takes another quick draw on the pipe before passing it to Hunter.

The quartermaster snorts in response.

Graveney closes his eyes, blowing out the smoke. Tries to let the exhalation settle him.

He's aching to leave Lindisfarne. They've been here more than a week, the ship languishing in the bay beyond the anchorage—keeping their distance from the house, no doubt, after what happened between the two boys. Time is standing still. There's a restless frustration burning under his skin.

This inaction has given him far too much time to think. To think about the prisoners. About his own shifting views. Thoughts he wishes he didn't have. Thoughts that nights at the tavern have been unable to wash away. He wants simplicity: a world where the Williamites are right and the Jacobites are wrong, and he never heard a Catholic prayer murmured on that merchant ship, or thought of his mother praying the rosary.

But he can't find that world any longer. He just hopes that once they're back out at sea, they'll be thrust back into conflict, and he'll be far too immersed in whether he's going to live or die to think about what that life might look like.

Graveney doesn't even know why he's entertaining these thoughts. Leaving Ward's crew is not an option. He's far too deep in debt to step away. Without this regular income, and an officer's position to boot, he'd be curled up on a street corner somewhere in Saint Giles, stealing from the markets to survive.

Creaking davits and footsteps, and Graveney knows Ward has finally returned to the ship. Despite the hounding of his officers, he'd been adamant that they remain on the island. For what purpose, Graveney cannot quite tell. As far as he's aware, Ward hasn't found the courage to face the family in the house again. There seems to be no reason to them being here beyond the captain wallowing in his own bad decisions.

"Here we go," Hunter murmurs to Graveney, scratching at his thready white beard. "About bloody time." He clambers to his feet, leaning on the saloon wall for support, the pipe dangling from his other hand. He shuffles across the deck to meet the captain. Graveney leaps up to follow.

"Come on, Henry," Hunter says firmly, clapping the captain over the shoulder. "We've been here long enough. We've business to attend to in London, aye?"

Ward doesn't speak at once. He looks pale and drawn, with shadows under his eyes and a new slump to his shoulders. Still, his hesitation is something of a victory, Graveney supposes. Yesterday, when he and the other officers had raised the issue of leaving, Ward had lopped off the conversation and marched away without so much as a coherent response.

It had taken days for Graveney to get the full story out of

him about what had happened at the house that night. Tucked away in the parlour with a bottle or two of whisky, he and the other officers had had no thought that anything was amiss until Ward had sent them out into the night to search for the cabin boy.

Ward turns to look back at the island, his eyes glassy and faraway. The ruins of the priory are washed by cloud, like a shipwreck in murky water. "I'll have an answer for you shortly," he says. Disappears into the saloon before either man can ask any more questions.

Hunter watches after him. "The man's going to stay here. I'm telling you." He shoves the pipe back into Graveney's hand. "He's going to stay here for the woman in the house. There'll be no more privateering for him. Just you watch."

The comment catches Graveney off guard. For all the captain's brooding, he'd not considered the possibility that Ward might step away from a life at sea. The thought is jarring. Doesn't quite seem to fit. Henry Ward seems like a man who does not exist outside of the confines of his ship. But Graveney knows Abigail Blake has gotten under his skin.

The notion of Ward putting an end to his privateering is an uncomfortable one. But why? Ward's leaving wouldn't mean the rest of the crew would be put out of work. Ward could just send the *Eagle* out with a newly appointed captain and collect the income due to him as the ship's owner. There's nothing about this that makes that street corner in Saint Giles any closer to a reality.

Hunter trudges back towards the saloon as the drizzle gives way to steady rain. "He's a changed man. And you ain't been yourself lately neither."

Graveney thinks to laugh it off. *What are you talking about, old man?*

He hesitates. A moment too long.

Hunter snorts. "You're still wound up over them French prisoners."

Graveney shrugs, trying to make light of the situation. "The ransom could've been made by just holding the *Fortune's* captain and master."

Hunter leans a gnarled hand up against the wall of the saloon, preventing the younger man from passing. "And? What else?"

"There's nothing else."

Hunter snorts. "Bull. You've been on about this for weeks. Something's got you, I know it." He raises thick grey eyebrows, a new look of suspicion in his eyes. "What're you hiding, John?" The words feel far too accusatory. Feel like a threat.

Graveney is relieved when the saloon door creaks open and Ward appears in the doorway. Eyes vacant as he says, "We're to sail at first light."

CHAPTER THIRTY

At first, the house seems impossibly empty. Quieter; unfilled—unfulfilled. A place so weighted by death and loss.

Abigail had chosen not to bury Oliver with Samuel. Had not claimed a place for him at Saint Aidan's, forever beside his father.

In the weeks following Oliver's death, she finds herself questioning, again and again, why she had made this decision. Perhaps she could not bear to go back there so soon, to the churchyard where she had watched her husband's coffin disappear into the earth. Perhaps it just highlighted the cruelty of being forced to bury her son less than a year after she had buried her husband.

No, it was more than that. It was the knowledge that Bamburgh had never been Oliver's home, as it was Samuel's. But it was also the dull knowledge that Samuel and Oliver had never had the kind of relationship Abigail imagined a father and son ought to have. They had never had that innate connection that Nathan and Samuel had shared, that warmth, that easy affection. In her frustration, her anger at her husband, Abigail had told herself Samuel had not tried hard enough. But she knows in truth that Oliver had not allowed it. Even as a young boy, he had never been the kind of child to build close relationships—at least with anyone other than herself. She will never know the kind of man he would have grown into.

Well, she knows. But she can tell herself otherwise.

A part of her had feared that no one would attend her son's burial. Perhaps she had cut herself off from the village too much. Perhaps Oliver had been too challenging a child for people to wish to mourn him. Perhaps word of the accusations Abigail had flung at Mairi had filtered through the village.

But in the end, she had not buried her child alone. The tolling of the church bells had brought much of the village to Saint Mary's, and many of the same people who had attended Samuel's burial had also been there for Oliver's, including Mairi and Elias Mitchell. Abigail and Mairi had not shared a word beyond rote condolences and murmured thanks. It was far more than Abigail had expected.

In the weeks after his brother's death, Nathan is even quieter than usual, retreating to the distant world of his star maps and telescope. On more than one occasion, she catches him standing outside his brother's room, back pressed to the wall, and a look in his eyes that is at once both vacant and overflowing.

But then, unexpectedly—or perhaps not—he awakens. When they sit down to dinner—the three of them lost within the endless acres of the dining table—he tells her about comets and constellations and moons circling distant planets. She had no idea he knew about such things. Had no idea his and Samuel's love for the skies had extended into such far-reaching parts of the universe. As though encouraged by her brother's intellect, Eva's questions gain a new depth. She asks about seasons and sunrises and the world beyond the island—and how has Abigail missed her daughter turning from an infant into this bright young girl? Oliver's loss is a searing pain inside her, but it makes her even more painfully aware of how much she had been neglecting her other children.

Eva asks many more questions about Oliver's death than she did about her father's. She is nine months older, endlessly more curious. Abigail gives her the simple lie-that-has-become-the-truth she has been giving the villagers. Another fatal bout of smallpox. It's easier to tell Eva her brother died in the same manner as her father. Easier to put it into a neat box, pare it down into something her four-year-old mind will understand. The truth of Oliver's death is one she will never need to know. Abigail will make sure of it.

Lying has always come easily.

She begins to go back to the village. A church service. A visit to the apothecary, the post house. Walking Nathan to the coach that will take him up the coast to the grammar school. Abigail knows her children deserve better to than to live out their lives imprisoned in Highfield House, and there has been no sign of the thieves in the four, five, six weeks since Oliver's death. And while Abigail knows her friendship with Mairi is in pieces, Mairi's civility the day of Oliver's burial has given Abigail the strength to believe nothing will crumble if she dares to show her face in the village again.

Oliver has been gone almost two months when Donald Macauley chases Abigail out of the church after Father Dering's Sunday service. The autumn is careening toward winter, great sacks of cloud hanging low over the ruins of the priory and turning the sea to slate.

"The Baron of Milgate," Macauley says, voice low.

It's a name Abigail has barely thought of in the turbulence of the past two months. But suddenly her thoughts are back in Bamburgh, circling around thieving rings and mud-streaked alleys, and Jacobite donors with overflowing pockets. She swallows hard. Forces herself to keep her composure.

"What about him?" She dares to look at Macauley; an attempt to make light of his comment. The moment she meets his accusatory grey eyes, she regrets it.

Mrs Calloway glances in their direction, a faintly concerned look on her face. Abigail gives her a faint nod, gesturing to her to take the children back to the house. She dares to look back at Macauley. He strides towards the empty far corner of the churchyard, shadowed by the ruins of the priory. Reluctantly, Abigail follows.

"At a meeting among the rebels last night, the Baron asked what his donations were being used for," Macauley tells her. "Says he's donated over two hundred pounds to the cause this year." He pins her with hard eyes. "Our records show he's handed over far less than that amount. And on a number of occasions, he handed the money over to you."

Abigail forces herself to keep her voice level. "What are you implying?"

Macauley snorts. "You know exactly what I'm implying."

She swallows heavily. "I must say, this is all quite flimsy evidence to confront me on."

"Is it? Lord Milgate made the rest of the donations to Mrs Mitchell. And I'm far more inclined to consider you a thief than her."

Abigail tightens her hands into fists. "Why is that, exactly?"

Macauley looks caught off guard by her question. He says, "Where is the rest of the money, Mrs Blake?"

Abigail opens her mouth, the truth on her lips. But something stops her. She knows how lucky she has been that the thieves have not seen fit to come after her. She had almost begun to believe she had put the whole sorry mess behind her.

And if she speaks of them now? If she tells Macauley of the thieving ring and he goes tearing into Bamburgh to take back the Jacobite money? If she does what she promised Lizzie she would never do, and tells people of the ring's existence? She will go back to those long, fearful days of locking herself away in the house. Of fearing for Nathan whenever he is out of sight at school. Of herding Eva inside at every flicker of movement in the garden.

Even after all she has lost, there is still so much they could take from her.

"I took the money," she blurts, before she can change her mind. "I needed it. I was struggling after my husband's death. My settlement was far too small..." It's a neat, convenient story, this faux truth Henry Ward had arrived at. But she knows pity is not about to sway a man like Donald Macauley.

"I can get it back to you," she rushes, before he can get a

word out. "Every penny." It's far too much money. *Every penny* will leave her almost destitute. She can manage it, she tells herself. Just. She has the settlement, and the income from the tenants in Chelsea. And, she thinks distantly, she has Henry Ward, and his safe at the Bank of England overflowing with privateering wealth.

But does she? Eight weeks since Oliver's death. Eight weeks and three days, and she has not seen a sign of Henry. Has not heard a word from him. Certainly, he has gone this long without visits before, but these are extenuating circumstances. Surely she must be in his thoughts.

Henry is keeping his distance out of respect for her, she tells herself. Perhaps out of his own guilt. He will give her the space she needs to mourn her son, and then he will return. Surely. Surely he has not disappeared forever. Surely he is not that kind of man.

Isn't he? Somewhere at the back of her mind, an unwelcome voice reminds Abigail of how little she truly knows of Henry Ward.

She finds her gaze drifting instinctively across the water. Finds it empty but for the fishing ketches and dories that usually dot the anchorage.

"Repayment," Donald Macauley says, the word yanking her away from her thoughts of Henry. "Do you really think that is all it will take?"

Fear runs through her. Because she knows that, whatever brand of justice Donald Macauley has in mind, it will not be lawful. How can it be, when he is raising funds for an illegal cause?

"Donald Macauley." Mairi comes striding towards them, eyes darting between him and Abigail. She plants her hands on her hips. "What's all this about?"

"Just addressing some pressing accusations of theft within the Jacobite movement," Macauley says pointedly.

"I see." Mairi's eyes meet Abigail's for a fleeting second. A weighted look. "Leave her be, Donald. She's done nothing wrong. Has the poor woman not been through enough?"

Macauley chuckles. "Ought to know you'd side with her, Mairi, given you were the fool who took her out visiting with you in the first place. I'm sure Elias would like to hear all about Mrs Blake's thievery. No doubt he'd have plenty to say about his wife's choice of friends."

Abigail glances at Mairi and catches the flicker of fear in her eyes she does not manage to hide.

"I can make it up to you," Abigail hears herself say. "I can give you something far more valuable than the money I took from the Jacobites."

"Oh yes? And what might that be?"

"Information. About the Jacobite leanings of a prominent Whig politician. His party would pay handsomely to make sure that information never got out."

Macauley's eyes narrow. "How do you know about that?"

"I read it in a letter. From a Scottish nobleman. A Williamite spy." She hears a sharp inhalation from Mairi.

Macauley rubs his bristled chin, considering her. "How do I know that's not a lie?"

"It's not a lie."

He gives a humourless laugh. "That information's not enough. I need the letter."

"I—" Abigail stops herself from admitting such a thing is impossible. Admitting she no longer has the letter.

Macauley seems to catch hold of her hesitation. "Can you

get me that letter?" he asks. "Or was this all a load of rubbish?"

Irritation flickers inside her. "I told you, it's the truth." And then, before she can stop herself: "I'll get you that letter."

"Good," Macauley says finally. "Then you can consider your debts repaid."

Something turns over in Abigail's stomach. "I need a few days."

With each word, her heart beats faster. How can she promise such a thing? The letter is in the hands of the thieving ring. Or lying at the bottom of the sea.

No. Not at the bottom of the sea. Oliver had told her he had given it to Lizzie's mother. And Oliver never lied.

But is the letter being in the thieves' hands really any better than it lying on the ocean floor? In both cases, it is completely unreachable. But right now, all she can cling to is this look of interest in Donald Macauley's eyes. A look that gives her hope she may avoid being hunted down by the Lindisfarne Jacobites.

Macauley nods. Barks out an instruction for her to bring the letter to his farmhouse once she has it. And if nothing else, Abigail knows she has bought herself a little more time.

A little more time to do what, she is unsure. Flee to London and her mother, who still thinks Abigail is married with three children?

Mairi watches Macauley trudge out of the churchyard. She turns to face Abigail, her face unreadable.

Abigail wraps her cloak around her body, trying to slow her heart. "I don't know how to get this letter," she admits. "The thieving ring has it. Oliver gave it to them before he died. In exchange for them staying away from us."

It had worked, she thinks suddenly. She had berated Oliver for his naivety in thinking he could coerce Lizzie and her mother into staying away. But it had worked. The thieves had stayed away as he had promised her they would. Abigail feels something squeeze in her chest.

Mairi is silent for a long moment. Abigail can practically hear her turning her words over in her head, sifting through the validity of them. Finally, she says, "I can help you get the letter back."

Abigail shakes her head. "I couldn't ask that of you. It's far too dangerous. The thieving ring, they—"

"I know," says Mairi. "I know." Two older women look their way as they pass, and Mairi takes Abigail's arm, tugging her out of the churchyard. She pulls her into the shadows beneath shopfront awnings on Church Lane. "I can get into the thieving ring," she says finally.

Abigail's lips part. She doesn't speak; just lets Mairi's words fall into place. "You are involved with them," she hisses. It's not shock she is feeling. It's not shock at all. Just anger. Hot and fierce. "Were you the one who sent them after me in the first place?"

Mairi's silence is all the answer Abigail needs.

No, of course it's not shock. Because when she had first told Mairi about the thieving ring, Mairi had not asked questions. Elias and Donald Macauley had not come seeking more information about these thieves who were targeting the Jacobite cause. Had not come asking about when it had happened, or what she had seen. Of course they hadn't. Because Mairi had not spoken of the ring to anyone. Why would she? Why risk revealing her own involvement?

Mairi toys with the lacing on her shortjacket. Eyes down, she says, "I'm sorry. I never intended it to go as far as it did. Young Lizzie, she was under pressure from some of the men in the ring for not bringing in enough coin. I sent her your way after you went to see Lord Milgate. I knew they'd be especially pleased with Lizzie if she handed over money intended for the Jacobites. And I knew you'd not hurt her."

Abigail smiles wryly to herself, thinking of the way she had shoved Lizzie up against the wall of the house. Thinking of how close she had come to hurting her. "Why?" she demands. "Why in hell would you do such a thing? You and your husband are staunch Jacobites."

Mairi lets out her breath at Abigail's raised voice. "My husband is a staunch Jacobite," she says in a sharp whisper. "I've little choice but to go along with what he believes. At least outwardly."

In spite of herself, Abigail feels a fragment of her anger give way.

Mairi presses a hand up against the wall of the shop, as though to support herself against the truths she is about to admit to. "The Jacobite cause was never mine," she says. "It was always Elias's. Since the Revolution, it's all he's talked about. And after Dunkeld, it just consumed him. He came home from the war to a newborn daughter and barely even looked at her. Was far more fixated on the men who'd been lost than he was on poor Julia. He's been like that ever since. Barely a kind word for the children. Never one for me." She shakes her head, lost in her own thoughts. "He forced me into the fundraising. But why would I wish to raise money for a cause that took my husband from me?" Bitterness in her words now. "Helping the thieving ring feels like a way of taking back some small piece of what's owed to me."

For a long time, Abigail doesn't speak. She feels betrayed. She feels angry. She feels afraid. Feels the ocean of grief that has been a constant for every minute of this year surge and roll inside her. She wants to walk away. Never go near Mairi Mitchell again. But she knows she has little choice. She needs to get that letter back from the thieves—in the desperate hope they have not sold it. And the only way she will do that is with Mairi's help.

"Meet me at the Pilgrims' Way tomorrow morning," Mairi says, before Abigail can find a response. "We're going to Bamburgh. We're going to get your letter back."

CHAPTER THIRTY-ONE

Today, there is no easy chatter as Abigail and Mairi cross the Pilgrims' Way in the wagon. Today, there is just a stilted wordlessness, filled with all the questions that are storming around inside Abigail's head. Mairi has not brought her baby with her today, and his absence feels notable. Feels like they are heading into danger.

Despite the November chill, it's a hideously bright day, with sun pouring into the wagon and making the wet sand of the Pilgrims' Way shimmer in the light. This does not feel like a day that ought to be filled with sunshine. There ought to be clouds and shadows and rain that keeps prying eyes out of the streets.

"Tell me everything you know about the ring," Abigail says finally. They have almost crossed onto the mainland, and it is the first time she has opened her mouth since she climbed into the wagon.

Mairi looks down into clasped hands. Much of what she tells Abigail is the same as Oliver had told her: a ring of thirty or more, active in Bamburgh and the surrounding villages. Their thievery ranging from simple pickpocketing to embezzlement. Many of them widows and orphans of the Jacobite movement, seeking whatever meagre retribution they can muster.

"The day you sought me out in the village to see how I was faring. The day you first spoke to me about raising funds for the Jacobites." Abigail presses her lips together at the effort of keeping her composure. Her control comes from a need for answers, rather than any desire to be polite. "Did you only do that in the hope I'd join the cause?"

"No," Mairi says hurriedly. "Of course not. I swear it. I only wanted to make sure you and the children were coping after Samuel's passing." There's a look of such intensity in her eyes that Abigail cannot help but believe her. However reluctantly. "When I spoke of the fundraising that day, I had no intention of involving you. The thought had not even crossed my mind. You were the one who showed an interest in the movement."

"So you thought you'd invite me along and send the thieves on my trail?"

Mairi doesn't answer. Does not need to answer.

Abigail blows out a breath. "I don't understand. If you do not want the Jacobite cause to succeed, why bring me with you to raise more money? Why not just give the ring a cut of what you yourself are taking from the donors?"

Mairi picks at something beneath her thumbnail. Avoids Abigail's eyes. "It's what I've been doing for years," she admits. "A lot of the money the ring takes helps the women and children left behind by the war. I wanted to take from the Jacobite cause, yes. But I wanted to help the people that needed it too." She begins to gnaw at her thumbnail. "I could tell Elias was becoming suspicious about the amount of money I was handing over. And I was afraid he'd find out that the records did not match what the donors were handing over—as Donald discovered with you and Lord Milgate. I thought that if I brought you along, I could still get the money to the ring for the people who needed it. And I could hand over enough from the donors that Elias and Donald would no longer question me."

Abigail does not answer immediately. Her anger is far too raw, far too sharp to cobble together anything coherent. And she knows that if she does not take a moment here to breathe, to consider, she will say something she will regret.

Perhaps she will not regret it that much.

"And here I thought you were trying to make a friend of me," she says finally. "Trying to help me get past the loss of my husband." Her words come out dripping with bitterness. She does not attempt to hold it back. "Have you any idea of the trouble you've caused me and my family?"

"I'm sorry," says Mairi. Her freckled cheeks are flushed with shame. "I truly am. Causing you and your children trouble was the last thing in the world I meant to do." When Abigail doesn't speak, Mairi leans forward, pinning intent eyes on her. "This letter. How did you get your hands on it?"

"That's no business of yours," Abigail says tightly. "You just need to help me get it back."

Mairi nods resignedly. "Of course." She sits back on the bench, chastened.

Abigail leans against the side of the wagon, pulling her cloak tight around her. Her body rattles with the movement of the wagon. It feels as though the darkness inside her is pulsing, trying to find an escape. "Oliver said he gave the letter to Lizzie's mother. Do you know her?"

"Yes. Ailith. She lives at the far end of Church Wynd. I can get into the place without difficulty. She'll welcome me in." Mairi speaks quietly, gently, as though ashamed of all she is saying. "Ailith is one of the ring's record-keepers. She's smart. Well-educated. But she married beneath her and lost everything after her husband died at Killiecrankie. She keeps a box safe under one of the flagstones beside the hearth. Keeps the takings there until they can be divided up between the ring members. I'm sure that will be where she's keeping your letter."

"Oliver gave her the letter more than two months ago. She might well have sold it by now."

"No." Mairi shakes her head. "She's not sold it. It's far more valuable for them to keep it."

Abigail purses her lips. "She's told you about the letter before, hasn't she."

It is not a question, but Mairi nods anyway. Guilt in her eyes. "I knew of the letter. But I didn't know it came from you and Oliver until you told Donald about it yesterday." She shifts awkwardly on the bench seat. "Ailith and the others are holding tight to it to get themselves out of a difficult situation," she says. "In case the redcoats come looking." She looks squarely at Abigail. "We'll get the letter back. I promise. And we'll see to it that Donald doesn't come after you again."

It's risky, Abigail knows, trusting Mairi like this. The women in the thieving ring are friends of hers. Women whose families have become broken and disillusioned by the Jacobite cause, just as Mairi's has.

But Abigail knows she has no choice. She has promised

Donald Macauley the letter, and she must find a way to deliver.

"I'll call on Ailith first," says Mairi. "Do her best to get her and Lizzie out of the house. There's a cloth window that leads from the alley into the kitchen. You'll be able to get inside through there."

Abigail nods.

Mairi looks at her pointedly. "Make sure you put everything in the house back just as you found it," she says. "I can't have Ailith getting suspicious of me. She can't know the letter's been stolen until I'm long gone. I can't have anyone from that ring coming after me. Or my children."

CHAPTER THIRTY-TWO

She wishes Oliver were here. Of course she does; she wishes it every minute of every day, with a desperation she did not know she was capable of.

But right now, she wishes it even more than usual.

Because Oliver would know what to do. Would know how to handle these people.

She closes her eyes, fighting back a swell of self-loathing. How can she be thinking such things? If Oliver were here, she ought to be keeping him as far away as possible from such things. Perhaps if she had kept a closer eye on him from the beginning, he would not have gotten involved with the thieves in the first place. Would not have given them the letter. Would not have become the kind of boy to take a knife from the water and wave it around and—

No. She is not going down that deep, dark tunnel of regret. Not now. It will do no one any good, and she needs a clear head if she is going to do as she needs to.

Abigail waits on the corner of the Wynd, crouching at the

corner of the cottage opposite Ailith and Lizzie's. She can see Mairi on the doorstep, speaking to someone unseen. Mairi is smiling, laughing, waving a hand around as she speaks. Then she and Ailith step out of the cottage and head down the Wynd towards the village.

Abigail hesitates. Where is Lizzie? Is she still in the house? Was Mairi unable to convince her to leave?

She has no idea. Either way, this is her only opportunity to get the letter back. Abigail reaches into her pocket for Oliver's knife. Hates that there's a part of herself that longs to use it.

She hurries across the narrow street towards the cottage, shoes sighing through the mud. Squeezes herself down the narrow gap between Lizzie's cottage and the next. Towards the back of the house, she sees the narrow window covered in its colourless cloth.

Abigail stands motionless for several moments, listening for any sound inside the house. She hears the shout of a young boy from the other end of the street. A dog barking in the distance. Nothing from inside the house.

She takes the knife from her pocket and slices carefully along the bottom of the cloth, severing it from the nails holding it to the window frame. She pulls back a corner and dares to peek inside.

A thick gloom hangs over the cottage. A crooked table, cluttered with unwashed stew bowls and a burned-out candle, takes up most of the space. A grate holds a dwindling fire, pots and a kettle resting on the blackened stones of the hearth. The air is soured with the smell of old meat and wet wool. Ash and unwashed bodies. Abigail's gaze darts across the flagstones. Which of those hides the box safe?

Her gaze travels to a narrow doorway at the far end of the room. The bedroom, she guesses; there are no sleeping mats or washstands here in the kitchen. She holds her breath, waiting for Lizzie to appear. A cold wind whips suddenly through the alley, fluttering the loose cloth over the window.

When there is nothing but silence and stillness, Abigail hoists herself up onto the window frame. She swings her legs awkwardly over the sill, skirts tangling around her calves. Lands with a soft thud on the flagstones of the kitchen.

Fingers tight around the knife, she edges towards the grate. Kneels beside the fire, running the knife around the edges of the flagstones to find the loosened tile.

In the far corner, she feels it. Feels the blade of the knife slide beneath the stone. The smallest tile, thankfully; light enough to prise up with the knife to reveal the small ditch dug into the earth below. A wooden box sits inside the hole, fastened with nothing more than a simple latch.

Abigail leans the loose flagstone up against the wall and pulls out the box safe. Shoots a glance over her shoulder. Then she turns back and opens the box.

There's little in the safe beyond a small pouch of coins, and a spring watch she suspects is worth pennies. But there between them, lying on its side, is Henry Ward's brass box. Abigail lets out a murmur of relief she is unable to hold back. She snatches it out of the safe and opens the lid. There is the letter, neatly folded. She fastens the clasp again and buries it in her pocket.

Abigail shoves the safe back into the hole. She wrestles the flagstone towards her, easing it downwards. Cringes as it groans against the floor.

The sound is replied to by a volley of snoring, coming

from what Abigail assumes is the bedroom. A man's snoring. Far too deep and loud to be Lizzie's.

The sound freezes her for a moment, then she flies into action, leaping to her feet and rushing back across the cottage. She heaves herself up through the window, landing heavily in the damp earth of the lane beside the house.

She stops for a moment, gathering her breath. *Run.* She has the letter. Has made it out without being caught. But the cloth of the window is fluttering in the breeze and the moment Ailith sees it, she will know someone has been here. She will suspect Mairi had lured her out of the house to allow thieves into the cottage.

There's a part of her that doesn't care. A part that's telling her to run, regardless. To put her own safety first. After all, Mairi had put Abigail's family in danger from the thieving ring. Why not do the same to her?

But it's this internal argument Abigail has been fighting against her entire life. This need to betray, to retaliate, to put her own selfish needs first. Mairi might be guilty of deceiving her, but her four young children are not.

Abigail fumbles with the window cloth, hurriedly yanking it downwards and hooking the torn edges over the nails on the sill. It's a sloppy, temporary solution. But perhaps it will save Ailith and Lizzie—and whoever is sleeping in that bedroom—from immediately discovering someone has been here. Perhaps it will buy her and Mairi a little time.

Abigail hurries back towards the anchorage, keeping the hood of her cloak pulled up to hide herself. She has no thought of how long Mairi will be, or where she has gone, but she can hide herself in the wagon until she shows herself.

As she is approaching the anchorage, she hears, "Mrs

Blake."

She holds her breath. Keeps striding past the harbourside tavern.

"Mrs Blake!" Footsteps come thumping towards her, forcing Abigail to look up. Lizzie stops walking as she reaches her, breathless. "Aye, I thought it was you."

Abigail's heart is suddenly thundering. Had Lizzie been in the house too? Has she followed her here from the Wynd? Or has she just crossed her path in the street?

The look in the girl's eyes is not a threatening one. It's something far closer to pity. And something else too. Sadness?

"Is it true?" she asks. "What happened to Oliver?"

Abigail swallows heavily. Is it true? There's never been any truth about *what happened to Oliver.*

She wonders what Lizzie has heard, and from who. From Mairi, she supposes. Unless there are others on Lindisfarne entangled in the ring.

She gives Lizzie nothing more than a faint nod. Digs her hands into her cloak pockets—one tight around the box, the other around Oliver's knife.

"I'm sorry," says Lizzie. "I truly am." There's a depth to her voice Abigail has not heard before. A genuineness. "He was a good person."

Abigail lets out her breath. "You met because he was teaching you to pick the pockets of funeral-goers."

Lizzie's lips part. "Aye, but..." She trails off, shifting uncomfortably.

"Oliver was not a good person, Lizzie," says Abigail, hearing her voice crack. "But neither are you and I. That's why we both understood him as we did."

Lizzie hesitates for a moment. Gives a faint nod. Then, though she has just glimpsed a part of herself she would rather not acknowledge, she turns and hurries back into the winding streets of the village.

CHAPTER THIRTY-THREE

Abigail and Mairi barely speak on the way back to Lindisfarne. As they rattle out of Bamburgh, Abigail can see the tide beginning to creep towards the castle. She wills the coachman to hurry so they can get to the Pilgrims' Way before the rising water cuts Lindisfarne off from the mainland. The last thing she needs is to be stranded off the island in Mairi Mitchell's company.

Abigail grips the brass box until her knuckles whiten. Henry's box. Henry's letter. He has no idea of all the strife it has caused her. Will she ever get the chance to tell him?

"Was there any trouble?" Mairi asks finally. It feels as though she has been trying to gather the courage to ask the question since they had first climbed into the wagon.

"Nothing I couldn't handle."

Abigail toys with the lock on the front of the box. What had Oliver used to open it, she wonders? It's a question she will never have the answer to.

The moment she steps onto the island, she thinks, she will

go to the Macauleys' farm. Hand over the letter. And then? If ever the thieves were going to come for her, it will be now. Now, that she has broken into Ailith's house. Stolen from the box safe. Taken back the precious letter. And been seen in the village by Lizzie.

Run away. Leave this place. The thought swings at her suddenly. Surely staying here is the height of foolishness. But she cannot bear the thought of returning to London and the grip of her mother's talons. More than that, she cannot bear the thought of disappearing without another word to Henry Ward.

She needs to see him. Needs to speak to him. Needs to tell him that sending him away that night was a mistake. And she needs to find out if *there is a place for you in my future* is still a reality. Because right now, the possibility of that future is all that is keeping her afloat.

Yes, she can leave him word for Henry with his buyer, telling him of her whereabouts. But she knows there's no certainty he will return to Lindisfarne now, after she had sent him away. And she could not bear the uncertainty of never knowing if he has read her words.

She shakes Henry out of her head. Dwelling on that future—or lack thereof—right now will only cause her to make mistakes.

"Can I trust Donald Macauley?" she asks Mairi suddenly. "If I give him this letter, can I be certain he'll not come after me and my family?"

Mairi nods. "Aye. You can. He's something of a brute, but he's a man who keeps his word."

Abigail nods brusquely. It does not feel right to thank her. They sit in silence for the rest of the journey.

Abigail is on her way to the Macauleys' farm when she sees him. At the sight of him, she freezes, hand clenching around the brass box.

She has seen Noah Murray on Holy Island many times before, of course. Had heard of his wife's death, his son's disappearance. Had felt some indifferent, obligatory pity for the tragedy of him. Beyond that, she has barely paid him a second glance.

Now, the sight of the Longstone lightkeeper has her breathless. This is the father of the boy who had killed her child.

A tangle of emotions threatens to overwhelm her. She wants to fly at him, hurl abuse, hurl her fists. Blame him for everything.

She wants to tell him his son is alive.

His son is alive when hers is not.

She can tell him no such thing, of course. Could never face the questions that would come. Not least because she has no idea how to answer them. Really, she has no piece of useful knowledge to give the lightkeeper about his child; cannot even assure him the boy is still alive. If Henry Ward has had his way, there is every chance he may not be.

The man is headed in the direction of the anchorage, a brown woollen cap pulled low on his head and a large tarred greatcoat swamping his body. Dark hair hangs loose down his back, grey-flecked stubble across his cheeks.

He looks up as he crosses Abigail's path. Glances at her, as though feeling her intense gaze on him. He says nothing, and it occurs to her that he likely has no idea who she even is. Certainly, they have never exchanged a single word. Noah

Murray is known to everyone on Lindisfarne, of course; the man who had built his home on the pellet of Longstone, and keeps the beacon blazing to light the dark sea. Who is she but the woman who haunts the house on the head?

She closes her eyes. Tries to breathe against the tide of fresh grief the sight of the lightkeeper has brought.

He strides past her, and before Abigail knows what she is doing, she says, "Your son. I've seen him." This has to be done, she realises. She has no real knowledge to give him, nothing that can assure him of his child's safety. But she can give him a glimmer of information. A glimmer of hope. And what she wouldn't give to have a glimmer of hope for her lost son.

Noah stops walking. Turns back to face her. His eyes are widened, lips parted. "You've seen Finn?"

"I have. But not… It's been many weeks."

"Where?"

She tightens her fingers around the box containing the letter. "He was here on the island. Sailing as a privateer's cabin boy. But he's not… He's not a part of that crew anymore."

"Why not? Where is he now? Where'd he go?" She hears the urgency, the desperation in the man's voice.

Abigail draws in a breath. She could tell him everything. Tell him all that happened that horrible night. And what will that achieve? The information will not help the lightkeeper find his son.

She knows the weight of being the parent of a lawbreaker. She does not want Noah Murray to carry that weight too.

"I don't know where he is," she says. "I'm sorry. But he is alive." At least, he was on that bleak September night.

The lightkeeper's eyes bore into her, and for a long time,

he doesn't speak. Abigail feels the fierce urge to turn away, to escape the intensity of his stare. But she feels rooted in place. Finally, Noah nods. "Thank you." There's disappointment in his voice, and weight. But perhaps that fragile glimmer of hope too.

Abigail replays their conversation over and over in her head as she passes through the village. Regrets it with one step, is glad to have done it with the next.

Out ahead of her, she can see the narrow path leading to the Macauleys' farm. She slows her pace. Her encounter with the lightkeeper has made her rattled and tearful, and the last thing she wants is to face Donald Macauley in such a state. For all she tries to convince herself of her own strength, she knows Macauley would not have to try too hard to tear her down today.

As she tries to find the courage to continue on towards the farm, she hears: "Mama!"

And when she turns to sees Nathan and Eva behind her with Mrs Calloway, it takes everything in her not to sprint to their sides. She is not sure she has ever been so glad to see them. Having her children close feels suddenly so fleeting, so fragile. So precious.

They hammer towards her and she bends to gather Eva into her arms, gesturing for Nathan to come close. Doesn't bother to wipe the tears that spill without warning down her cheeks.

Mrs Calloway trots down the road to catch up with them. "Have you more errands to run, Mrs Blake?" she asks. "Shall we see you back at the house?"

Abigail gathers up the brass box she had dropped on the

path in her hurry to embrace her daughter. "No," she tells the nurse. "I shall take the children home myself." She shoves the box into her pocket and clasps her fingers around Eva's. "I can finish the rest of my errands in the morning."

CHAPTER THIRTY-FOUR

Nausea has her tearing out of bed to the chamber pot and she knows she cannot deny it to herself any longer.

Abigail tells herself it's grief, it's fear, it's anger. And yes, perhaps it's all those things. But she also knows Henry Ward's child is stirring inside her. Somewhere in the back of her mind, she has been aware of this for days. Weeks, perhaps. Has not found the strength to accept it. But she knows there is little point in pretending any longer.

Her youngest child, conceived as her eldest had died.

She closes her eyes. Breathes. Presses her forehead against the cool stone of the bedroom wall.

Run away. Leave this place.

Does she have any other option? Never mind the fact that she had stolen from the thieving ring yesterday—it will only be a matter of time before the villagers come to see she is carrying a child that cannot be her husband's. She can only imagine what they will think of her then. And she refuses to bring shame to Samuel's good name.

Really, *run away* is all there is. All there can be. But how can she disappear without telling Henry about his child?

She hunches beside the bed, watching dawn light squeeze through the curtains and pick out the shapes of her bedroom. Rain is pattering against the windows, and she tries to let the calm rhythm of it soothe her.

She hovers by the chamber pot until the sickness has passed, then splashes her face at the washbin and rinses her mouth. Ties a robe around her to ward off the chill of the house and empties the chamber pot into the garderobe. She has no intention of leaving the task for Ruth, and facing any questions that might arise.

As she is making her way back to her bedchamber, in an attempt to force out another hour of sleep, a knock at the door echoes through the house. Abigail panics. Who would be here at this time? The sun has barely risen, and the rain has grown louder against the windows. Ruth has not yet arrived, and the house is cold and lifeless.

Abigail finds Mairi on the doorstep. Her cheeks are flushed, eyes wild. Rain drips off the brim of her bonnet. She steps inside without waiting to be invited.

"The letter," she says, breathless, "have you given it to Donald yet?"

"No." Abigail pushes the door closed behind her, silencing the lash of the sea. "I planned to take it to him this morning."

"You can't give it to him. Please."

"Why?"

Mairi paces back and forth across the foyer, barely looking at Abigail. Rainwater trails off the hem of her cloak, leaving a silver trail across the flagstones. "One of the Northumbrian

Jacobites was arrested late last night," she says. "He was intercepted carrying messages meant for the movement in London."

Abigail swallows heavily.

"There'll be more arrests," says Mairi. "For certain. The redcoats know the movement is active up here again. If Donald and Elias are arrested and they have the letter, they'll use it to blackmail the authorities for their freedom."

Abigail frowns, not understanding. "That could save their lives."

"It will draw unwanted attention to this village," Mairi says bitterly. "It will put far too many people in danger. Perhaps even those who are not involved in the cause." She winds her hands into her tartan cloak. "If Elias is caught, he ought to be punished. It's not right for him to put others in danger for his own safety." She looks at Abigail with piercing green eyes. "You must think me a terrible person for doing this to my husband. But I've been trying to get Elias out of the movement since Dunkeld. For the good of our children. He'll not do it. Won't even listen to all I have to say." She turns away, scrubbing a hand across her face and leaving a smear of mud against one cheek. "Heaven, what you must think of me to be saying all this after all you've lost. But I—"

"Mairi." Abigail snatches her arm to stop her pacing. "I don't care what you want for your husband," she says tautly. "But I promised Donald Macauley that letter. If I don't hand it over like I promised, I'm afraid of what he will do to me. To my children." She looks desperately at Mairi. "I can't lose anyone else."

"I'll see to it that Donald doesn't come after you. I swear it."

"How?"

"I don't know," Mairi admits. "But I need you to trust me. I don't want my husband to get his hands on that letter. I don't want him to know anything about it."

I need you to trust me. Abigail almost laughs. She does not trust Mairi an inch. Nor does she have any faith in her ability to keep Donald Macauley at bay.

But it doesn't matter, she realises suddenly. None of it matters. Not anymore. Because *run away* is all there is.

"Tell Donald I could not get the letter back," Abigail says brusquely. "Or tell him I lied about its existence. Let him think I stole the money for my own purposes. It doesn't matter what he thinks of me. Or my family. I cannot stay here any longer."

Mairi frowns. Her voice softens. "Abby, you don't need to leave." Guilt in her eyes, her words. "I'll see to it that Donald and Elias—"

"I do need to leave. For many reasons." She pins Mairi with a look that tells her not to ask questions. "I just need a few days to put things in order. Can you keep Donald away from me until then?"

Mairi hesitates. After a moment, she nods. "Of course. If that's what you need." Her lips part, as though debating whether to ask more questions. But she just lurches forward, pulling Abigail into her arms. Abigail stiffens in her embrace. "Take care, Abby." Mairi's voice wavers. "And I'm sorry for everything."

Not handing the letter over to Macauley feels dangerous. Foolish. But Abigail can't deny there is something faintly steadying about having it tucked back into her nightstand where it should always have been. Somehow, it gives her space to breathe.

Donald Macauley might come for her. The thieving ring might come for her. But she will not have to admit to Henry Ward that she cannot be trusted. And right now, this feels like the most pressing thing of all.

She sits at the desk in her husband's study. Barely any trace of Samuel in here now. The scent of his tobacco has faded, the indentations on the chair have been replaced with her own. Perhaps he is still here, if she looks hard enough. Perhaps he has faded because her thoughts are circling around another man.

No time for guilt now, or for reminiscence. Samuel is gone. Oliver is gone. She has another son or daughter on the way, and she needs to ensure her child grows up knowing their father.

Henry will not come to the house; she knows that now. Or at least, she fears it. In any case, she does not have the time to wait around for his ship to reappear; for him to fight past his regret and return to her doorstep. She cannot wait for the Jacobites, or the thieving ring, to beat him to the house. And she cannot wait for the child inside her to grow, and betray her as the woman who had taken to bed a man who is not her husband.

She will tell Henry, yes. Will write him a letter and tell him everything, raw and unfettered. And she will find out if her lost son had been speaking the truth when he had said that Henry Ward loves her.

She stares down at the blank page. She will make two copies of this letter. Will ask Henry's buyer to hold on to one copy, in case the *Eagle* comes north again to sell their cargo.

The second, she will send ahead to London. Deposit it in the bank safe, in her son's name.

The plan is sound—or at least as sound as it can be. As secure a way to get word to Henry as she can manage. Not secure enough, of course. It will never be secure enough. Not unless she can look him in the eye and tell him everything face to face. But she has no time. No choice.

How does she go about a letter like this one? Straight to the point, or meandering around the issues?

She wants Henry to know all of it: of his child, of her feelings for him, of the way she wishes—needs—that future they had discussed to become a reality. The way she has no choice but to leave Lindisfarne. Not a single piece of it feels like the kind of information she ought to be conveying through a letter. *No time*, she reminds herself. *No choice.*

In the end, she decides on the same openness and honesty she has committed to each of her previous letters to him. It is so much harder given she is intending, unlike the others, for this letter to actually reach him. But once she begins to write, the words pour from her quill, filling the page with a sea of sloping letters and careless inkblots. She tells him of the thieving ring, of her true reason for stealing from the Jacobites. Tell him of the adventure his little brass box has been on. She tells him of the child she is carrying inside her.

She sets the quill back into the ink and leans back in her chair, suddenly drained. She reads over the letter as the ink dries. Soon, she thinks, she will repeat the process. Will write Henry a second letter to send on to London. But not today. Today, already, she is worn through with emotion and exhaustion. Getting the letter to the office of Henry's buyer feels like a monumental undertaking. But it must be done.

She folds and seals the page. Tucks it in her pocket and stands to fetch her cloak and bonnet.

CHAPTER THIRTY-FIVE

Ward wakes drenched in sweat, the bedsheets tangled and lying on the cabin floor. He has no recollection of what he had dreamt about—all he knows is it has left him with a sense of dread pressing down on him.

Daylight is flooding through the windows, and he reaches for the spring watch on the stand beside the bed. Almost noon. He's only slept three hours.

He sits up, scrubbing a hand across his eyes. His body feels weighted with lead, but he has no desire for more sleep—not if that sleep is going to be peppered with unidentifiable horrors.

He'd had nightmares like this as a much younger man; the same imageless, formless dreams that would cause him to wake in terror. Back then, he'd put it down to the stress of not meeting his father's rigid expectations. Now, though he has no conscious recollection of what he has been dreaming about, he's fairly certain it features Oliver Blake's glacial blue eyes staring lifeless at the ceiling of his bedchamber.

JOHANNA CRAVEN

No more sleep. Since Oliver's death—since the night Abigail had cast him from her house with that look of blame in her eyes—Ward has learnt to exist on whatever scraps of sleep he can snatch—not that he has ever managed to cobble together more than a few consecutive hours when he is at sea. In any case, they will be coming up on Lindisfarne soon.

Ward goes to the washbin and splashes his face with cold water, trying to slough away that lingering anxiety. There's a restlessness in his chest he knows has little to do with his nightmares, and everything to do with the choices he is on the verge of making. He turns towards the bank of windows in the stern of the ship, trying to soak in a little sunlight. The flimsy rays that struggle into the cabin bring little warmth with them. Little light.

He pulls on a fresh shirt and rakes his fingers through the waves of his hair, tying it into a loose queue at his neck. When he has his boots and breeches on, and has managed to conjure up a little steadiness, he opens the door of the great cabin.

Instinctively, he opens his mouth to call for Finn. Stops himself at the last moment. More than two months since his cabin boy has been gone, and the ache of the loss has not yet begun to fade. He marches down to the ward-robe, seeking out Quartermaster Hunter. Does his best not to think of his cabin boy, and where he might have ended up.

Ward takes Hunter back to the great cabin. Locks the door behind them. "I'm handing command of the ship over to you," Ward says, before either of them have even managed to take a seat at the table.

Hunter nods slowly. There's no shock in his eyes.

Little wonder. Ward is well aware of how distant and

distracted he has been since Oliver's death. He's made more than one bad decision at the helm—sailed headlong into dangerous weather; gone after targets far more heavily gunned than the *Eagle*. He's mildly surprised they've returned from the latest voyage in one piece. Suspects they wouldn't have if Hunter hadn't stepped in to make his captain see sense on more than one occasion.

Ward slides onto the bench at the table, nodding for Hunter to join him. "You'll need to apply for your own commissions," Ward says. "And you'll be free to choose your crew as you see fit. Take whichever of the men you wish."

Hunter scratches the white bristles on his chin. "When?"

"I'll be leaving the ship when we land in Northumberland tonight."

Hunter raises his bushy eyebrows. "These men still have four months left on their articles of agreement."

"Yes." Ward nods, feeling a tug of shame. The men will not be happy at having their agreements cut short, of course. He wishes he could make himself care a little more. But he knows now, with deep certainty, that this life is not the one he wants.

When he was a younger man, trying to scrape together a life that would please his father, he had wanted success at any cost. But he has had that success now, and he feels nothing but hollowness. His father is long in his grave, and still Ward is fighting to prove himself to some outside entity.

It had been a thrill once, this existence. But now it just makes him think of death and loss. Just makes him think of how precious and fleeting life is, and how he must find the strength to turn towards what he truly wants.

The thought of existing without the sea is a strange and

hazy one. But he has full ownership of the *Eagle*, and for that, he will be paid a cut of Hunter's takings. Coupled with the money locked away in his account in London, it will be plenty to build a good life for him and Abigail. For Nathan. For Eva.

He has no idea how Abigail will react when he knocks on her door tonight. He knows there is every chance the sight of him will send her back to that dreadful night two months ago, and she will cast him from her home once again.

Even though Ward knows this is a distinct possibility, the only way he can find the strength to do this is to trust that the life he longs for will become a reality. He must make the necessary arrangements with Hunter. Must pack his belongings and prepare to leave the ship. Prepare himself to face whatever criticism he will receive from the crew when they learn he is to slice their agreements in half.

Somewhere in the back of his mind, he is toying with the alternative. Entertaining that bleak vision of what his life will look like if Abigail turns him away. He will not stay in England, that much is clear. He will take the *Eagle* to faraway colonies. Operate out of the Caribbean. And perhaps his bitterness, his despair, will reshape him. Rub shoulders with buccaneers. Blur the line between privateering and piracy.

No. That is a line he never wishes to cross. He pushes the thought away.

"What of the sale of the cargo?" Hunter asks. "Will you see to that before you leave?"

"No." He needs to do this now, before he changes his mind. "I shall leave that in your hands. Divide the takings between these men, and then you'll be free to choose your crew as you wish."

Abigail trudges through the mud of the dunes to deliver the letter. Wind whips up from the water, stinging her cheeks and turning the tip of her nose numb.

Her eyes dart as she crosses the open greenery. She is wary of Donald Macauley appearing to string her up for not handing over the Jacobite letter. Mairi had promised to keep him away from her, she reminds herself. Plus, he himself had given her a few days to produce the letter. And before those few days are up, she will be gone.

This thought, this resoluteness, keeps her moving forward, trudging over the wet grass with her skirts pulled high above her ankles.

She will deliver the letter to Henry's buyer, then return to the house and begin to pack. What else? A second letter to Henry, of course, to be left in the safe in London. But that can be written on the long journey south. She must write to the grammar school notifying them that Nathan will not be returning. Must write to Samuel's lawyer, asking him to see that the house in Chelsea is vacated. Letters of reference for Ruth and Mrs Calloway, along with their final payments. As for the possibility of leasing Highfield House, she will make a decision about that later. She doubts Samuel's lawyer will have any luck finding tenants to fill such an isolated and sea-blown wreck. She has never been able to see the allure of the place, the way Samuel and his cousin could. Perhaps, she thinks, you must have the Blakes' blood coursing through you to see the magic in Highfield House. No part of her will be sad to leave the place behind.

It all makes simple sense, this plan. All makes simple

sense, as long as she doesn't think too hard on the contents of the message she is leaving for Henry. All she is telling him. Asking him. All the vulnerability she is showing him. This was a far less terrifying thing when she was determined to keep him at a distance.

Then of course, there is the issue of her mother. Abigail has no thought of how she will even begin to explain everything that has happened in the past year. Perhaps it's for the best that Susanna believes her still tucked away up in Northumberland with her husband and three children. Perhaps it's best that their lives never intersect again. Abigail shakes the thought away as soon as it arrives. It's far too cruel a thought—a thought that comes from the very part of herself she is afraid Susanna's presence will bring out into the light.

Abigail stops walking as she passes the castle. A ship is approaching the island. Three-masted barque—at the sight of it, her heart is racing. Henry's ship? Dare she hope for that? It feels as though she has willed him here.

She hurries into the village and clambers up towards the abandoned fort on the Heugh. Squints into the wall of cloud, watching the ship grow closer. And as the barque slices through the silver-grey water, she sees it—sees that regal eagle figurehead, its wooden wings frozen in flight.

Her breath is suddenly rattling against her chest in a frantic mix of relief, excitement, nerves. Because now she has a chance to tell Henry everything face to face. Now she will not have to cast this most personal letter into the depths of his buyer's office and hope it somehow makes it into Henry's hands. Now, she will be able to see the look in his eyes when she tells him everything she needs to tell him.

About the child. About her plans to leave Lindisfarne. Every true and honest detail of her entanglement with the Bamburgh thieving ring and the lies she had let him believe.

She will tell him of the life she wishes to build with him. And she will hope with every inch of her being that it is a life he wishes to be a part of. Hope he'll not look down on her for all she has been involved in. He will see past it, surely. He loves her, doesn't he? Oliver had said so.

She casts one last glance out at the ship, then turns and hurries back to the house.

Goes up to her nightstand and opens the brass box. She folds the message she had written to Henry and crams it into the box beside the Jacobite letter. Fastens the lid again and slips the box back into her nightstand.

CHAPTER THIRTY-SIX

John Graveney had feared this. These were unfounded, irrational fears at first: fears that Henry Ward might choose to leave the sea behind. Fears that Ward's leaving might mean the end of his own short-lived life at sea.

Graveney had told himself that when it all came down to it, Ward wouldn't leave. He was a man who belonged on the ocean. A man who surely only felt alive when his lungs were full of salty air.

And besides, even if he did... *Even if he did*, there was no reason Graveney himself would be out of work. Hunter would become captain, and Graveney was sure he would keep him on as boatswain. He's good at his job. Reliable. Organised.

Over and over, Graveney told himself he would not become penniless. He would not die on that street corner in the London slums, or at the hands of Amos Sheffield when he could not repay his gambling debts. He would not have to resort to a life of running, of looking over his shoulder, of wondering when Sheffield might show his face. Or his pistol.

And then that conversation with Hunter the day of the Blake boy's burial. The suspicion in the quartermaster's eyes had been all too blatant.

What are you hiding, John?

In the two months since, Hunter has barely exchanged a word with him, beyond barked, necessary instructions on the smooth running of the ship. Graveney has caught the quartermaster's sideways glances; is well aware of the murmurs he's been exchanging with Ward.

Hunter's distrust of him is glaring.

Graveney does not know, for certain, what it is Hunter thinks him guilty of. French sympathies? Jacobite sympathies? He would not be wrong.

Whatever it is, it doesn't matter. All that matters is that, if Hunter takes control of the ship, he will surely not be offering Graveney a berth upon it.

Tonight, Ward has gathered the entire crew on deck. The ship is moored in the bay beyond Emmanuel Head, but in the thick cloud and darkness, Holy Island is just a vague shape in the gloom.

Henry Ward is climbing onto the poop deck. Is telling his crew their articles of agreement will be cut short tonight. Telling his crew he will he handing control of the ship over to Quartermaster Hunter.

The words echo and roll inside Graveney's head. His body is suddenly blazing, and he curls a hand around the gunwale to keep himself upright. He stares up at Ward, trying to catch his eye, but the captain has a distant look about him, as though a part of him has already left.

Voices erupt. Questions fly out of the men's mouths;

questions about payment, about Hunter's plans for new articles of agreement, about whether those not chosen in the new crew will be given passage back to London. Too many questions in too many angry voices.

"Mr Hunter will arrange the sale of the cargo tomorrow morning," Ward says, without emotion. "And each man will be given the share of the payment due to him." He sounds distracted. Looks distracted, his gaze darting regularly out in the direction of the island. The house.

Hunter steps up to join Ward on the poop deck. He looks out across the heaving mass of men, his eyes hovering on Graveney for a moment too long. "I'll be offering new agreements shortly," Hunter says loudly. "The men I choose'll be given the option to continue on to the North Atlantic for another voyage with the *Eagle*."

"And what of those you don't choose?" This man's voice is laced with bitterness.

Yes, thinks Graveney. What of those you don't choose?

Distant memories swing at him of a stomach so empty it made his legs feel hollow. Of that bruising London cold, with no money for coal to keep it at bay.

Really, Graveney thinks, a life on the streets is a generous assessment of the situation. When he fails to repay what he owes, he's far more likely to face Sheffield's bullet than he is a life on the streets. He knows that, what he is really facing, when Henry Ward leaves the ship and he loses his place in this crew, is death.

That reality swings towards him, making his chest tighten. Ward steps down from the poop deck and begins to stride towards the saloon, with not even another glance at his rioting crew. Hunter opens his mouth to speak, but his words are lost over the shouting. And the crew moves towards the saloon door as one, charging after their captain.

Abigail stands at the window of the study and peers out at the ship. She can see the *Eagle's* lamps glittering through the thick bank of cloud. Why has he not come yet?

She tries to shake the unease away. Henry is the captain of his ship. No doubt he has other matters to attend to. Or perhaps he is waiting until later tonight to come to the house, so he can be sure her children are asleep. It is still several hours from midnight.

Abigail has set a lamp on the windowsill, its light beaming steadily through the study window. A beacon, making it as clear as possible to Henry that he is welcome here. She wishes there was more she could do. Prays she has the chance to tell him in person how much she regrets sending him away.

She had intended to pack up the house. She has not yet even made a start. She has managed the letters of recommendation for Ruth and Mrs Calloway. Has half-written the letter to Samuel's lawyer. But her productivity has been stolen by thoughts on Henry Ward, and all she has to tell him.

She needs him to come now, before she loses her courage.

Abigail turns away from the window. Rakes her fingers through the hair that hangs loose on her shoulders. Focus, she thinks. She has far too much to do to waste the night pining at the window. Henry will come when he comes. And he *will* come, surely. The ship would not be here otherwise.

The thought nudges her into action and she leaves the

study for her bedchamber. She kneels, peeking under the bed in search of her travelling trunks. It has been more than twelve years since she has used them. Once, she had imagined the entire rest of her life would be spent up here in this wild top corner of the country.

She straightens at a sound from outside the house. The faint sigh of footsteps. Someone is here. But it's not relief that she feels. Because these footsteps are coming from the side of the house furthest from the sea. No one from the ship would be approaching from this direction.

She rushes back to the study and snuffs the lamp at the window. Curses her foolishness. With the lamp blazing so brightly, she has made herself a beacon. For Henry Ward, or for Donald Macauley, or for whoever else might wish to come here to Highfield House tonight. For whatever reason they wish to come.

She reaches into her pocket. Wraps her fingers around Oliver's knife. It has become such a part of her, she often forgets she is carrying it.

She moves through the building, dousing the rest of the lamps. Blackness falls over the house in waves. It's an almost impenetrable dark; the only hint of light travels from the coals still glowing in the parlour grate. Abigail moves instinctively through the lightlessness. Even sightless, the house feels so familiar, so knowable.

Footsteps again, much closer to the house this time. The dull murmur of voices. Abigail hurries upstairs. She may have made it clear that she is here in the house. But she will not make herself so easy to find.

Shouting. Men shoving and surging through the door of the saloon. The flash of a pistol here; a cutlass there.

Animals.

Ward supposes he cannot blame the crew for this. A few months ago, he would never have considered doing something as shameful as abandoning his own ship before the men's agreements are through. He has to admit, he's not proud of any of this. But it's what he must do. Going back to Abigail is not even a question.

He shoves away the man at his shoulder and climbs onto the table of the saloon. Slides his pistol from his pocket. He does not raise it. Does not threaten his men. But the sight of it in his hand sends a hush through the men. They stop shoving each other through the saloon door. Their shouting falls quiet.

"My decision has been made," Ward says, his voice loud, but controlled. "And I suggest you all remember that Mr Hunter is yet to choose which of you he wishes to take on. I'm sure I do not need to remind you that violence is prohibited by this ship's articles."

His warning causes a fresh murmur to ripple through the men. Ward climbs off the table and pushes his way back out onto deck. Hunter strides out behind him.

"I trust you're not going to just abandon ship with the crew in such a state," his quartermaster says tautly.

Ward lets out a short, humourless laugh. He has to admit, it's a tempting prospect. "Of course not. I've more decency than that." There are payments to arrange for the men, and ship's papers to go over with Hunter. Besides, he's barely even begun to clear the contents of his great cabin.

Ward picks up the spying glass dropped on the deck by

the crewman who had abandoned his lookout post. "Get the anchor watch back in place at once," he barks to Hunter. He lifts the spying glass to his eye, trying to pull the shape of Highfield House from the darkness. He cannot see it. The landscape is black; the house has disappeared. As though it never existed. Had he seen a lamp in the windows earlier tonight? Perhaps. Or perhaps just his imagination. He has been cursedly preoccupied.

Unease tugs at him. Urges him to go straight to shore. Find her, in amongst all that blackness.

Ward looks at the house through the spying glass again. Tries to talk himself out of his unease. He is overreacting, surely. Abigail and her children are asleep in bed with the lamps doused. Nothing more sinister than that.

Nonetheless, he would feel better if he knew that for certain.

He turns at the sound of Graveney's footsteps. His boatswain is heading towards Hunter with an uneasy look in his eyes. Ward claps him on the shoulder. "I need you to take a message to the house, John. Tell Mrs Blake there's trouble on the ship and I'll be there as soon as I can."

CHAPTER THIRTY-SEVEN

Abigail pulls back the curtain of her bedroom, daring to peek out onto the dunes. She can just make out two figures moving through the darkness. A man and a woman, she thinks, draped in dark cloaks.

They are coming for her, surely. They must be members of the Bamburgh thieving ring, come to punish her for taking back the letter. Why else would anyone be here? No one comes to Emmanuel Head, other than to come to the house, at least not at this time of night.

It's not panic that overtakes her, but a strange, almost dizzying calmness. A sense of going past herself to reach this inevitability she has been waiting for since she first got entangled with the Bamburgh thieves.

Of course there is no surprise that they have shown themselves now. She knows it would not have taken Lizzie and Ailith long to realise they had been robbed. And Lizzie had seen Abigail in the village the day of the theft. Surely it had not taken her and her mother long to put the pieces together.

So there is no surprise to this. But she has not been quick enough to leave the island, Abigail sees that now. She ought to have ignored formalities such as recommendation letters and legal correspondence. Ought to have just taken her children and run, the moment she had returned from Bamburgh with the letter in her pocket.

Her need to write to Henry, telling him everything, had delayed her. And she sees now how foolish that was.

Still. There is no time for regret. No time for panic. Right now, the best thing she can do is remain calm. The thieves are outside the house, yes. But so is Henry Ward. And he will come for her. Because he loves her. Oliver had promised.

She grips the bedpost tightly, trying to order her thoughts. How will the thieves try and get into the house? Through a window? Every door is locked tight. Surely they cannot know of the passage in the walls. Even she did not know of the thing.

Unless Oliver told Lizzie about the passage. Told her of the tunnel that leads into the house from beneath Nathan's bedroom window.

Abigail rushes across the hallway and throws open the door to Oliver's room. A part of her is grateful for her urgency, because it does not allow her to feel the grief she knows would be careening into her otherwise. She has not set foot inside the room since Oliver's death. Still, his books are scattered across the desk, his clothes hanging in the wardrobe. Still, his blood is staining the floorboards. The coat belonging to the boy who had killed him is still bunched up in one corner of the mattress; the cabin boy's abandoned boots still tipped over beside the bed.

But Abigail does not think of these things. She just thinks of the double-barrel priest hole beside the fireplace, and the passage leading down, down into the walls. Easy access in and out of the house for anyone who knows how to find it.

She throws her weight against the bed, trying to slide it towards the fireplace. Trying to block the opening of the hole. It groans against the flagstones. Barely moves an inch.

Before she can try again, a volley of breaking glass comes from the ground floor and echoes up through the house. Abigail swallows her murmur of fear.

Get the children. Leave the house through the passage.

These thoughts are all she can manage.

Henry's ship is in the bay. She will get to him. She has given away the rowboat, and has never learnt to sail or swim. But somehow, she will get to him.

She flies down the hallway towards Eva's room. Can hear footsteps inside the house now. The soft click of boots on flagstones.

Abigail holds her breath. Looks down the stairs into the sea of darkness. On the edge of her vision, she sees movement; shapes at the bottom of the stairs. They catch sight of her, and suddenly the two figures are rushing up the staircase, stealing away the last of her calmness. Abigail darts away from Eva's bedroom and snatches the fire poker from Samuel's study.

She charges back into the hallway. Meets the intruders at the top of the stairs. Abigail can just make out enough in the darkness to know the woman is Ailith. Beside her is a man Abigail does not recognise. She holds the poker out in front of her. The nose of a pistol emerges from the dark, held out in the man's hand.

"Where's the letter?" he asks. His voice is deep and Scottish.

She hesitates. A click of the pistol. "Nightstand," she croaks.

The man keeps the pistol trained on her. He nods towards Ailith. "Go."

Ailith shoves her way past them. Abigail hears her throwing open the doors to first the dressing room, then her bedchamber. Hears her clattering blindly through the darkness, searching for the nightstand.

Suddenly, there are more noises downstairs. The thump of someone jumping through the broken window. Boots crunching over shattered glass. Abigail holds her breath, unable to take her eyes from the pistol levelled with her face.

A pale globe of lamplight breaks the darkness.

"Mrs Blake?" The voice rising up from the entrance hall is not Henry's. One of his crewmen? His footsteps quicken, intensify, and it causes the man with the pistol to falter.

Before the thought enters her head, Abigail is swinging the poker, knocking the pistol from the man's hands. It clatters against the floorboards. Henry's crewmate—Mr Graveney, she realises distantly—rushes up the stairs towards them. He grabs at the man, hauling him from the landing and heaving his body down the staircase. The lamp in Graveney's hand shatters, and blackness spills over the house again. Abigail hears the dull thumps of bodies falling. Drops to her knees in a desperate search for the pistol.

She feels a sharp pain as Ailith lurches into the passage and grabs a fistful of her hair; yanks her away from the weapon. Instinctively, Abigail hunches, curls in on herself, a protective arm wrapped around her middle. Ailith stands over her and Abigail can just make out the brass box in her hands.

"Go," she manages. "Take it and go." She will not her fight for this. Will not put herself in danger for that cursed brass box. Surely, Henry will value his unborn child over his letter. Will value *her* over his letter.

Ailith meets her eyes for a second, then rushes down the staircase with the box. Abigail watches her disappear. The Jacobite letter. The letter she had written to Henry, telling him every piece of her heart.

It doesn't matter, she tells herself. Henry is here, just out in the bay. Soon, they will stand face to face and she will tell him everything.

He is here, isn't he? Why has Graveney come to the house instead? Has something happened to Henry? Has he not returned home from the Channel? Fresh panic rushes at her.

As she gets shakily to her feet, her fingers find the pistol. She tucks it into her pocket and edges downstairs.

"Mr Graveney?" Her voice disappears into the sudden stillness of the house.

"Down here."

Abigail steps slowly down the staircase. Graveney is standing at the bottom of the stairs, looking down at the limp figure of the man from the thieving ring.

Abigail swallows heavily. "Is he dead?"

Graveney nods.

"Are you hurt?" she asks.

"Nothing I'll not shake off. I had the element of surprise on my side."

"Thank you," Abigail murmurs. It does not feel like enough. She knows that, in all likelihood, this near stranger has just saved her life. But speaking it makes it too real.

Graveney looks up at her, then down at the body. "What was that about?" he asks. "Who were they? What did they want?"

"They—" She stops herself. She has no idea if Henry has told his crewmen about the Jacobite letter. All she knows is that he had told her to keep quiet about it. Keep it safe. She has failed on so many counts. "They were just petty thieves," she manages. "They must have known my children and I were alone in this house."

Graveney nods faintly.

Abigail's eyes draw downwards to the body. The man has fallen face-down, and in the pale light, she sees a thin trail of blood snaking out from the body.

She has to go. She has to go, she has to go.

The thought circles through her head without pause. She has delayed for too long, and now a man is dead.

Less than an hour back to Bamburgh on horseback, she thinks. Less than an hour before Ailith gets word to the rest of the thieving ring about what Abigail Blake has done.

But what if Ailith and the dead man were not alone? What if there are more of them out here? Abigail knows she cannot count on *less than an hour back to Bamburgh*. It is far too dark to be certain the dunes are empty.

If—when—the thieves find out one of them has been killed in her house, they will be back at her door. And there is no telling what they will do to her in retribution.

She needs Graveney's help. She cannot risk Nathan or Eva getting out of bed and seeing a dead man at the bottom of the stairs. Especially not after all they have been through these past months.

"Help me," she says huskily. "Please. I need to remove the

body."

Graveney nods. "Is there somewhere we can bury—"

"No. I can't have him buried here. What if someone sees you? What if they come looking—"

"All right," Graveney says. "All right." He glances out through the broken window. "I can take him out in the longboat. Take him out to sea and dispose of the body before I get back to the ship."

Abigail nods, despite the sudden rolling in her stomach. There's something inevitable about this, she thinks dully. About her becoming the kind of woman who sees dead men tossed into the sea. She feels a pull of self-loathing. And she says, "Thank you."

Graveney rolls the body over and hauls it from the floor. Slings the figure over his shoulder. Abigail hurries into the parlour, lighting a single candle with the tinderbox on the mantel. She takes it back to the entrance hall. Its pale light illuminates the line of blood snaking across the flagstones. Abigail pulls off her shawl and tosses it onto the floor. Uses it to wipe the blood from the stone. Let there be no trace of this night left for whoever steps into these halls next. She has no thought of who that might be.

Cupping the tiny flame with her hand, she leads Graveney down the narrow passage toward the servants' entrance. Shoves on the door at the end of the corridor. It opens with a creak, cold air billowing inside.

"This will take you out onto the dunes," she says, voice low. "Do you think you can get to your longboat without anyone seeing you?"

Graveney heaves the body from his shoulder and sets it down beside the door. He steps out into the night, scanning the dunes. "It's quiet," he says. "No one out here as far as I can tell. But it's far too dark to be certain."

Abigail nods wordlessly. She sets her bloodstained shawl on top of the body. And then she asks that which she has so far been too afraid to: "Henry. Is he alive?"

"Aye. He'll be here as soon as he can."

She lets out a breath of relief she was not aware she was holding. "Take me back to the ship," she says suddenly. "My children and I need to leave this house at once. It's not safe for us here."

Graveney hesitates, eyes darting between her and the dead man on her doorstep. "I can't," he says. "I'm sorry. The men are brawling over the captain's new conditions. You don't want your children around that, aye?"

Abigail feels her hope shatter. "No," she manages. "Of course not." She swallows hard. She cannot wait for Henry. She needs to leave now.

She looks up at Graveney, meeting his eyes in the candlelight. "Will you give Henry a message?"

"Of course."

Her thoughts race. There is so much she needs to tell him. But she will not spill her heart to this man from his crew. Will just give him the bare facts.

"Tell him I need to leave at once. Tell him to come to the lodging house in Beal as soon as he is able. I shall be waiting for him there."

Graveney nods. "Of course."

"Tell him—" Abigail hesitates. *Face to face*, she thinks. But she needs him to understand the urgency of this. Needs him to understand everything that is at stake. Needs him to come to the lodging house, knowing the life that awaits him. "Tell him he is to be a father."

Something almost imperceivable passes across Graveney's eyes, but he keeps his face level. "I see." He nods. "I shall pass on your message." He looks at her squarely. "Take care, Mrs Blake."

CHAPTER THIRTY-EIGHT

Abigail rushes back upstairs to her bedchamber and pulls a pouch of money from her nightstand. Shoves it into her stays. She grabs her cloak from where she had tossed it on the end of the bed, fumbling with the hooks as she swings it around her shoulders.

Henry will find her, she tells herself. He will find them, and he will help them start again. Once they are off this island, they can begin to plan their life together.

With the candle in hand, she steps out of her bedchamber, not looking back. She strides down the hallway, keeping her eyes averted from Oliver's room. At the back of her mind is the knowledge that she is leaving her son here on Lindisfarne, alone. Guilt knifes her; not just for leaving him, but for allowing him to become what he had. Allowing him to die the way he had.

She pushes open the door to Nathan's room.

"Mama?" Nathan is already sitting up in bed when she steps into the room. How long has he been awake? How much had he heard?

She fights the urge to pull him into her arms. "I need you to get dressed, my love," she whispers. "Quickly. Can you do that for me while I fetch your sister?"

He looks up at her with wide eyes. Nods. Does not ask questions. Abigail swallows the lump in her throat. She sets the candle on the mantel.

"Good boy. I'll be back in a moment."

She hears his faint footfalls as he goes to his wardrobe, pulls open the squeaking door.

Two doors down the hallway, Eva is breathing deeply in sleep, one hand curled beneath her cheek, her dark hair fanned out on her pillow. Keeping her wrapped in her blankets, Abigail scoops her into her arms, careful not to wake her.

She hurries back into Nathan's room. He has buttoned his breeches and waistcoat; is fumbling with the silk neckcloth he wears to school. "Just your coat, Nathan," she tells him. "Just get your coat and shoes. You don't need anything else."

Obediently, he tosses the neckcloth on the bed and snatches his coat from the wardrobe. Wrestles his arms into it and buttons it crookedly. Sits on the floor to pull on his shoes. On his way past the window, he grabs his telescope from its wooden stand.

He hurries to Abigail's side. Stands close, not touching.

Down the stairs; one step, the next, the next, candlelight painting long shadows over the walls.

And as they make her way towards the door, Abigail is suddenly aching for it: for this house; her prison, her protector. This house, where she had brought her children into the world, where she had fallen in love with her husband, where she had built herself into something close to a decent person.

But there is not a scrap of choice to any of this. Not a single way to stay. And it's this that keeps her walking. Keeps her leaving her house behind.

"Take hold of my skirts," she whispers to Nathan. Leads him down the passage of the servants' entrance and slips through the side door. She blows out the candle, letting the full intensity of the darkness fall over her and her children.

She does not look back at the house. Does not look out at Henry's ship, glittering in the bay. She just has to trust that he will come to the lodging house. Has to trust that this life she has laid out for him is a life he wishes to live.

"Where are we going, Mama?" Nathan asks. His voice is a murmur, but she hisses to him to be quiet, instantly regretting it.

"We need to leave," she says. "I promise I'll tell you more soon. But right now, I just need you to do as I say."

He looks up at her with a thousand questions in his eyes. Does not ask any of them. He lifts his face upwards, seeking out the glimmers of starlight between the clouds. Clutches his telescope to his chest.

The path to the village is invisible in the thick darkness, the rugged grass of the dunes far too uneven to navigate without light. Abigail hears the dull thud of hooves. Sees the glow of a roe deer's eyes. She freezes, several yards from the house, listening for any sound of humanity. Is Ailith still on the island? Are there others from the ring seeking to punish her for all she has done? She cannot even think about who might be hiding in the dunes. All she can focus on is getting off this island.

When the silence returns, Abigail keeps walking, Eva slung over her shoulder and Nathan stumbling along beside her with a fistful of her cloak. They follow the coastline in the dark; follow that line of white water that will guide their path to the Pilgrims' Way. Abigail can tell the tide is rising. They need to hurry if they are to make it off the island tonight.

Her arm aches under Eva's weight, her long legs dangling down past Abigail's hips. She is growing too big to be carried.

As Abigail tries to shift the weight of her, Eva wakes and begins to murmur—murmurs that turn to wails as she takes in the layers of night pressing down them. Abigail tries to murmur soothing words, but can find nothing. All she has inside her now is panic. Out ahead of them, the Pilgrims' Way stretches out dark and endless, the sea invisible, a constant sigh. How deep is the water? How high has the tide risen?

Hide in the village. Wait until morning.

No. She has made too many enemies for that. Father Dering, surely, would help her. But there is no certainty she will get to the vicarage without coming across Donald Macauley or Elias Mitchell, or any of the other Lindisfarne natives with a Jacobite alliance. Men who believe she has stolen from their cause. Men who will punish her before they help her. Men who will curse her family's name.

Abigail takes a breath. Grabs Nathan's hand tightly, ignoring the way his fingers stiffen and try to escape her own. She steps out onto the Pilgrims' Way, feeling her shoes sink into the damp sand. One step. Another, another. And now here is the water, rushing up against her ankles. Soaking through her stockings, tugging at her skirts. Another step. Another.

Water at her shins now, her knees. It's a cold she has never experienced. A cold that blazes and burns and has her gasping. A murmur of shock escapes her lips. She pulls Nathan close to her, gripping hold of his coat. Pushes forward as the water tugs at her skirts, tries to pull her back onto the island.

"Just keep going," she says. Is not sure if she is speaking to Nathan or herself. "Just keep going."

Another step. Another, into and through the rising tide.

CHAPTER THIRTY-NINE

Graveney does his best not to think as he heaves the body into the water. Does not think about how easily—and how soon—it could be his body being disposed of by Amos Sheffield and his men. He does not look back at the dark circle of water where the man had disappeared. Close enough to the moment of death, he thinks, for the body to sink quickly to the bottom. For the man to just vanish from the world without a trace. Is this what will happen to him? Will Sheffield's men fling his body into the Thames when he cannot pay his debts? Will he be washed out into the ocean, with no one any the wiser? He swallows a sudden swell of sickness.

He pulls on the oars, stifling a groan. Pain is roaring through his shoulder after his tumble down the stairs. The *Eagle* is just a few yards ahead of him now, lit up in pools of lamplight. Out on Emmanuel Head, the house has vanished into the darkness. The tide is rising, he realises, and it occurs to him he had not even thought to make sure Mrs Blake and her children had a way off the island. Perhaps he ought to go back and find her.

The thought is pushed away by the cold reality of all that is going on aboard the *Eagle*. He can still hear angry voices drifting out across the water. Can tell nothing has been resolved since he had left. Hunter, is seems, has not managed to take control of his men.

Hunter, who believes him a Jacobite traitor. Hunter, who will never allow him to remain a part of this crew.

Graveney tries to tell himself this is for the best. Because each time they fire at the French; each time they steal from the Jacobites, he knows it will come with guilt. A memory of his mother. But the only conclusion he can come to is this: what kind of life is it to be penniless and starving? To live each day in fear that Amos Sheffield will hunt him down and demand payment for debts he cannot pay? What kind of life is it to die at the end of a gambling man's cutlass?

The ship is still heaving when Graveney climbs back aboard. Men are strewn about the deck, locked in heated conversations with Ward, with Hunter, with each other.

Ward looks up as Graveney approaches. Strides across the deck towards him. "Did you find her?" he demands. "Is she safe?" His eyes flicker across the water towards the darkness containing the house.

And sometimes, Graveney thinks, sometimes a man has to do what is right for himself and himself alone. Sometimes a man has to put his own needs first.

Besides, he knows Henry Ward. Henry Ward is not a man who settles down to raise children. He is a man who fights for his country. And he'll realise that, Graveney thinks. Once he's sailed out from under Abigail Blake's spell, he'll realise

314

that the helm of the *Eagle* is where he belongs.

"The house was empty," says Graveney. "Not a soul about. Looks as though no one has been there in some time." He meets the captain's eyes in an attempt at sympathy. "I'm sorry, sir. She and her children have left."

CHAPTER FORTY

She has her answer.

When she had finally made it to the lodging house in Beal, Abigail had intended to stay awake all night. Stay alert, stay watchful of anyone who might have followed her off the island; wait for Henry. But exhaustion had pulled her down, and as she had drifted off to sleep, she had imagined being woken by Henry's knock at the door. Or perhaps, implausibly, by his breath tickling her skin as he leant over the bed, kissing her cheek and telling her she was safe.

In the end, she had been woken only by waves of nausea, to find the candle burned out and a grey dawn light slinking through the gap in the curtains.

Wrapped in blankets, with her sodden clothes drying by a restoked fire, she had gone to the window. Sat there, watching the sky lighten, exhaustion making her body ache, and the child inside her making her stomach roll. And she had looked out across the sea. Watched the *Eagle* pass. Disappear.

Henry Ward has not come for her.

THE RISING TIDE

Abigail sees now that she had made herself believe in a different reality. Made herself believe in all that Oliver had told her. Made herself believe that Henry Ward loved her. That he would want this life she was offering.

Had she truly imagined she might lure a man like Henry away from the sea and into some dour, city-bound domestic life?

Perhaps she is as adept at lying to herself as she is to others.

Sitting at the window, she had watched the ship disappear with a necessary sense of detachment. And, perhaps, inevitability. Because her tryst with Henry Ward has always been a little too make-believe. A little too fanciful to be reality.

With a sense of empty resignation, Abigail had stumbled back into bed beside her children. Fallen into a deep, dreamless sleep.

Late morning now—she can tell by the white light peeking through the curtains. Beside her, Eva and Nathan are sprawled across the bed in their underclothes, still breathing deeply with sleep. Abigail watches them dazedly, her mind filled with flashes of the crossing: water at her ankles, her knees, her waist. Hauling one child in each arm as she struggled through the deepest water at the heart of the Pilgrims' Way. Fearing that her decision to leave would end in all of their deaths.

But then the water had begun to grow shallower and the lights of Beal had begun to grow brighter, and the prospect of living, surviving, had begun to feel within reach.

In the early afternoon, with her skirts still slightly damp and her children still sleeping, she goes downstairs to find the

317

innkeeper and make her arrangements. A wagon to Berwick, where they will find a coach down to London.

A piece of parchment, please. Ink pot and quill.

She writes the letter upstairs in their room while the innkeeper arranges for the wagon. Writes that long-overdue letter to her mother.

Her words are succinct. Samuel and Oliver dead from smallpox, herself carrying a child. She and her two youngest children on their way to the townhouse in Chelsea.

Her words are heavy with fresh grief, though it is not grief for her husband, who has been gone almost a year now. Not that her mother will ever know that. Nor will anyone else in London. She will return to the capital in her mourning clothes, and speak of her departed husband with emotion thickening her voice, as though he has only just left them. And the child growing inside her? Well, how could that be anything but Samuel's child? She knows Eva and Nathan are too young to question it. Knows herself an adept enough liar to let this become the truth.

And so, it will be like this:

This part of her life, she will never speak of.

The house, she will never speak of. The island, she will never speak of.

Most of all, it is Henry Ward that she will never speak of.

He has made his decision. And so she has made hers.

She will lock away the part of herself that makes dangerous, impulsive decisions. Lock away the memories of this past year, and the emotions that come with it. From now on, her sole focus will be making a good life for her children. Ensuring they know nothing of the mistakes she has made, the foolish things she has done.

Rain is falling when the wagon begins to pull away from the lodging house, tapping steadily against the thin wooden roof inches above her head. Abigail sits bundled in the blankets the coachman has left on the bench seats for them, trying to ease away the last of the water's chill. Eva, still in her nightgown, is curled into her lap with her head against her mother's chest. Nathan sits close by her side, his telescope lying across his knees and a faraway look in his eyes.

As the wagon rattles down the muddy path, Abigail cannot help but look out at Lindisfarne, bathed in cloud on the other side of the Pilgrims' Way. She cannot see the house, hidden away on the far corner of the island. Is glad for it. Now that she has made her escape, she has no desire to look back.

She will never return to Northumberland—this she knows with a certainty that reaches her bones. Silence will fall over Highfield House now; the kind of silence that seems impossibly fitting. The fires she had left simmering will turn to cold ash, the food in the cupboards will become dust. Her garden will be torn at by birds and trampled by deer, and overrun by scree and wild grasses. As for all the clothes and books and pieces of lives they have left behind, the loss of them will make space for something new. Something better.

Nathan's house, she thinks distantly. It will become Nathan's house now. The manor, and all the struggles Holy Island has brought this family, will fall upon his shoulders. And for this, she pities him. Best, she thinks, that he never return either, to this tidal island; to this world of thieves and Jacobites and privateers.

Best he turn his eyes forward and build a life on more solid ground. Let every piece of this past fall away.

ABOUT THE AUTHOR

A lover of old stuff, folk music, and ghost stories, Johanna Craven bases her books around little-known true events from the past. She divides her time between the UK and Australia, and can be very easily persuaded to tell you about the time she accidently swam with seals on Holy Island.

Find out more at www.johannacraven.com.

Printed in Dunstable, United Kingdom

63608986R00190